## Prologue

Pale face, bulging eyes, head lolling backwards. How had it come to this? I'd let myself get carried away in a moment of weakness, made a split decision, a poor choice – years of restraint down the drain. A careless reaction I should have been able to rise above. But the fear, the certainty that one would become two, then another and another, led to a self-fulfilling prophecy. Once an addict, always an addict, no matter how much time has passed.

Oh, but it was magnificent. There was no better feeling, no more satisfying way to calm the urge. How could I have forgotten? Why did I resist when it was so much easier to give in? Risky, but worthwhile. And all the little tricks I had used to keep my desires at bay were no longer enough. Part of the experience wouldn't do. I wanted all of it.

She came back. Silly girl. Left and then returned with a feeble excuse, I didn't believe. Too friendly by half that one. Annoyingly accommodating, endlessly helpful. Wasn't she ever told to mind her own bloody business? Perhaps she was and ignored the advice. The girl wasn't too bright, that's for sure, or she'd have realised who she was dealing with. No, not an intellectual by any means, but someone with a fierce sense of right and wrong. And something else – street smarts. Whatever it was, it gave her a window into something that no one else saw. An inherent feeling that things were not as they seemed. Somehow, she suspected, and just when I thought she'd left forever, she returned.

I'd gone to the shops and might have been out longer if I'd remembered my card. I had opened and closed a bag and fumbled in my pockets, a hot flush of embarrassment mottling my neck. Leaving the basket on the counter, I had asked the shopkeeper to put it by – I'd be back in a moment. He had glowered, eyes heavenward, while the woman behind tutted loudly, and I'd left feeling stupid, just as I had back in the day. In those formative years when personalities were shaped, and consciences moulded. Detentions, slaps, rules, pain. *Shut up. Stop thinking about it.*

Thank God for that little slip. Five more minutes, and it would have been too late. The girl had only suspected something was wrong, but if I'd taken any longer, she'd have known for sure. So close to catastrophe. But as it was, I'd returned and found her interfering in my life, checking her suspicions but not quite finding the evidence she sought. A good thing – she wouldn't have stomached it. I found her kneeling, ready to check, about to unwrap, unbind, and reveal the truth she thought she wanted to know. She heard me arrive and cast an anxious glance my way but had no solid reason to fear me. So, I smiled with a forced friendliness light-years away from my true feelings.

She tried to stand, and I could have, should have, let her leave. Taken the chance that she didn't recognise what I was. But old habits die hard. I made small talk about the weather, spotted a cord on the counter, and reached for it,

# THE GIRL IN FLAT THREE

JACQUELINE BEARD

VINCI
BOOKS

Vinci Books

vinci-books.com

Published by Vinci Books Ltd in 2025

1

The EU GPSR authorised representative is Logos Europe, 9 rue Nicolas
Poussion, 17000 La Rochelle, France contact@logoseurope.eu

Printed and bound in Great Britain by Clays Ltd, Elcograf S.p.A.

## By Jacqueline Beard

Denman & Tallis Cotswold Crime Thrillers

*The Girl in Flat Three*

*You'll Never Escape Me*

snapping the corner of my nail down to the quick. Searing pain made me wince, but I didn't care. The game was afoot. An equal match – I wasn't strong, but with the benefit of foresight, I was quicker.

Twisting the cord around her neck while she faced away, I missed the pleasure of seeing her bulging eyes as I dodged, turned, and manoeuvred past her thrashing limbs. She writhed and moaned, and I forced her to the floor, face down, with my foot on her back, riding her like a horse as I tugged on the reins, the cord biting deeply into her tender neck. A rattle, a gurgle, and it was over. I relaxed my stranglehold, and she flopped to the floor with a gasp like a dying fish. I stood, exhausted, my hands ridged with rope burns, fingers shaking. Now another problem. Where to put her?

I kicked her over with a shaking foot. Bloody froth speckled her lips, and bloodshot eyes stared from her head. She'd wet herself, and the stench of ammonia from the urine-covered floor made my eyes water. Not tears. Oh no. She had it coming. Too nosy for her own good. A sudden urge gripped me with fearsome force. And once I'd acknowledged it, I couldn't contain myself. My hands clenched as I tried to fight it. Better not here, if at all. But it was too late. I walked to the drawer as if in a dream. Seizing a knife and steel, I swiped it, metal grinding against metal, to a sharp, lethal edge. Then, kneeling in front of the dead girl, I drew the blade lovingly from knee to ankle, expertly paring a thin layer of skin.

Blood prickled the surface but did not bleed out as I'd kept a layer intact. An excitement rose inside me, a longing, a need for more, and I sliced more urgently, slapping the peeled flesh onto the floor, frenzied, careless now – blood splattering the tiles, the knife, my thighs. I'd need to clean the mess away, and soon. But not right now. It could wait.

Fear battled triumph with heart-stopping shivers of uncertainty. Or was it pleasure? I wasn't sure anymore. But I knew how to put it right – at least in the short term. It had been a long time, but if memory served, there was a bottle of wine at the back of the kitchen cupboard. I uncorked it and raised a glass to the only living witness of my crime.

# Chapter One

The sickly smell was back again – a pungent aroma drifting around my kitchen like a malodorous wraith, its origin leaving me baffled. I had torn the place apart, emptying cupboards and drawers, trying to find the source of the problem. It didn't take long to look. Most of my possessions lay unpacked in supermarket boxes in what the letting agent laughingly referred to as the second bedroom. Boxroom, more like. I could probably wedge a bed in there if my life depended on it, but not much else. And why would I bother? I was unlikely to have steady streams of visitors to my flat, being new in town and unemployed. Thankfully, the letting agent had already taken up references before the unfortunate incident a fortnight previously that saw me marched out of Froggatt and Co by the Managing Director's PA. I can still feel the ghost of her hand on my shoulder and remember the triumphant sneer on her face as I shook it away. She didn't believe my story. Nobody did. But that son of a bitch in the sales department tried to touch me up, and nobody gets to put their hands on me unless I want them to. Certainly not a creep like Curtis Newton.

I flexed my hand, balling it into a fist as I had when I punched him in the nose, remembering the satisfying crack as it snapped. I hadn't meant for it to happen, but my well-honed military instincts had kicked in automatically. Forgetting where I was, I had reacted as if I was still a Royal Air Force policewoman, keeping the base safe. Act quickly, think clearly, and don't let them get to you – my mantra then and now. Unfortunately, the acting bit was always a few steps ahead of the thinking. And I was quick to anger. Had I calmed down and used my brain, I might still have a job and not be fretting about how to make the rent this month. But my fist was out and in Curtis Newton's face long before I'd considered the benefits of going to the HR department and reporting him for the misogynistic pig he was. So, Curtis bloody Newton got away with it while I got the sack.

I ruminated about the unfairness, which was still raw, as I scrabbled on my hands and knees in front of kitchen cupboards which had seen better days. But no matter how hard I tried, the smell was as elusive as my prospects of getting an employment reference suitable to secure another job. Ten minutes of fruitless searching passed, and I gave up. I got to my feet and opened the window, setting it on the widest latch. The window frames were ancient, like the building. My apartment wasn't awful by any means, but previous upgrades had relied on painting over or repairing existing structures rather than replacing them with new ones. So, my kitchen resembled something from the 1950s with a Belfast sink and blue painted units. It only needed a gingham tablecloth and an old-fashioned transistor radio for the full effect. But I knew the flat was a fortunate find, becoming re-available suddenly when the scheduled new occupant pulled out. The rent was cheaper than most. I hadn't much money for a holding deposit, and things could have been far worse.

I was lucky to find something close to the centre of Truscombe without it being on the High Street. A light sleeper at the best of times, my idea of hell was settling down after the pubs closed with all the drunken banter that followed. So, the flat suited me well, apart from the smell which still turned my stomach. I couldn't take it any longer and decided to shop for an air freshener.

Grabbing my jacket and bag, I opened the door to a compact landing opposite Flat Number Four, apparently occupied by a middle-aged couple I hadn't yet met. And judging by their raised voices the previous night, making their acquaintance wasn't a priority. But now was not the time to consider meeting the neighbours. It was lunchtime, and all was peaceful. The occupants were out, probably working if that's what they did to generate an income.

I clattered down the stairs, wondering when the management company would finish much-needed work on the stairwell. Bereft of a carpet, which must have been there at one time as a couple of clunky brackets were still in place, the rail also needed substantial sprucing up. I glanced at the shabby hallway, remembering the splinter I'd picked up from the banister the previous day, and rubbed the inflamed lump on my thumb. I reached the bottom just as the door of Flat One opened, and an affable-looking man I had first seen yesterday appeared.

"Hello," he beamed. "How are you getting on?"

"Well," I said. "The unpacking is coming along nicely." It wasn't true. I'd hardly started and had spent my time pointlessly searching for an elusive, noxious smell. But people don't want the truth when they ask how you are. Life is all about niceties, and a banal response keeps everyone happy. So, I smiled and continued my fictional account of how well I was settling in.

"Good for you," he said, and I was about to sail past when I heard a mewl and felt soft fur around my bare legs as a black cat weaved between them. I leaned down to tickle its ears.

"Sinbad," said the man.

"I'm sorry?"

"The cat, he's called Sinbad. And I'm Frank." He extended his hand, uncertainly smiling as if he wasn't sure whether I would return the handshake. "Saskia Denman," I said, grasping it firmly. He'd made an effort, and so would I. Frank turned around and picked up a small pot plant, which he balanced on an insubstantial plastic tray containing several others. And when he stooped to pick it up with both hands, it bowed and wobbled.

"Can I help?" I asked, imagining the mess if half a dozen pots came crashing onto the tiled hallway.

"I'll manage," he said, negotiating his way past the cat. I moved towards the front door to hold it open for him, and as I glanced at the entrance to his flat, I saw a small grey-haired woman sitting in a wheelchair at the end of the passageway.

"Thank you," he said as he passed through the open door. I followed him out, and he placed the tray beside a newly dug flower bed at the front of the house. The rear garden, which I could see from my bedroom, was large and a significant draw in choosing the property. But the front garden was only a few feet deep, with two lawned areas on either side of a path leading to the road.

"It's good of you to bother," I said, appreciating his efforts at keeping the property tidy for everyone. After ten years in the military, mess and muddles bothered me, even though my flat currently looked like a bomb had gone off inside it. But I knew it wouldn't be like that for long. I just needed time.

"We all muck in," said Frank, withdrawing a trowel from his jacket pocket. He glanced at the front window of his flat, smiled, and nodded.

"That's my mother," he said, and I followed his gaze, seeing that the grey-haired woman had wheeled herself into a position where she could watch him. I followed suit, waved, and smiled, but she did not respond.

"She can't walk or talk," said Frank sadly. "Age is a terrible thing."

His ironic remark belied the fact that Frank was no spring chicken himself. But on closer inspection, he was more likely in his sixties than seventies, as I had initially thought. Like me, Frank was slim, but his hair was sparse, and a comb-over effect did him no favours. Still, aside from a brief hello to one of the young men in Flat Two, I hadn't exchanged so much as a word with the other residents, and finding a friendly face, however old, was a good start. I wasn't a people person, but anyone, no matter how insular, needs some form of human contact.

"I'll be off then," I said, making towards the path. Frank grunted something I couldn't hear, and I left him to it.

---

I returned to Bosworth House with a pair of cheap air fresheners from Truscombe's newest pound shop and placed them strategically in the kitchen, where they battled with the pre-existing smell. The open window had little effect, and I searched through the food cupboard I'd stocked yesterday for something to force down, despite my queasiness. I settled on a tin of Bombay potatoes and heated them in a saucepan with a wobbly handle before tipping the cooked mess into a bowl. Sitting on a saggy couch in the living room overlooking Mortimer Road, I watched the passers-by as I finished my evening meal. The Bombay potatoes tasted good with the additional benefit of overpowering the kitchen smell. One lit candle later, I felt relaxed and ready to re-organise my life.

Emptying one box, then another, I eventually found the dregs of my military career beneath an old, dog-eared rug. I shoved my discharge paperwork into a drawer and hung a framed picture of my passing out parade on the wall. I stood in front of it, looking at the fresh-faced girl I was back in the day – young, hopeful and a world away from the jaded cynic I became.

I straightened the picture, creating an even more lopsided effect, and almost returned it to the box. It was more trouble than it was worth, reminding me of happier times and a life filled with promise. Then, I felt a familiar shortness of breath and reached in my pocket for my inhaler, sucking it back for immediate relief. Damn that little blue bottle and its counterparts in my medicine cabinet. But for my barely controllable asthma, I'd still be in Cyprus, living in the Sergeants' mess at RAF Kyrenia just down the corridor from Greg Sanders. I wondered how he was doing. The last I'd heard, he was chancing a career-ending relationship with Chloe Singh, the unfaithful bastard.

I sat down, momentarily overwhelmed by an unusual bout of self-pity, and let it wash over me. I allowed it to fester for a few minutes, rehearsing everything I wish I had said to Greg but didn't, before letting it go. Then I popped a tin of gin and tonic and knocked it back in a few gulps. It did the trick and settled me long enough to vegetate in front of the television in a low-lit room for a few hours without paying much attention to the programme.

I must have fallen asleep and woke with a start in the small hours. It was July, and the weather had been warm and dry, but the flat felt freezing, making me shiver. I picked up the remote control and switched off the television, bringing silence to the room. The side table lamp cast a woefully inadequate pall of light over the middle part of the small square lounge. It was my third night in the new flat, and I should have been getting used to it, but the deafening silence cast tendrils of fear into my overactive brain. My loneliness rose to the surface in a bubble of despair. I had no nearby family, no partner, and barely any friends. I wondered what I was doing with my life. And why a building containing six flats was as quiet as a mausoleum? Idle thoughts turned to fear, and dread slithered through me as it did back in my childhood when I climbed the steep steps of my grandmother's house, waiting for the bogeyman to plunge his razor-sharp knife into my back. Summoning courage that came more naturally during the day, I rolled off the couch and crept towards my bedroom, dimly lit by the pale moonlight. I closed the curtains, turned on the closest sidelight, and slipped fully clothed under the duvet. But I had made a mistake. The door was still ajar, and patchy moonlight shadowed the view from my bed towards the living room, making monsters from furnishings and demons from doors. Sleep would be impossible if I didn't close it, so I gave myself a pep talk and got out of bed. But as I reached the door, lighting my way using the torch on my mobile phone, I stopped dead in my tracks at a sound in the distance – the faint keening of someone moaning in pain. It was coming from one of the flats.

## Chapter Two

I woke late Saturday morning looking like death warmed up. The blood-curdling sound had only lasted a few short minutes, but it had been enough to tickle my fevered imagination into a night of insomnia and worry. I had tried to stick with the sidelight but gave up in the early hours of the morning, switching on the main bedroom light and one in the hallway, which made sleep near impossible. After three hours of tossing and turning, I plugged an earbud headset into my mobile and listened to a podcast which bored me into oblivion. But at least it got me through the night.

The sun was high by the time I finished showering, and I donned a pair of leggings and trainers before taking them off again. For a fleeting moment, I considered going for a run, but I was tired, apathetic, and unprepared to set myself up for failure. Instead, I ventured into the kitchen and popped a crumpet in the toaster before slathering it with butter. The so-called furnished flat hadn't come with a dining table, so I reclined on the couch and scrolled through TikTok while I ate. Then I put my plate in the sink and leaned across the windowsill to see what was happening outside. The rising sun had spread over the lawn, across a bench and onto a small, paved terrace, casting a warm glow that made the garden look inviting. Having nothing better to do on a weekend morning, I picked up the latest Lawrence Harpham mystery and headed outside. The weather wasn't as warm as it looked, and I regretted my decision not to bring a light coat, but I was out now and too lazy to take the flight of stairs to my flat, so I made the best of it. I settled down and opened my book, where a receipt doubling as a bookmark held my place and started reading. Half an hour flew by. The garden warmed up, and the ragged early morning clouds drifted away, leaving clear blue skies. I tipped my head back, closed my eyes, glorying in the sun's warmth on my face, and was about to resume reading when I heard someone clearing their throat.

My eyes snapped open to see the young dark-haired man from Flat Two, who also carried a book. "Mind if I join you?" he asked.

"Er, no," I muttered. I did mind, and I'd been enjoying solitary tranquillity unlikely to be improved by an awkward, stilted conversation with a stranger. But it wasn't socially acceptable to say so, and I didn't. "Go ahead," I said, in what I hoped was a friendly tone.

"Dhruv Patel," he said, offering his hand. "What are you reading?"

I showed him the cover of my book, and he nodded as if he was familiar with the author. "Good one," he said. "But I prefer thrillers. You should try this."

Dhruv gestured, and I nodded approvingly, but not so much that he felt obliged to give me further details.

"You're new," he said. "I saw you arrive on Wednesday. It's about time they filled your flat."

"Was it empty for long?"

"Three or four months. Milligan and I looked around to see if it was worth swapping, but we decided not to in the end. I mean, there's nothing wrong with it," he added as if trying not to offend. "But it wouldn't have given us any more room."

"Are the flats different sizes?"

"Apparently. The ground floor flats are slightly bigger than the first floor, but I didn't know that until I saw yours. It's the first time we've been in one of the mid-level flats."

"Are the other residents friendly?" I asked.

"Sure," said Dhruv. "But we rarely go in for coffee or anything. Well, Mill and I don't. Perhaps the others do. For all I know, they are having dinner parties every night and don't invite us. It's not like we'd ever find out. Anyway, I'm talking too much. Would you rather read?"

"No," I said. Dhruv could talk for England, but I found his enthusiasm and desire for conversation both endearing and exhausting. He was the sort of guy you could chat to for hours without having to try too hard – a perfect foil for an introvert.

"Tell me about the others," I said. "Who else lives here?"

"Well," said Dhruv, leaning back and stretching out with his book balancing on his belly. He crossed one tanned ankle over another as his tailored shorts perfectly accentuated slim, athletic legs. "There are six flats, two on each level."

"So, two at the top as well? I wasn't sure. It's hard to tell how it all works from the front."

"Yes. The second-floor flats are studios. You know the type of thing – a bedroom and living room in one. It's alright if you're single, although I couldn't do it. I'd rather room share. And above that is an attic."

"Across the entire house?" My mind drew mental floor plans.

Dhruv shrugged. "Could be. I don't know. It's always locked."

"Doesn't matter. I was just curious."

"Anyhow, Frank and Veronica Lewis live at Number One."

"I know, I've met them. Well, I've met Frank. And Sinbad too."

Dhruv laughed. "Frank's nuts about that cat. I caught him hand feeding slices of beef to Sinbad in the hallway last week. The poor thing is getting fat."

"Sinbad didn't seem phased about the size of his waistline when I saw him," I said. "I waved to Veronica while helping Frank outside, but she didn't wave back."

"She's not all there," said Dhruv. "I don't mean that disrespectfully, but I don't know the latest politically correct term for dementia or whatever it is she has. Frank's a nice chap, though, and very handy. If you want a shelf putting up, he's your man."

"And you live opposite?"

"Yes. Mill and I share a flat and a bed. Sorry if that's blunt, but it saves you wondering. We've been together for four years and finally got engaged last month. He's going to make an honest man of me." A platinum band inset with a diamond sparkled on Dhruv's ring finger.

"Congratulations," I said.

"Well, thank you. It hasn't been an easy ride, what with our differing backgrounds. Perhaps I'll tell you about it over a glass of wine sometime. Now, where was I?"

Dhruv made a show of trying to remember, and I couldn't help smiling at his earnest face. Deep brown eyes sparkled beneath a floppy fringe, and his mouth turned naturally upward. Dhruv bubbled with good humour, and I couldn't help wondering why he wasn't on friendlier terms with the other occupants. I had only known him a matter of minutes and already felt inclined to ask him back for coffee. He seemed like a man I could trust in a crisis.

"Now, your immediate neighbours are the Fosters," he continued. "You must take them as you find them, and I won't say too much. But good luck trying to work them out."

"Why?"

"They're out more than they're in, and neither is particularly chatty."

"That suits me. I like it quiet."

"Quiet? Ah. As I say, you must make up your own mind."

"Actually, can I ask you something?"

"Go ahead."

"Did you hear anything last night?"

"Over Milligan's snoring? I wish."

"Seriously. I couldn't sleep, and I thought I heard a cry, well, more like moaning – someone in pain, perhaps."

"Sorry. I slept like a baby. A dozen burglars could have broken in, and I'd have been none the wiser."

"No matter."

"I'll ask Mill if you like?"

"It's okay."

"So, Brendan Marshall is in Number Five and Velda Ribeira in Six. Both are single, as far as I know. Brendan shares the odd chat. Velda, not so much. And now you know almost as much as I do."

"Thank you," I said, beginning to feel more orientated. Six flats, three couples, three singles. Nine people, including me. I could cope with that. "Very helpful."

"Now it's your turn." Dhruv shifted in his seat, crossed his leg over his knee, and turned to face me.

"My turn?"

"Yes. Who are you, and where are you from? Don't spare the gory details."

He smiled perceptively, knowing there must be a tale to tell. After all, most women in their mid-thirties are up to their knees in nappies and schoolwork or at least partnered up. I was neither. I gave him a short, sanitized version of my life, including my RAF police career, which satisfied him up to a point. And then he asked a further question and hit pay dirt.

"Where do you work now?"

I sighed. The question was inevitable, but I had no intention of telling Dhruv or anyone else that I'd lost my job, let alone the events leading up to it.

"I don't," I say.

"Oh?"

"I'm in between jobs."

"Ah. I see."

"And you?" I shot the question out more to head him off than because I was in any way interested.

"Oh, insurance," he said vaguely. "Not very interesting, but it pays well."

"Any vacancies going?" I quipped.

"Not at my company," he said. "But I'm glad you asked. I know where there's a job going, and he's been looking for a while."

## Chapter Three

Nothing further materialised over the weekend. Dhruv was strangely reluctant to give me details about the job and wandered off almost immediately after our conversation, having agreed to take me to his workplace on Monday morning. I had spent Sunday alone and, with nothing better to do, had no excuse to procrastinate over the unpacking, which I finished that evening. Milligan and I had crossed on the stairs, and he'd said hello in a lilting Irish brogue, but Mill was quieter than Dhruv and did not extend the conversation. I had debated whether to try to break the ice but dithered too long. The moment passed, and Mill returned to his flat. Sunday was otherwise uneventful apart from a brief appearance by the Fosters. And when I say appearance, I mean I'd heard them – raised voices from Flat Four opposite, sometimes with a jovial edge but always loud. I'd tried to imagine what they looked like, and during the afternoon, when I was both bored and curious, I wasted time polishing the door furniture, which gave me an excuse to lurk in our shared landing. But neither Foster set foot outside, and I gave it up as a bad job, spending the rest of the day in front of the television.

Monday finally dawned, and I was up with the lark, feeling a sense of purpose for the first time in a while. I launched into a few downward dogs, and a couple of seated yoga poses before jumping into the shower and getting dressed. I still hadn't motivated myself to go shopping, and funds were getting low. The bread bin was empty, so I picked a speck of mould off the one remaining crumpet and tried not to think too hard about it as I smeared it with jam and quickly devoured the evidence. A cup of tea, a quick game of Candy Crush, and I was ready to meet Dhruv.

He was waiting at the bottom of the stairs with a leather bag slung over his shoulder and his mobile phone in his hand.

"Good timing," he said. "Let's go."

We ambled along, chatting about our respective week-ends, his more interesting than mine. I tried to probe him for information about the position while we walked, but he didn't bite, and I worried that the prospective job might be a colossal waste of time. But to a large extent, it didn't matter. I would be in the centre of Truscombe on a Monday morn-ing, close to the only two employment agencies and with no excuse not to get cracking on my search for a job. But agen-cies were a last resort. They would want references, and I certainly wouldn't be getting one from Froggatt & Co. I had already considered the prospect of securing casual work just long enough to get a reference, but waiting tables and cleaning held little appeal. I wasn't a job snob, but I had been proud of my RAF career, fully expecting to climb the greasy pole and not slip off the bottom because of a medical condition.

Dhruv interrupted my introspection. "This is it," he said as we turned into Prescott Street. He slowed and pointed to a sizeable Cotswold stone building set over three levels. "Follow me."

We walked through the front door and into a large reception area with a wooden staircase rising above. Doors led off to the side and rear. "I'm up there," said Dhruv, pointing to the ceiling. "My company is Boughton and Co. You won't have heard of us. We're insurance specialists, not your run-of-the-mill kind. There's a bridal shop on the first floor and a hairdresser through there." Dhruv pointed to the door towards the side.

"Which of them is looking for staff?" I asked.

"Neither. Come with me."

My heart sunk as Dhruv approached a tatty black painted door to the rear of the building. A corkboard hung to the side, its sole notice a faded handwritten paper marked in capital letters – HELP REQUIRED.

"It's not cleaning, is it?" I asked, hoping I didn't sound too ungrateful.

"Dhruv ignored me, knocked on the door and unlatched it. "Come inside," he said when I hesitated.

I followed Dhruv down a set of rickety stairs and into a basement lobby area with a door to a further office. Loud rock music assailed our ears and judging by the shadow cast on the opaque glass on the top half of the office door, the occupant was oblivious to our presence. Dhruv cleared his throat, but the noise drowned out his cough. Rolling his eyes with a smile, he slapped his palm on the office door and waited. The shadow moved into the corner of the room, the music stopped, and the door swung open.

"Dhruv. How are you? Shouldn't you be upstairs by now?"

Dhruv looked at his watch. "I've got a few minutes to spare. Meet Saskia. Saskia, this gentleman is Sean Tallis."

Sean extended his hand, and I shook it, wondering what I was doing there. The cluttered office, with its overfilled filing cabinets, stained chairs, and untidy paperwork, held no appeal. It reminded me of the old military police section immediately after an inspection when tidiness and order went to the dogs for the next few days. My eyes searched the room for clues to his profession, but nothing gave it away, and my radar twitched anxiously at the prospect of something illegal.

"I'll leave you two to it," said Dhruv, preparing to walk away.

"What do you mean?" Sean's expression changed from amiable to irritated in one fell swoop.

"Saskia's here about your notice."

"Hmmm?"

"Your job. The one you advertised outside."

"Oh, for crying out loud. No."

"Why not? You've been searching for months."

"For a bloody good reason, as you very well know. Sorry, Miss, whatever your name is. We've crossed wires here."

"No crossed wires from my point of view," said Dhruv, sweeping his fringe back. "Saskia needs a job, and you need help. Simples."

"But she's completely unsuitable."

"Excuse me. I can hear you."

"Stay out of it," snapped Sean.

"Going now. Have a wonderful day." I stomped past Sean and Dhruv, making straight for the door, fists clenched and trying to avoid another confrontation.

"Wait." Dhruv grabbed me by the shoulder as I swept past. "I'm sorry, Saskia. Sean has been complaining about the lack of help almost daily. I genuinely thought there was an opportunity. Sorry to have wasted your time."

"It's okay. I'll see you later."

"Bloody hell, Sean. That was rude." Dhruv's voice rose unfamiliarly.

"I wanted a partner, not a bloody secretary," snapped Sean.

I was still listening as I strode furiously through the door and into the lobby. My hand was on the doorknob, and I was about to yank it open when I noticed a plastic stand containing business cards. I snatched one and turned it over. "Sean Tallis, Private Investigator." The penny dropped, and I spun around on my heel and re-entered the room before flicking the business card towards Sean. It whirled through the air before rebounding off his coffee mug.

"Just so you know, I worked in the military police until six months ago. I'm as well-qualified for your crummy role as it gets. But don't worry. I don't want it. I'd rather sweep the streets." And with that, I finally left, flouncing from the building with a curious feeling of satisfaction and hoping that my snappy retort would teach him to make assumptions about women.

I had joined the Royal Air Force expecting a certain level of misogynistic prejudice, but it wasn't the case at all. Instead, I had encountered unexpected equality in an environment where I could progress as quickly and easily as my male counterparts. I'd sailed through the ranks until my asthma cut short my career, pipping a fair few of those who I'd trained with at RAF Halton to early promotion. I gritted my teeth as I remembered the day I ended up in the Station Medical Centre on the wrong end of a nebuliser. They'd treated me, turning a blind eye to the long-term career implications of asthma, but when the second major attack occurred, they acted. And that action marked the path towards civilian life – a route I'd never intended to take.

I slowed down and tried to forget my bitterness by walking toward the river, hoping the water's tranquillity would lift my mood. Two of the three nearby benches were occupied, and I couldn't face the thought of sitting next to a stranger. So, I sat alone on the third, staring across the water at a mallard duck gliding along without a care in the world.

Sean Tallis, Private Investigator, was an arrogant bastard who clearly needed help with his people skills. Why should he be sitting in an office in Truscombe deciding at a whim not to employ someone as well qualified as me while I couldn't motivate myself to get a proper job? And why did a small Cotswold town need a private investigator, anyway? I hadn't lived in Truscombe for long, but it was hardly a hotbed of criminal activity. Or was it? What was Tallis involved with that meant he needed extra help? A familiar prickle of excitement washed over me as it had in the heady Cypriot dog days of my RAF career. Computing was my passion – information gathering, counterintelligence, and cyber security came naturally to me. I missed the dopamine hit from a nugget of previously unknown information or something undisclosed that led to real progress. I would never pass a civilian police medical, so I hadn't bothered trying and had given up on the one part of my life with real meaning. And now I'd had another brush with my ex-profession in the form of a miserable private investigator. Sean Tallis might be a dick, but he was all that stood between me and a job I could enjoy. He wasn't interested, and I'd made my disgust at him embarrassingly clear. Still, at least I hadn't hit him, which left me in with a chance. I knew with certainty that I wanted to work in investigation again, even if it took a massive plate of humble pie to get there. So, I got to my feet and headed back to Prescott Road, wondering how to convince Sean that I was the help he needed.

# Chapter Four

There were two ways of dealing with Sean Tallis, non-confrontationally or with all guns blazing. I chose the latter. Striding through the building before I could change my mind, I wrenched open the latched door, took the stairs two at a time, and barged straight into his office without knocking on the door first. Sean stood shirtless by the barred window with a face full of shaving foam. The unexpected sight left me lost for words, and I stood guppy-like while my brain processed the scene.

Tallis raised an eyebrow but appeared less surprised than I was. "Ever heard of knocking?" he asked.

"Just my luck," I said. Not a good start.

"What do you want?"

"To talk to you about your staffing situation."

"Give me a minute." Tallis wandered into a room immediately off the office, leaving me standing there listening to the gurgle of water and the faint buzz of a battery-operated razor. He returned fully clothed moments later, with no explanation for his previous state of undress.

"Sit."

I clicked my mobile to silent, perched on the chair and placed it face down on the table.

"Turn it around."

"Sorry?"

"The mobile."

I flipped it over, and he casually glanced at the screen, then steepled his hands and leaned forward.

"Calmed down, have we?"

My brain urged me to apologise, but my mouth resisted.

"OK. We'll take it as read. Were you really in the military police?"

I reeled off my service number, rank and name and the corner of his mouth twitched. "Well, well," he said. "Army or Air Force?"

"Air Force."

"Good. I've known a few snowdrops in my time. It shouldn't be hard to check you out if it's worth my while."

"You could try asking me," I said, dismayed at his reference to the white Royal Air Force Police caps, which implied genuine contacts.

"You're hardly going to tell me if you're unsuitable."

"How would you decide that?"

Tallis leaned back with a wry smile. "If you're too officious, set in your ways, or unnecessarily gung ho."

"What are you looking for?"

"Someone with initiative, while accepting the mundane, who's chilled but knows when to step it up a gear and who doesn't take offence easily. Above all, a grafter."

"I'm all of those things."

"So, you say."

"Fine. Speak to your friends. There are only four hundred of us. It won't be difficult."

"Why did you leave?"

"The RAF?"

Tallis nodded.

"They discharged me on medical grounds."

"Why?"

"Strictly speaking, you're not allowed to ask me that."

"Do you want the job?"

"Are you offering it?"

"Not unless you answer."

I reached into my handbag, rummaged for my inhaler, and held it aloft between my finger and thumb.

"Asthma?"

"Yes."

"Can you run?"

"Very well. I'm perfectly fit, and my asthma is more or less under control."

"What was your last posting, and when did you leave?"

Sean Tallis reached for a pen, scribbled my name and medical condition on a notepad and waited expectantly.

"God. Must we?"

"Yes, if you don't want me to assume you've got something to hide."

"RAF Kyrenia and I left six months ago."

"How do you spell it?"

"As it sounds," I replied, losing the will to cooperate. I felt the job slipping out of reach, knowing that the painful subject of my short employment at Froggatt and Co would soon be up for discussion.

"Coffee?" Sean asked unexpectedly. I swithered for a moment, desperate for a caffeine hit but not wanting to prolong the agony. Sean decided for me and walked towards a desk at the back of the office where an evil tar-like brew percolated on a low heat.

"Milk, sugar?"

"Both."

He shoved a chipped mug towards me with no regard for the coffee ring he'd created on the desk. I picked it up and, risking burned lips, took a gulp, but it was lukewarm.

Sean noted my expression and shrugged his shoulders. "It's been on the go since seven o'clock," he said, glancing at his watch.

"An early start?"

"Par for the course, right now."

"Hence your need for help."

"From the right person." Sean conceded nothing as he scrutinised me. "So why haven't you worked since you left the RAF?"

"I have."

"Is today a holiday, or are you pulling a sickie?"

"Neither."

"Bloody hell, Saskia. It's like pulling teeth. I'm not wasting any more time unless you're more forthcoming."

"Alright. I had a job for a few months, and I don't have one now. And before you ask, there's no chance of me getting a reference."

"Why?"

I explained and waited for Sean to wind up the conversation and politely show me the door. But he didn't.

"Sick pervert. Serves him right," he said.

I breathed a sigh of relief. "It wasn't my finest hour."

"Whatever you say. I've no problem with it. No woman should expect to put up with that sort of behaviour."

For a moment, I wondered if he was winding me up, but the look of disgust on his face appeared genuine. He paused and spoke again. "I am an overworked Private Investigator just about making ends meet. My life is a vicious circle of early mornings, late nights, and little social life. I can't afford a partner, but the business won't grow without one. It can and should with a second pair of hands, but I won't lie. I've got through three potential partners this year, and none have worked out."

"Why not?"

"One didn't listen, one couldn't get to work on time, and the last turned up two days running as high as a kite."

"You're taking on the wrong people."

"Obviously. In an ideal world, I'd like another copper. But the job doesn't pay enough."

"Is there any point in continuing this conversation if you can't afford to pay me a salary?"

"I didn't say that. I can offer a small amount."

"What?"

"Not much more than minimum wage."

"I'll take it."

"I haven't offered it."

"How about a trial?"

"Unpaid?"

"Seriously?" I think about the mouldy crumpet I forced down for breakfast. My time should have been worth something, but Sean held all the cards.

"Look, we might not get along. I work better alone. It's this or nothing. Your choice."

"Alright. Where and when."

"Tonight. Meet me here at six o'clock. Dress down, keep it casual."

"Right." I wondered what I had let myself in for.

# Chapter Five

I arrived home to find a letter by my front door lying on top of a leaflet about Domestic Violence. I was about to open it when I realised the letter wasn't mine. Though correctly addressed to my flat, it was intended for Miss Gretta Smith. I took it inside and tossed it onto the kitchen work surface to deal with later. Someone in the block would know what to do with it.

I switched on the kettle and retreated into the living room to escape the smell. But I was only there for a moment when the doorbell rang, startling me. Clutching my chest, I ventured towards the door and slid the cover over the eye hole to see Dhruv's fiancé loitering outside.

"Hello," I said, opening the door with a relieved smile.

"Hi", he replied. "Sorry to be a pest, but you wouldn't have a plaster, would you?"

"You mean a band-aid?"

"Exactly."

"Come in. My first aid kit is still in a box, but I'll have a look if you don't mind waiting for a moment."

I showed Milligan into the living room, and he limped down the hallway before taking a seat on the couch.

"I hope you don't mind me bothering you?" he said.

"Not at all. What happened?"

"I don't know. The phone rang when I was half asleep. I work shifts, you see. And as I walked towards it, I stood on something sharp. I cleaned my foot and went back to bed. But I've been up for half an hour, and it hurts like hell."

"Poor you."

"Thanks."

I left Milligan alone while I searched one of the few remaining unopened boxes and returned moments later, clutching a green bag.

"It's a full medical kit," I said. "Take what you need and drop it back when you've finished."

"I will," said Milligan.

"Can I get you a drink?"

He hesitated. "Go on then."

I returned to the kitchen where the kettle had boiled and risked adding milk before taking both mugs, a spoon, and a packet of sugar I'd lifted from Costa to the living room.

"Thanks," said Milligan, clutching his drink with both hands.

We sat in awkward silence for a moment, and then Milligan spoke. "How did you get on this morning?" he asked. I shot him a quizzical look and Mill grinned. "Dhruv tells me everything," he said. "He's a fixer. As soon as you mentioned your military police career, he mentally matched you with Sean's investigator job."

"It's a pity he didn't mention me to Sean Tallis first. Or tell me the job was for a private eye. A bit of warning might have prevented a very frosty reception."

"Yes. Sorry to hear it went badly. Dhruv's known Tallis for a few years," said Milligan. "He's a tricky character. If Dhruv had said too much, Tallis would have refused to see you."

"So, he brought us face to face, knowing it could all go to rat shit?"

"Dhruv works in mysterious ways. The million-dollar question is, did Sean bite?"

"I don't know yet. I'm meeting him for an unpaid trial session later."

"A word to the wise – don't do a second without payment," said Milligan.

"I won't. Do you know Sean well?"

Milligan shook his head. "Not really. I see him occasionally if I call in to collect Dhruv from work. And he's been to the flat once or twice."

"Pity. I'd like to know more about Sean's background. Forewarned is forearmed."

"He's ex-police," said Milligan. "Left about five years ago to set up his own business. It's been rocky, so Dhruv says, but Sean's a decent enough chap once you get past his gruff exterior."

I raised an eyebrow. "If you say so."

Milligan stopped talking, and I searched my mental list of socially acceptable topics fit for small talk. But I wasn't in the mood for chatting, and Milligan was evidently a fellow introvert. He cleared his throat and muttered something about settling in, and I waffled for a moment about the trials and tribulations of moving. We were both relieved when he pushed his tea away and stood.

"Don't take offence. I never finish a cup," he said.

I followed him back down the hallway, and he wrinkled

his nose as we passed the kitchen, making me feel obliged to explain.

"Excuse the smell. It's been here since I arrived. I don't know what it is."

Milligan did not reply. There was nothing polite to say. I let him out, but as he was leaving, I noticed that the neighbouring door was wide open. Nobody was around, and the flat was strangely silent.

"Odd," I said.

"They'll be around somewhere."

"Should I shut it?"

"I wouldn't. Perhaps the Fosters are downstairs. It's not as if anyone can get in without a key."

"The postman did," I said.

"He can't."

"I found a letter on my doormat earlier, but it's not for me."

"Where?"

"I left Milligan on the doorstep while I retrieved Gretta's letter.

He took it and frowned. "Ah. She lived here before you, but Gretta's long gone."

"Do you have a forwarding address?"

"No. Best take it to the letting agent."

"I wonder who put it here?"

"Good question. I didn't know the postie had a key, and we've all been around long enough to know that Gretta left. I suppose someone was too lazy to walk the few yards to the letting agent's office."

"That will be it," I said. "I'll do it. No time like the present."

I said goodbye to Mill, grabbed my keys and sauntered

down to the Bayliss & Finch office, where I handed the letter to a young lady sitting behind the front desk. She thanked me, but the telephones were ringing, and she was alone, so I left her to it and walked back to Bosworth House. I was thinking about my encounter with Sean Tallis as I climbed the stairs and almost sailed back into my flat without noticing that the front door of Number Four was still wide open. But a faint noise from inside alerted me, and I turned around to hear a low but undeniable groaning as if the occupant was in pain.

---

I stood still on the landing, hoping that someone would emerge from the open doorway of Flat Four, but they did not. I should have high-tailed it back downstairs to find Milligan, but after hearing a second groan, I felt compelled to act. And like the implausibly foolish victim of a slasher movie, who takes the least sensible option, I went inside.

Passing the kitchen, a mirror image of mine minus the smell, I made for the hallway. The noise had stopped, and the ticking of an old-fashioned mantle clock lured me into the living room. I walked towards the window and peered outside but was none the wiser for doing so. The Foster's twee living room was unappealing, their floral-patterned three-piece suite too busy on the eye. They'd somehow fitted a large mahogany wall unit along a narrow wall, where it gloomily lurked, overshadowing the other furnishings. A Persian-style rug lay in the centre of the room, competing with the other fabrics. My head hurt just looking at it.

A low wail interrupted my reverie, panic gnawing at my insides. I did what I should have done when I first entered and called out loudly. "Hello. Is someone there?" Silence. "Hello. Can I help?" Nothing. Waves of adrenaline pumped through my veins, and my heart thumped heavy and fast. "I'm coming through," I said, still rooted to the spot. But nobody replied, and the moaning stopped almost as soon as it began. I clenched and unclenched my hands, willing myself to move, dizzy with jagged memories of a bomb scare in my old life five years earlier.

Thoughts of anxiously waiting, excitable sniffer dogs, followed by a controlled explosion, swirled through my head. Nobody died, and I saw no physical injuries – but that sound, that unmistakable blast of air still lived with me. It made me think about what might have been and swooped over me whenever I felt uneasy. There, but for the grace of God.

I pushed away all thoughts of fate and found the will to walk towards the bedroom, the most likely source of the noise. Tiptoeing slowly through the tiny landing, I passed a closed bathroom door and waited momentarily, listening for signs of life. I couldn't bring myself to try the handle. Taking so resolute an action filled me with inexplicable fear. Instead, I headed for the bedroom door, which stood ajar, and touched it with my finger until it was open wide enough to see. Then, I slowly peered inside.

The unopened blackout curtains left the Fosters' bedroom dark, and it took a moment for my eyes to adjust. I half-expected to see a shape in the bed if one of the Fosters was unwell. But the chintzy covers matched the curtains, giving the same cluttered effect as the lounge and were too tidily made to cover a sleeping body. I crept through the room until I could see the other side of the bed, craning my neck forward in case someone had fallen over. But there was nothing untoward save the offensively tan-coloured carpet. Relieved, I departed, having looked everywhere except the bathroom. And if the Fosters had taken unwell there, they were on their own. But as I passed the built-in double wardrobe, I felt an irresistible urge to open the door and gave in to it. Inside, a large chest freezer buzzed noisily beneath carefully ironed clothes hanging from the upper part of the wardrobe. With my heart in my mouth, I reached for the handle.

"What the bloody hell do you think you are you're doing?"

I froze as a high-pitched voice shrieked at me from down the corridor. I cautiously moved my head to see a well-groomed woman in her mid-forties striding towards me in platform-heeled sandals brandishing an umbrella like a weapon.

"Nothing, I'm your neighbour," I said.

"You broke into my house."

"No. The door was open."

"Liar. I locked it myself this morning when I left for work."

"Perhaps your husband unlocked it?"

"Lance is in Worcester today. He set off before I did. Why are you in my flat?"

"I heard a noise," I said lamely.

"What noise?"

"A moaning, as if someone was in pain."

"I don't believe you. Where is my silver?"

"What silver?"

"Don't treat me like a fool. Pieces have been disappearing for weeks. I thought it was Lance up to his tricks, but now I find you in my flat where you've no business to be."

"How can I be responsible for your missing stuff? I only moved in last week."

"So, you say. But you must have viewed the flat. Did you get your hands on it then?"

"No, I didn't. I'm not in the habit of wandering into strangers' homes and stealing things. You're not thinking straight."

"Don't take that tone with me, or I'll report you to the agent."

"Look. I'm sorry. Let's not get off on the wrong foot. My name is Saskia Denman, and I live opposite."

"I know who you are," said Kitty Foster coldly. "Now, why are you poking around in my closet?"

"I just wondered where the noise came from, and I opened the door on auto-pilot. But why do you keep a freezer in there?" I pointed to the wardrobe with a shaking hand.

"None of your damned business."

"Could something have got inside?"

"Don't be ridiculous," she said. "Now get out."

"Look. I'm sorry, but your door was open. Ask Milligan in Number Two."

"Just leave." Kitty Foster lowered the umbrella for the first time and stepped aside to let me out. A flushing mess of embarrassment, I slunk past her and out of the flat. Moments later, I heard the door slam behind me.

## Chapter Six

I arrived at 14 Prescott Street a little before six o'clock and proceeded to the front door, meeting unexpected resistance when I tried to open it. Pressing my nose to the glass, I peered inside, straining to see through the blurry window into the silent, unlit hallway. Sighing, I leaned against the side wall and casually checked my emails, hoping I didn't look like a potential employee whose new boss had just stood her up. Five minutes later, I was still waiting and cursed under my breath as I realised that Tallis might have offered me the job solely to teach me a lesson in manners. If he had, he wouldn't get away with me leaving quietly. I futilely hammered on the door, knowing he wouldn't be able to hear from the basement, then remembered that I had swiped a second business card from the corkboard earlier that day. I quickly found it and called the number on my mobile, which only rang twice before a gruff voice answered. "Tallis."

"It's Saskia."

"You're late."

"The door's locked."

"Ah. Good point. Wait there."

I stood for another five minutes, becoming increasingly irritable. Impatient by nature and with a low tolerance for poor timekeeping, my day had already turned to crap after my confrontation with Kitty Foster and was getting markedly worse. Though tempted to bolt, I stayed, knowing that Tallis was my best hope of a meaningful career. And just as I zoned out while deleting unwanted pictures from my mobile, I heard the rattle of keys, and Sean Tallis opened the door.

"Ready?" he asked.

"Yep."

"Follow me."

We turned the corner and walked a few yards to the rear of the building, where Sean's vehicle was waiting. He gestured to the passenger side, and I let myself in, stopping short when I noticed a box on the seat. I picked it up and placed it in my lap as Sean entered the driver's side.

"What do you want me to do with this?" I asked.

"Ah, forgot about that. Stick it in the footwell, if you don't mind. No. Not yours, in the back."

"I've got plenty of room down here."

"I dare say. But open the box and then tell me if you still want it by your feet."

I eased the lid free to reveal a Tupperware container of something that, at first glance, appeared to be food. Closer inspection revealed that the brown mass was moving. I shoved the lid back on.

"Mealworms," said Sean, grinning.

"Gross. For snacking on?"

"Not for me. My geckos."

"You're kidding."

"Nope. I share my home with a large tank of lizards."

"Each to their own," I said, stashing the box as far away behind me as I could reach.

"Where are we going?" I asked as Sean took a sharp right across the flow of traffic.

"Marsh Green. And I hope you've junked your plans for the rest of the evening."

"I didn't have any."

"Good. Now, for some background. When the Truscombe police are under-resourced and overworked, they turn to me. Did I mention that I'm an ex-copper? My fifteen years' experience trumps their junior officers, and with current employment issues and recruits thin on the ground, skills like mine are in short supply. The senior officers know me, I'm trusted, and, more importantly, there's a budget for my services. So, it makes sense for them to send the mundane stuff my way. Understand?"

"It's not rocket science."

Sean flashed me a glare, and I apologised. "Sorry. Yes, it makes sense."

"I'm on a stakeout for the second night this week. It happens a lot, and I badly need help keeping on top of routine jobs. But it's dull and not ideal for a woman. And I don't mean you can't or shouldn't get involved. I'm not misogynistic, and my reluctance to assign females is my problem, not yours. But walking away from my responsibilities bothers me. Do you know what I mean? Outdated feelings of chivalry and all that."

"I understand." His earlier reaction made sense now. I wasn't precious about gender roles and could hold my own in a crisis. Sean didn't need to worry about my safety, but his concern didn't offend me, either.

"Have you worked surveillance before?"

"Of course. But not usually from a car. Is that what you do?"

"Mostly, but not always."

"I can look after myself, Sean. You're the boss, but you can trust me to work alone." The words sounded unconvincing even as I uttered them, probably because my earlier encounter with Kitty Foster had left me shaken. I was neither brave nor decisive in my actions during her onslaught.

"And you're trained in self-defence?"

"You'd better believe it," I said, this time on more solid ground. Self-defence training had been a regular part of my military life and would still be second nature in the right circumstances.

"Nearly there," said Sean, driving unexpectedly towards a parade of shops. He parked the car and turned to face me. "Have you eaten yet?"

"Yes."

"Lucky you. I haven't had time, and I'm starving. Do you want something from the chippy?" I glanced towards the queue of people snaking from the shop, and my heart sunk. More waiting. "No, thanks."

"Sure?"

"Alright, a bottle of water. Make it sparkling, please."

"Won't be long."

Sean slammed the door and strode towards the chip shop, then disregarding the queue, he disappeared inside. Five minutes later, he returned carrying a plastic bag.

"Friend of a friend," he said, seeing my quizzical look. "Hang on to this. It's not far."

Sean pulled away while I sat with the thin plastic bag on my lap, feeling the warmth of his supper through my jeans. A deep-fried chip smell permeated the car, making me feel peckish, and I regretted my hasty decision to refuse his offer of food. Our journey ended almost immediately.

"This is it," said Sean, parking the car opposite a purpose-built block of flats on the edge of Truscombe. "That's Marsh House."

"Nice building," I said, admiring the contemporary architecture. Though modern, with large glass windows, the sympathetically constructed Cotswold-style stone building complemented the surrounding properties.

"It's not bad," agreed Sean. "Pity about the inhabitants."

"Really? It doesn't look that type of place."

"I'm being unfair. Most of the tenants are fine. It's just one in particular who doesn't deserve to live among decent law-abiding people, but there's nothing we can do about it now that he's out of prison. See that window," said Sean, pointing to the far end of the building where a half-drawn curtain hung limply over the glass. I nodded.

"That's where Robbie Sutherland lives with his girl-friend. And this is his photograph," said Sean, opening the glove compartment and withdrawing a dog-eared picture of a dark-haired, heavy-set man with a throat tattoo.

"Shouldn't be hard to spot."

"Exactly. So, keep an eye out while I eat," he continued. "Here, take this." Sean passed me a bottle of water, still not sparkling as I'd asked. I said nothing but opened it and sipped while Sean tore open the packet and dug into cod and chips.

"Want one?" he asked.

I took a chip and ate it, immediately feeling hungry. "Aren't we a little obvious out here?"

"He doesn't know we're watching him."

"Even though the same car appears in the same place every night?"

"Which applies to everyone else who lives here. I half wish Robbie was aware. Applying that kind of pressure might give us an idea about the other matter."

"What's that?"

"Amy Swanson," said Sean.

"Hmmm. Sounds vaguely familiar. Who is she?"

"A missing girl. And part of the reason we're here."

"Foul play?" I asked as Sean offered me another chip.

"Hmm," he murmured, crunching the battered cod.

"What's Amy Swanson got to do with Sutherland?"

"Hold your horses."

Sean shovelled down another mouthful of his chip supper, opened a caffeine drink, and gulped it down. Then he balled up the paper and shoved it into the plastic bag.

"That's better," he said. "Look." Sean nodded towards the window with newly drawn curtains. "Someone's home."

"What are you expecting to see?"

Sean took another slug of his foul-smelling drink. "There are two parts to this surveillance. Robbie Sutherland is out on licence from Leyhill after a second offence. He served six years for rape, and they released him. Then, Sutherland re-offended by exposing himself in a public place and spent another eight weeks inside. He got out a fortnight ago under a supervision order. One wrong step, and he's back inside."

"And where do you come in?"

"Sutherland is allowed to work – manual labour at Kennington quarry. It's a regular source of employment for prisoners. The owner also had a chequered past and is sympathetic to reform. Anyway, ex-cons have no honour, and one of the other men has ratted him out as a drug supplier. Crack cocaine through the county lines. But there's no proof. Not one iota."

"Perhaps there's nothing in it. Sex offences are a world away from drugs."

"And Sutherland takes regular drug tests as part of his supervision order," said Sean. "Clean as a whistle."

"I'm surprised the police are bothering."

"So was I, but Kim Robbins said the information was good, which makes me think that the other prisoner is an official informant."

"So, your man is a dealer but not a user?"

Sean nodded. "If it's true, he's in it for the money. His girlfriend's not too bright and has the hollow-eyed look of an addict. Anyway, we've heard there will be a drop somewhere in Marsh Green this week. It's easy to monitor Sutherland at the quarry, so if the rumour is true, it's likely to happen here in the evening."

"Surely, this is a police matter?"

"It's all about costs," said Sean. "With no proof and the word of a self-interested snout, it's not in their interests to pursue it. And we're not talking about drugs with a high street value. If not for Amy, they probably wouldn't bother."

"Amy Swanson. The missing girl?"

"Yes. Assuming she hasn't voluntarily disappeared."

"Don't they know?"

"No. And that's the problem."

"Tell me about it."

Sean sighed. "I haven't decided whether to keep you yet," he said, scratching the side of his nose. I recognised the negative gesture. Sean's body language spoke volumes about his discomfort in dealing with me, and I retorted in kind.

"And I haven't decided whether I want to work for you."

"Touché. Are you prepared to sit here watching the building for the rest of the week for something that might not happen?"

"Of course."

"You have a car, right?"

"Yes, I own a car."

"I still don't know." Sean pursed his lips.

"What would convince you?"

"Ah, sod it. Let's take your employment as read for now. Look, I'll tell you everything I know about Amy. I presume you haven't read about her in the papers?"

I shook my head.

"I'm not surprised. There were only a few articles, and only then because her sister contacted a reporter. Anyway, Amy Swanson moved into Marsh House four months ago. Except she didn't."

"I'm sorry?"

"She moved her furniture, which arrived in a removal van early in the afternoon, opened up the flat, and took possession in the normal way. Then she spoke to one of her neighbours and went back inside. Amy must have left sometime later that evening, never to return."

"That's fairly conclusive. I can't see much room for doubt."

"For anyone else, perhaps, but not for Amy. She was bohemian, something of a free spirit. Amy hopped in and out of jobs, never struggling to find one, and often moved home on a whim. She wasn't from Truscombe and arrived here a few years ago after living in a caravan park on the outskirts of Evesham for a year. Before that, she stayed in various parts of Cornwall, where her family lived. Amy was rotten at keeping in touch, and the family often went for weeks or months without contact. But they cared and eventually realised they hadn't heard from her for a while. Then Rachel Swanson turned up at Truscombe police station."

"Rachel?"

"Amy's sister. She'd received a rare letter from Amy several months before saying that she was moving to a flat in Marsh Green and Rachel came to find her. With only three letting agents in Truscombe, the chances of finding Amy were good unless she had rented through a private landlord. Fortunately, Rachel visited Truscombe Lettings first, and they'd let the flat to Amy on a tenant-find basis. The agent didn't hold a key but contacted the landlord. Rachel met him at Marsh House, and he let her inside."

"What did she find?"

"Very little. Amy had straightened a few things out and moved some boxes around but hadn't opened them. Rachel checked through her possessions but found little, which didn't surprise her, as Amy wasn't materialistic. Amy kept some personal papers, suggesting she'd been planning a break with an unnamed friend. The sister assumed she'd gone ahead with her trip and let matters lie for a few weeks longer."

"Still nothing?"

"No. Amy never returned."

"Did she work?"

"Yes, but casually. She'd signed a zero-hours contract and worked when they needed her."

"I'm surprised she earned enough to pay rent."

"Amy wasn't a shirker but wouldn't let anything tie her down – it wasn't in her nature. After a few weeks of calling and receiving no answer, her employer assumed she'd lost interest in the job. It wasn't unreasonable. Amy was like that."

"So, is there a crime here or not?"

"The police don't know. I doubt it would have gone any further, but the sister grew increasingly concerned and made a nuisance of herself. Knowing Sutherland's history and having the justification of potential drug dealing, my contact, Kim Robbins, asked me to monitor his movements at the property."

"Seems a bit haphazard," I said.

"It is, but at least the police can tell her sister they're doing something. Since Rachel discovered Amy was sharing a building with a convicted rapist, she's threatened to tell the press."

"So, this is all about public relations?"

"Essentially. But we might catch the slimeball pushing drugs if we're lucky."

"What about Amy? Is her stuff still there?"

"At the flat? Not any longer. After the rent stopped, the landlord kept it for a while and then put her things in storage. Someone else lives there now."

"Did anyone look for Amy?"

"To a point. The police spoke to a neighbour and checked the building, including Sutherland's flat. He was out, but his girlfriend was very cooperative."

"So, you don't expect to find Amy?"

"I'm not even sure that she's missing. Not at the hands of someone else. Look, Sutherland is a pig who can't keep his dick in his trousers. But abduction isn't his thing. It doesn't fit at all."

"Then why are you bothering?"

"I'm doing what it takes to pay the bills," said Sean, shaking his head. "I don't know what it was like in the RAF police, but private detective work isn't glamorous. It's all about making money – this isn't television."

Sean downed the last of his drink and crunched the can.

Then he slid back in his seat and reclined while watching the curtained window of Robbie's flat.

"Are we here all night?"

"'Fraid so. He'll leave for work at five, and then we can go home."

Sean yawned, and I glimpsed his drawn face and the black bags under his eyes.

"Why don't you doze for a few hours, and I'll wake you if anything happens?"

"Tempting," said Sean.

"Go on."

He did. And I spent the next few hours casting my gaze between Sutherland's flat and my mobile phone screen.

## Chapter Seven

We left Marsh Hill House just before five after a night of intense boredom. Sean slept for a few hours while I read an online newspaper, and we swapped over at about three o'clock in the morning. It had been some time since I'd worked nights, notably a stint of guard duty at RAF Kyrenia that lasted for a week. Though tedious, they'd rostered us into guardhouse shifts, followed by Land Rover patrols, interspersed with rest periods. With Sean, I endured eleven hours of boredom with little to no relief until the thought of a till job at the local supermarket became increasingly attractive.

With the shift over and too tired to eat, I stumbled straight into my bedroom as soon as Sean dropped me off, donned my pyjamas, and fell asleep to a daytime television programme. I woke in the early afternoon, feeling oddly guilty that Sean would have only had a few hours of sleep before returning to the office for midday. But he hadn't made a big deal about it, only asking if I was still interested enough to join him for another shift at Marsh Hill House later.

I showered, changed, devoured a sandwich, and sat down to watch the news when the doorbell sounded, followed by a gentle knock. Sighing, I muted the television and answered it. A young woman in her mid-twenties stood on my doorstep with a pot plant in her hand.

"Hello, I'm Velda Ribeira," she said shyly. "I live in Flat Six upstairs. This is for you."

"Thank you," I said, taking the proffered plant with a sinking heart. My flat lacked greenery for a good reason – plants withered and died at my hands as I steadfastly forgot to water them.

"I thought I should introduce myself," she continued. "Work's been mad, or I'd have done it sooner."

"Good of you to bother. Would you like to come inside? I've just boiled the kettle."

"If I'm not interrupting anything."

"No. I've just come off nights and I'm free for a few hours." I ushered Velda through, feeling like a proper human being again. Articulating my gainful employment made it feel real. However reluctant Sean was to agree on terms, at least I was no longer unemployed, and I made a mental note to ask him for a formal contract.

"Nice picture," said Velda, pointing toward a large watercolour of Kolossi Castle I'd hung in the kitchen. The sun-kissed symmetrical fortress stood solidly beneath a cobalt Cypriot sky, and for a moment, I felt desperately homesick.

"Isn't it?" I said. "Happy days. Coffee or tea?"

"Whatever you're making with milk and a sweetener."

I dropped a tea bag in each mug and searched my cupboards for the jar of granulated sweetener I had purchased, God knows when. I didn't dare check the sell-by date, unscrewed the lid, and took a spoonful.

Velda uncomfortably shifted as she waited, and I caught her wrinkling her nose.

"I don't know what it is or where it's coming from," I said, pre-empting her question about the revolting smell in my kitchen while wondering if it would ever go away.

"Perhaps it's the drains?" she said unconvincingly.

"I've looked. Are yours okay?"

"Fine," said Velda. "I've saved a copy of the latest local magazine if you want to look up the number of a plumber."

I considered the paltry amount remaining in my bank account. "Don't worry. I'm sure it will disappear, eventually. Come through. You can't smell it over the air freshener in the lounge."

Velda wandered through and perched on the edge of the sofa, crossing her shapely legs, and cupping the mug in her hands. A fawn knee-length dress hugged her slender frame, and a pair of leaf-shaped earrings bobbed beneath tight black curls. "So, how are you finding it?" she asked.

"The flat? A little different from my last place in Gloucester. Can't say I miss the noise."

"Is that why you moved?"

"Not really. I fancied a change and didn't expect to lose my job the minute I signed the contract."

"Bad luck," said Velda, but she didn't pry. Two days ago, I wouldn't have mentioned my unfortunate employment with Froggatt and Co, but knowing I had a job suddenly made talking about it easier.

"How long have you been here?" I asked.

"About eighteen months. I arrived after Milligan and Dhruv. I hear you've met them?"

"Yes. Both. Nice guys. Mill's a teacher."

"I know. And an enormous improvement on those at my school. Mind you, I didn't help myself, but I was a different person back then..." Velda's voice petered away as if dismissing an unwanted memory.

"I like Mill and Dhruv."

"Me too. But it's good to have another woman in the building."

"Don't you see much of Kitty Foster?"

Velda pulled a face. "She's not very friendly. I tried to talk to her, but she didn't seem interested in getting to know me. Or anyone else, for that matter."

"Same here." I opened my mouth to tell Velda about yesterday's encounter with Kitty, but I didn't want her to think I was a nosy neighbour and resisted the urge to over-share.

"Where do you work?" I asked, searching for a new topic of conversation.

"At Cavendish Colours," she replied, referring to the well-known clothing store that had just opened up on King Street.

"Very nice. But didn't you say you'd been in Truscombe for a while?"

"I worked in the Worcester store and commuted but living here is much better. Now I've time for a social life."

Velda beamed, and her eyes sparkled beneath long eyelashes, probably false. Immaculately groomed, Velda cultivated her appearance – not a hair out of place and with healthily glowing ebony skin. I bet she hadn't come straight from a night shift like me. I wondered what she thought of the bags under my eyes and spots on my chin without a scrap of makeup to conceal my flaws. The comparison between us was badly one-sided in Velda's favour, and for a moment, I felt resentful of her seemingly well-ordered life.

"What will you do with it?" I asked.

"Sorry?"

"Your newly found social life?"

"Let me show you. Look at this." Velda reached into an impossibly small designer purse and retrieved a mobile phone clad in a garish holder. She flipped it open, scrolled for a moment, and presented me with an image of a handsome, clean-shaven man posing with his chin on his fist. "What do you think?"

I hesitated, not knowing what to say. The man in the picture was undoubtedly good-looking but bore a superficial resemblance to Velda and could have been anyone from a brother to a lover.

"Gorgeous, isn't he?" she asked, and I mentally ruled out the brother option.

"Very nice."

"Glad I swiped right."

"Ah. Internet dating?" I'd considered this myself but lacked the motivation to download the app.

Velda nodded. "It's the best thing I've done in a while."

"Have you met him yet?"

"Twice. We had coffee the first time we met and shared some tapas the next. I'm thinking of asking him back for a meal."

"What's stopping you?"

"My flat's a studio," she said. "I don't want to give him the wrong impression."

"Can't you make it look like a living room?"

"To a point, but he'd soon notice the lack of bedroom door."

"Bring him here if you like," I said. "I work nights. In fact, I'm out later tonight if you can arrange things quickly enough."

"But you don't know me."

"True. But I know where to find you if it all goes wrong."

Velda squirmed uncomfortably.

"That was a joke. I don't have any valuables. There's nothing you could damage. Feel free, if it helps."

"It's kind of you, but I'd rather wait until we know each other better."

"Fair enough. What will you do instead?"

"What would you do?"

"Suggest a curry, perhaps? Maybe at the Balti Gujarat. It's casual there. No pressure."

Velda's nervous giggle suggested agreement, and she quickly grilled me about the restaurant's location, implying enough regard for him to plan the occasion carefully.

"What's your young man's name?" I asked, sounding as if I were her maiden aunt.

"Benjamin. I don't know his last name yet, but he's a photographer by trade."

"Well, good for you."

"Thanks." Velda drained her cup and stood. "Must go," she said. "Nice to have met you."

"Likewise. Drop by and let me know how it goes."

Velda beamed. "I will."

---

I closed the door on Velda and took the opportunity to catch up on my emails, which I hadn't checked since moving. Plugging in my laptop, I flipped the lid open and then started the ritual of deleting all the crap emails from websites I hadn't bothered unsubscribing from. I took a cursory look at the P45 sent from Froggatt & Co's outsourced payroll provider and consigned it to the 'keep' folder to avoid its constant presence in my inbox. Which only left a few emails, one from my audiobook provider and two others. I flagged one to remind me to cancel the audio as I could no longer afford it and turned my attention to the emails from Root and Branch family tree DNA website. I could afford this even less but would sell a kidney before giving up my subscription.

Legend has it that Royal Air Force recruits come either from a military family or a broken home. It didn't apply in my case, as far as I knew. My family wasn't broken so much as entirely unknown. I had lived with my adoptive mother since I was two years old and was in foster care for eighteen months before that. A happy, conventional childhood left me unconcerned about my origins until Mum died of cancer just before I joined the RAF. Life as a new recruit was exciting enough to take the edge off her loss, and it wasn't until I came home from leave six months after she had passed away when my brother Connor handed over a box of her possessions. Inside was a series of letters between Mum and Auntie Doreen, during which it became apparent that Connor was not my genetic brother as we had thought. Connor's adoption was all above board, and Mum had kept his adoption certificate. But my entry into the family resulted from an informal arrangement, details of which were not forthcoming. Mum's husband was dead, Doreen was in a dementia home, and I had nowhere to turn to find out more. Ironically, having no one to ask heralded the point at which I started to care. So, I joined Root & Branch and invested in two DNA kits. The tests confirmed my suspicions. Connor and I shared no matching DNA, and although I had a slew of fourth cousin results, they weren't enough to provide any clues about my origin. Consequently, all DNA emails set my heart racing, hoping against hope that I would discover more.

This time, both emails were disappointing. One was an unwelcome increase to my subscription, the other a reminder to check the website for new matches. I did, and over half were for private trees, with the others being low matches or with rudimentary family trees too small to help my search. I shut my laptop in disgust and contemplated preparing a proper meal for dinner instead of snacking. But just as I picked up a cookbook, my mobile rang. It was Sean.

"Are you busy?"

"Not particularly."

"Kim Robbins has summoned me to the station. Want to come?"

"Why?"

"I thought I might introduce you. Forget it, if you've something better to do."

"I haven't. I'd love to, but I'll need to change."

"I'll pick you up in ten minutes."

"I'll need more time," I said, but the line was already dead. Damn it. I hadn't washed my hair, which looked like rats' tails. I rummaged through my dressing table and found an old tin of dry shampoo. Spray, brush, spray. It looked alright if I didn't touch it. And it had been years since anyone had run their fingers through my hair so nobody would notice the chalky residue left behind. Forgoing jeans, I settled for a smart pair of chinos and a white shirt with a light jacket over the top. I'd lost my toenail the previous month after stubbing it on a filing cabinet and selected a pair of covered wedges instead of my usual summer sandals. Then I jammed a pair of pumps into my handbag in case we went straight from the police station to Marsh Hill House.

A message from Sean buzzed on my phone. "Come straight away. I've parked on a double yellow." Sucking a mouthful of toothpaste from the tube, I locked my flat and went downstairs.

# Chapter Eight

"Smart," said Sean as I climbed into the car.

"Too overdressed?"

"Not at all."

Sean lowered mirrored sunglasses over his eyes and pulled away, his khaki tee-shirt rippling in the light breeze from the open window. He seemed underdressed, casual for a police station visit, yet his branded jeans were on trend – immaculate and pricey. He stroked his stubbled chin as he indicated left while selecting a playlist marked 'rock'. The lyrics to 'Don't fear the Reaper' thundered from the stereo.

"Sorry," said Sean, turning the volume down.

"What's happening?" I asked.

"Dunno. Donovan Grainger called with a message from Kim."

"Who's Donovan? Who's Kim?"

"Inspector Kim Robbins. She's my contact. Donovan is her lackey – a not too bright, arse-licking grunt."

"You don't like him then?"

"He's best ignored. Kim's alright. We worked together as sergeants. She got a promotion not long after I left."

"Why?"

"Because she passed her exams." Sean stared at me as if I was half-witted.

"I meant, why did you leave?"

"That's a story for another day. Hold on to your hat." Sean floored the accelerator as he shot past a cyclist who had been holding up the traffic. We veered left just in time to avoid a vehicle coming the other way. The driver blared his horn and flashed his lights, aggressively holding up his middle finger as we passed. Sean grinned wolfishly. "Take a chill pill, mate," he said, forcing an insincere smile.

"Are we late?" I asked, clutching the passenger door handle.

"Nope. But I don't have the patience for cyclists."

We drove on, exchanging small talk for another five minutes, and then Sean stopped the car outside Truscombe Police station, parking in a space marked 'visitors.'

"Come," he said, and I followed behind, trying to keep up with him as he strode through the double doors. Sean approached the police desk and slapped his hand on the counter. A young police constable jerked his head up, startled, and then a slow grin spread across his face. "Sean, mate. How are you doing?"

"Good. Is she in?"

"Just stepped out for some grub. Back in five. You can wait here."

"Rustle up a couple of coffees?"

"No, mate. I'm on duty."

"Come on, Tom."

Shaking his head, the PC picked up the phone and punched a number. "Yeah, Becky. A couple of coffees in reception and one for me. Oh, come on. You owe me. Yes, I know, and I'm calling it in. Cheers, thanks. See you in a moment."

"The drinks are on their way," he said, winking.

"Good man."

"Sean picked up a copy of Police Magazine and flipped a few pages. "Feeling the Pressure," he said, pointing to an article. "They should try running a bloody business. That's pressure."

I nodded but didn't reply. Sean was letting off steam, not looking for a reasoned debate. I stared at the giant cork-board to the side of the desk and the range of neatly pinned notices. It felt unfamiliar, a far cry from the ordered chaos of our unit in Kyrenia. Too tidy.

"Bloody hell," said Sean, checking his watch. "It's nearly four thirty, and we're back at Marsh Hill in ninety minutes. Won't have time for food at this rate, and she's off stuffing her face."

An auburn-haired policewoman appeared, holding paper cups in each hand.

"Shit," she said as a trickle of coffee seeped down her wrist. Sean jumped to his feet and took the drinks from her.

"Thanks, love," he said to the police constable.

"Don't call me that," she hissed, stomping back up the corridor.

"Don't mind her," said Tom.

"I don't care. I've got coffee."

Sean handed me a cup, and I wondered whether I wanted it enough to drink it without sweetener. But Sean was tapping on the table with his free hand and wearing an impatient scowl on his face. I decided I'd rather deal with him while caffeinated and sipped the scalding liquid. Not a pleasurable experience.

"About time," said Sean irritably. I looked up to see a slender woman striding through the doors. "Here," she said, tossing a packet of crisps onto the counter.

"Thanks, Ma'am."

"Sean, sorry to keep you. And you are?"

"This is Saskia, my new assistant."

It was my turn to scowl. The way Sean said it made me sound more like a secretary than a private eye.

"Thanks for the warning."

"You can speak freely in front of Sass."

"I'll be the judge of that. Come."

Kim Robbins moved purposefully towards the second set of double doors, reached the stairs, and took them two at a time. Sean followed, and I trailed behind, feeling like a spare part.

I arrived at the top of the stairs to see her disappear into a room further down the corridor. By the time I reached it, Sean was already inside and casually sitting with his long legs crossed at the ankle and his arm hanging off the armrest of a padded chair.

"Take a seat," said the woman, and I perched on a hard wooden chair next to Sean, wishing I felt more relaxed.

"Saskia, meet Inspector Kim Robbins. Kim, Saskia."

"Pleased to meet you."

"Likewise," she replied, looking anything but.

"What's the drama, llama?" asked Sean.

I inwardly cringed, but Kim didn't react.

"The tip-off. It's a dud."

"What, Sutherland?"

"Of course, Sutherland. Who do you think I meant?"

"What's wrong with it?"

"Our CHIS. It turns out they're old enemies."

"Doesn't mean it isn't true."

"I know. But resources being what they are…"

"Dammit, Kim. It's only a week, and we're halfway through it."

"Yes, I know. But the chief's on my case."

"Jesus. I need the work. You know this is personal, right?"

I saw their exchange of knowing glances and banked it for later discussion.

"If that were true, we wouldn't be using your services."

"Oh, Kim. If only you knew."

The inspector raised a well-plucked eyebrow but said nothing.

"Give it until the end of the week."

"I shouldn't, really."

"You'll regret it if the tip comes good."

"God almighty. Make sure it does. I'm too close to promotion to upset my superiors."

Sean winked. "It's never bothered you before."

"We're both older and wiser."

"Can I ask a question?" I said, fed up with their easy intimacy, leaving me frozen out on the side-lines.

"Go ahead." Kim Robbins stared confidently into my eyes.

"What's the latest on Amy Swanson?"

Sean scowled while Kim straightened a paper clip.

"Funny you should ask," she said. "Funny peculiar, I mean. Rachel Swanson made another appearance this morning."

"Painful," said Sean.

"Yes. Especially today. I could do without it."

"Today? Oh God, Kim, I'm sorry. I forgot."

"Don't fret. It was twenty years ago. But the press never

drops it. After all this time, you'd think they would have something else to report."

"Consider it a mark of respect."

"More like a slow news day. Look at this. They've surpassed themselves."

Kim reached for a newspaper slung carelessly by the side of the waste bin and thrust it towards Sean, who unrolled it. I couldn't read the smaller text, but the headline emblazoned across the page was unmissable. "Suicide Shame of Truscombe Superintendent – 20 years on and The Killer's Still at Large."

"Bastards," said Sean. "Lazy reporting. I'm sorry."

"Yes, well, there's nothing I can do about it. But if Rachel Swanson goes bleating to the press, I'm in for the same treatment as my father."

"I would if my sister was missing," I said.

"*If* being the operative word." Kim threw the now useless paper clip at the bin. It missed and bounced off the side.

"Better safe than sorry."

"If we knew where to start. We have made cursory checks."

"Where?"

"Call her off, Sean."

He narrowed his eyes but said nothing.

"It's not a criticism. I just wondered." I stood my ground. Kim might not like the question, but I'd make it hard for her to ignore it.

"We've searched the flat and spoken to the neighbour and Amy's employer. Her sister is worried, but even she admits that Amy could have gone off wandering, and her diary certainly suggests it."

"What about Amy's bank account?"

"She worked casually. Mostly cash in hand. Paid weekly, as and when. She didn't have a regular payslip."

"Yes, but did you check her bank account?"

Kim sighed. "She only used it sporadically."

"Recently?"

"Not recently."

"Since she left?"

"No."

"Then no wonder her sister is worried."

"Jesus, Sean."

"Sass. Enough. We'll talk in the car. Look, why don't you wait for me outside?" He handed me his car keys, and I snatched them, feeling exasperated. It must have shown on my face as he spoke soothingly. "I won't be long," he said.

"Nice to have met you." I flashed Kim a beaming smile, which didn't reach my eyes. Whoever she was and wherever she might be, Amy Swanson was a real person who deserved better than a cursory search to tick a few boxes. Her concerned sister was equally important and not the nuisance Kim Robbins portrayed. Resisting the urge to slam the door, I hurried to the car, slumped inside, and spent the next ten minutes imagining a pithy put down to punish Sean for silencing me. By the time he returned, I was so pissed off I'd eaten a whole tube of his mints.

---

"Finally," I said when Sean reappeared. He glanced at his watch.

"Dammit. Take away food again. Sorry. I didn't mean to spend so long with Kim. Do you need to go home first?"

"No," I replied. "But I can't face chips."

"Chinese?"

"Real food – anywhere I can get a salad."

"Fussy," said Sean. "I'd sooner eat mealworms."

He started the car and drove away while I wondered how he fitted in enough exercise to make up for his poor diet. Once on a straight road, Sean rested one arm against the open car window while driving one-handed, giving a clear view of his well-defined biceps. And from the look of his snugly fitting tee-shirt, he wasn't carrying any weight around his middle, either. Sean probably had a six-pack and a tonne of eager girlfriends to admire it. Well, let them. Sean wasn't my type, nor was any man who spent more time looking in the mirror than I did.

"Will this do?" asked Sean, pulling up at a small retail park on the edge of Truscombe.

"Sure. I'll find something in the supermarket. Coming?"

"No. There's a kebab wagon over there. That will do for me."

He went one way, and I went the other, returning with a pre-prepared pasta and pine nut salad I could ill afford. I ripped it open, hoping to wolf it down before Sean came back with an evil-smelling dinner, but I'd only taken a couple of mouthfuls before he returned. He ripped open the package with gusto and started eating.

"This is good. You should have had one."

"I'm alright."

"Your loss." Sean continued munching, then paused and turned to face me.

"Don't take it personally, by the way."

"What?"

"Kim Robbins. She's having a bad day."

"So, I gathered. But I bet Rachel Swanson's is worse."

"They've done what they can."

"I beg to differ."

"What would you do differently?"

"Speak to the neighbours. Find out where Amy was going. Stop pussy footing around Sutherland and ask him if he saw her."

"They did speak to the neighbour. And the Sutherland thing is coincidental. Yes, he's a disgusting individual who can't keep his hands to himself, but this doesn't fit his MO. Look, I understand how you feel, but there's not much they can do for someone with a history of going off alone. The budget will only spread so far. Surely it was similar when you were in the military police?"

"No. We got the job done. I don't think I ever heard the word 'budget' while serving in the RAF. Probably above my pay grade."

"Lucky you. Cost motivates everything today, which I understood less when I was in the police force than I do now. I'd love to take every case, but I must first work out whether it's cost-effective."

I finished the last of my pasta salad and dropped the empty carton into a plastic bag.

"Hang onto that for a moment," said Sean. "I'll get rid of it when I've finished mine."

"What was all that about Kim's father?" I asked.

"Mike Robbins? I'm surprised you don't know. Do you come from Gloucestershire?"

"I think so. I grew up here."

"Think so?"

I ignored his puzzled frown and tried again. "I've never heard of Mike Robbins."

"But you must remember the Skin Thief?"

"God, yes. I do. Wasn't he around at the same time as the Summerside Ripper?"

"That's right. But they caught the Ripper, as you know, while our man got away."

"Which is why I can't remember much about it. News of the Summerside Ripper overshadowed everything."

"And the Skin Thief only had two known victims – low for a serial killer."

"Does it even qualify?"

"Probably not. But the similarities between the murders left the police convinced one man was responsible for both deaths."

"What's this got to do with Kim Robbins?"

"Her father was the super in charge of the case. He hung himself in their garage when the case stalled. Too much pressure, they said. He held himself accountable."

"God, how awful."

"It was. Kim was only a teenager. But it set her on a police career path. She wanted to follow in her dad's footsteps and achieve what he couldn't."

"What? Catch the Skin Thief?"

"Not that. He must be long dead or in prison. Nobody could do what he did to those girls and walk away into obscurity for the next twenty years. No. Kim only wanted to prove that she could handle the job without falling apart. And she can. She's calm under pressure and a damn good cop. Her father would be proud."

"Did you know him?"

"No. But I know Kim. She's sound, Sass. If Kim says she's done as much as she reasonably can about Amy Swanson, then she has. I trust her."

I swallowed down my temptation to regurgitate my earlier argument. I still didn't agree that they'd done enough for Amy, but it was not the time to press my point. "How did he kill them?" I asked instead.

"One with a ligature and one with a knife," said Sean.

"Completely different MOs."

"Yes, but the perp removed strips of skin from both girls' bodies. And they never located the missing pieces, hence the Skin Thief moniker bestowed by our beloved press."

"I vaguely remember. It was pretty gruesome. I still don't understand why Mike Robbins felt responsible. It wasn't his fault."

"No, but the second girl was a school friend of Kim's from Truscombe Grammar. Mike Robbins knew the parents on a personal level. Both were teachers, one at the Grammar though not working there at the time of the murder, the other at a local primary school. Anyway, they socialised with the Robbins, and Mike played golf with the father, so you can imagine how much time they spent together. They never recovered from their daughter's death, and their friendship with the Robbins family inevitably suffered. Mike couldn't cope with failing his friend, and that was that."

"Did he leave a note?"

"Not as far as I know."

"Then how did they know why he'd done it?"

"Sheila. Kim's mum. It was a close marriage, and they talked a lot. He said he just couldn't come to terms with his failure. She never foresaw the suicide but spoke at the inquest about his state of mind – said he had regular night-mares in which the murdered girl was Kim. He couldn't get past it. I guess it was a form of PTSD."

"Poor man."

"Exactly. Anyway, it all happened a long time ago. Kim doesn't dwell on it and probably wouldn't have mentioned it, but Miles Savage extracts his pound of flesh every year, and as you saw, this year's article was particularly vicious."

"Is he the reporter?"

Sean nodded. "Ratty little creep. He was one of the original journalists when the murders happened. He probably should bear some level of responsibility for hounding Mike Robbins as he did. Miles is knocking on a bit now, and whenever it's an anniversary or a slow news day, he dusts off the story and brings it out into the open again. I'm surprised anyone cares after all this time, but there's always a flurry of online comments."

"People can be ghoulish about these things."

"Lacking in sensitivity," said Sean, displaying surprising empathy. He folded the paper around the uneaten part of his kebab and gestured for my plastic bag. I handed it over, and Sean tossed the bundle in a nearby waste bin. When he returned, he opened another foul-looking caffeinated drink and swallowed.

"Ready?" he asked.

"Yes. But why are we both going? Can't we take it in shifts?"

"With only one car?"

"I could go back and get mine."

"No. We're here now, and Sutherland will be on his way back from work shortly. Got to move."

"You're going to struggle letting go of this," I said as Sean pulled away and onto Marsh Hill Road.

"I won't. You can go solo tomorrow, I promise. It looks like the job is dead in the water, anyway."

"That's not what you said to Kim."

"I want the work. I'd have said anything. And if Kim were certain that it's a duff lead, she'd have pulled me off immediately. It wouldn't be the first time. Her reaction is more like a warning shot across the bows and one I take seriously. There's another point to this. I don't just want police work for the sake of funds. The investigations must be successful. There aren't many police forces willing to bring in private investigators."

"I'm surprised there are any at all."

"Thames Valley Police started the ball rolling a few years ago, bringing in PIs to work on sex crimes. It worked very well, and fortunately, the chief superintendent is all for it, funds allowing."

"No need to worry, then."

"Hopefully not. But let's crack on. Look ahead. Do you see what I see?"

I strained forwards, following Sean's finger. In the distance, a man emerged from a dirty grey-coloured vehicle.

"Dunno."

"That's him. Robbie Sutherland."

Sean drove slowly into the spaces opposite the flats, parked and waited for Robbie to walk into the building.

"Good. Time to rest. With a bit of luck, he'll stay in all night." Sean reached across the back seat and opened a copy of Practical Reptile Keeping. I raised a quizzical eyebrow, which he ignored, pressed the Kindle app, and started reading a thriller I'd downloaded earlier. We were in for a long night.

# Chapter Nine

I noticed Robbie first. Sean was half asleep with his magazine face down on his knees when the lycra-clad figure ran by.

"Whoa! Isn't that Robbie?" I asked, eyeing his tattooed neck.

"Shit. I didn't see him leave the building."

"I did, but I wasn't sure until he got closer. What will you do now?"

"Give it a second and follow him. He's running like a geriatric snail – I needn't rush."

"He's already out of sight."

"OK. Laters."

Sean shrugged on his jacket and strode toward the alleyway Sutherland had just entered. While I couldn't imagine the solidly built labourer having any genuine interest in keeping fit, it was equally implausible that he would risk breaking his supervision order by running drugs from his registered address. Still, he didn't look that bright, so anything was possible. But now Sean was away from the vehicle, and Robbie was on the move, I felt like a spare part for the second time that day. I found sitting in the car purposeless and decided to relieve my curiosity about Amy and her brief time at Marsh House by trying to find her apartment. I walked toward the building entrance, hoping there wasn't a security lock. There was, and I stood like a lemon for five minutes until someone emerged from the building.

"Sorry, forgot my key," I said, barging past before he could challenge me.

The well-lit Marsh House lobby led to several corridors, a range of mailboxes and a large staircase in the centre of the building. Knowing Sean would disapprove if I got too close, I avoided the top right-hand section where Robbie Sutherland's girlfriend might be at home. Starting at the opposite ground floor corridor, I familiarised myself with the layout, hoping it would be useful if I could find out where Amy had lived. The passage was silent – nobody stirred, and I hurried on, climbing the stairs to the first floor and once again, keeping to the left. As I reached the top of the stairs, a door opened, and a young couple appeared, the male dressed in a leather jacket and the girl with a face full of glittery make-up. They were on their way out for what remained of the evening.

"Are you looking for somebody?" asked the girl. My attempt to lean casually against the corridor wall while checking my phone had fooled no one. I looked out of place, and they knew it.

I risked the truth. "Amy Swanson," I said. "She moved here a while ago. I lost touch with her, but she lives in the building somewhere. Just not sure which flat." I shrugged my shoulders ruefully.

"Oh, I don't know her," said the girl. "Spud, have you heard of Amy?"

The man stroked a red-haired stubbly chin and pondered. "No. No, I don't think so."

"Sorry, love," said the girl and turned to go.

"Hang on a moment." The red-haired man waved his hand. "She's the one who moved in and out in the same week, Bella. Don't you remember?"

"Oh, yes. Silly girl. Wasted opportunity. It takes a bloody miracle to get one of these flats. There's somebody else up there now, I'm afraid. It took a while, but the landlord emptied her flat in the end. What choice did he have?"

"Do you know the number?"

"Umm. I reckon she was next door to Cherry on the second floor. Cher is number 17, so your friend would have been 16 or 18."

"Great, thanks. That's helpful."

They turned tail and went, and I followed them down the corridor, taking the stairs to the top floor and quickly locating number 17. The faded inscription on the white buzzer hanging loosely from number 16 read 'Colin Bailey', which by process of deduction made Amy's former flat 18. I debated whether to knock on the door, but it seemed pointless. The new occupant couldn't reasonably know anything, so I quickly sketched the layout for later use and returned to the landing. I was about to descend the stairs when I caught sight of the occupant of the first flat in the opposite corridor sitting outside her front door. She beckoned me over, and I initially ignored her, assuming I'd misunderstood her intentions. But she followed it up with a cheery, "yes, you dear."

I walked toward her, and she smiled. "Vera Cavendish," she said. "Are you new?"

"No. I don't live here."

The woman's smile faded; disappointment etched across her weathered face.

"Oh. I'm the unofficial welcoming committee. It seems I've got it wrong again."

"Were you expecting someone?" I asked.

"Yes. A new tenant in number 19. A young lady, so I'm told. I do like to make people feel welcome."

"That's kind," I said. I was about to leave when it occurred to me, she might have done the same thing for Amy. "Do you welcome all new tenants?"

"I try to if I know they're coming, but people don't always tell me. That man below," she said, jabbing the air with her finger, "called me a nosy neighbour. Bloody hypocrite. Sheila Bright, who lives on the ground floor, saw him looking through her balcony window. Eyeing up her smalls, she said."

"Dreadful behaviour," I replied, then moved swiftly on so she didn't dwell on it. "I was looking for my friend, Amy Swanson. But a nice young couple just told me she's moved on."

"I heard that too."

"Did you meet Amy?"

"No. I don't think anybody did."

"I heard otherwise. Apparently, Amy said hello to one of her neighbours the night she arrived."

"Did she? I'm surprised. I must have missed her. How strange. She wasn't there when I spoke to her cleaner."

"Cleaner?"

"Peggy Ramsbottom's daughter. I know her from bingo. Well, she came out of Number 18 and waved at me. I like to sit out here in the evening and watch the world go by, and it proper surprised me when Karen appeared unexpectedly.

So, we chatted about her mum, and she told me she'd come with the movers to clean the flat. Quite a handsome payment she was getting for it too. More than usual, she said."

"What does Karen look like?"

"Petite, brown hair. Got her mother's nose."

"Meaning?"

"Hooked. Why?"

"Well, I wonder if the neighbour saw Amy at all. Perhaps Karen said hello."

"Maybe she did. I don't see why it matters."

"Amy is missing."

"Oh no, my dear. She's just one of those girls who comes and goes at the drop of a hat – the flighty type if you take my drift. Well, she's your friend. I'm sure you understand."

"Her sister hasn't heard from her."

"And I haven't heard from mine in twenty years. Clearly, I'm not good enough." Vera scowled.

"Families are peculiar. Do you know if Cherry is at home?"

"Oh, yes. I saw her carrying groceries upstairs."

"Thank you," I said and reverse-tailed it back to Flat Number 17.

---

I'd been back in the car for twenty minutes when Sean returned wearing a self-satisfied expression.

"You took your time."

"Mission successful," he said smugly.

"What happened?"

"A short run, which, with a bit of luck, will be followed by a long stretch."

"Ha bloody ha. Seriously."

"Robbie made a drop – looks like drugs and a hefty amount at that. I waited until he left and photographed the package. Obviously, I didn't open it but radioed in, and they sent a patrol straight over. They'll wait and see who comes to collect it, but it shouldn't take long. He put it behind a waste bin."

"What about Robbie?"

"The daft git jogged back here. He's probably at home by now and none the wiser."

"Won't they bring him in?"

"Eventually. No need to rush. Robbie's not going anywhere."

"Well. That's it then. Can we go home?"

"Absolutely. Fancy a drink first?"

I considered it. "Go on then."

We drove to The Martingale Arms in Truscombe centre, handily located within walking distance of our homes. Sean ordered a pint of IPA, and I had a gin & tonic. "These are on me," said Sean.

We sat on a comfortable sofa beside an unlit open fire, and Sean regaled me with stories about his previous successful exploits as a private investigator. Sean, relaxed and in good humour, chatted easily. But after a while, he noticed my taciturn responses. "What's up with you?" he asked.

I stalled for a moment, not wanting to spoil the atmosphere, but although I knew Sean would be more receptive to my news in the morning, I couldn't wait any longer.

"I found out something important tonight," I said.

"Yes?"

"About Amy Swanson."

Sean raised his eyes heavenward. "Not now," he said.

"Sorry, but I must tell you."

"Tell me what?"

I swallowed. "I went into the flats while you were chasing Sutherland."

"Oh, for crying out loud."

"Just to look around, you know, get a feel for the place."

"As long as that's all."

"It wasn't. I bumped into a couple of people and chatted about Amy."

"So?"

"So, the neighbour didn't meet Amy Swanson the night she moved in."

"Yes, she did, unless she's changed her mind. It's on record."

"She only thought she met the girl, but she didn't. She met Amy's cleaner."

Sean took a mouthful of beer and leaned forward. "How do you know?"

I recounted my chat with Vera Cavendish and subsequent conversation with Cherry of number 17, which had yielded some surprising results.

"Are you sure?"

"Yes. I asked Cherry about the woman she spoke to, and she gave me a detailed description of Karen Ramsbottom."

"She might have been mistaken."

"What did Amy look like?"

"Short, blonde, slender."

"Well, Karen has dark hair and an aquiline nose."

"Bloody hell. I'll speak to Kim and find out exactly what

they asked the neighbour. They should have double-checked."

"Exactly."

"Still. It changes nothing."

"Of course, it does. Without this, there is no evidence to suggest that Amy ever arrived at Marsh House."

## Chapter Ten

I dreamed about Amy Swanson last night and woke to find the duvet on the floor where I had somehow tossed it off the bed during my restless night's sleep. The alarm went at seven o'clock, and I snoozed it five times before getting up and wandering sleepily to the kitchen to boil the kettle. I opened the fridge only to remember that I had used the last of the milk when I'd returned, slightly woozy, the previous night. Forgoing a shower, I dressed in joggers and a fleece, then braved a quick walk to the corner shop, where I gave into temptation and purchased a croissant one day north of the best before date. I sprinted up the stairs, trying to burn off the croissant calories in advance, and almost ran into a fair-haired man in his early forties carrying an overnight bag. He was a little ahead and turned to face me when he heard my tread, flashing a friendly smile before letting himself into the opposite flat. Much nicer than Kitty Foster, I thought, wondering whether she had told her husband about my unscheduled visit yet.

I made a cup of tea and watched the news while

contemplating the previous night. My revelation about Amy Swanson had put Sean off the idea of extending the evening, and, muttering an excuse about the needs of his geckos, he'd finished his pint and left. Feeling unusually comfortable for an introvert, I had ordered a second gin and stayed for another half hour. But two gins were all it took to feel the effects of the alcohol, and I'd wandered home feeling somewhat worse for wear. Hence the broken night and the several cups of tea. I couldn't concentrate on the news for wondering what would happen next and whether I would still have a job. Our surveillance was over, at least for the time being, and I did not have high expectations of Kim Robbins' approach to finding Amy Swanson. I was considering whether I could do any more alone when I heard a crash and loud shouting.

I leapt from the couch, almost spilling the dregs from my teacup, and wrenched open the front door. The landing was empty, and the sound had abruptly stopped. I loitered for a moment, waiting to see if it would start up again and was on the verge of retreating inside when I heard footsteps from above. I lingered for a while, pretending to pick something from my door mat to avoid looking too much of a nosy neighbour, and when I looked up again, a dark-haired man was smiling at me.

"Ah, you must be...?" He left the words unspoken, and I filled them in.

"Saskia Denman. Pleased to meet you."

"I'm Brendan Marshall, Flat Five. Settled in yet?"

I nodded. "Yes. All unpacked and with a new job, too. Off to a good start."

"Nice one. Well, I'm sure I'll see you around." Brendan headed for the stairwell.

"Hang on a minute. Can I ask you something?"

"Sure."

"Did you hear anything just now?"

"Like what?"

"Shouting. Something metallic dropped on the floor, perhaps? It sounded like a pan."

"No, I didn't, but don't be alarmed. It happens a lot." Brendan nodded towards the Fosters' front door.

"Great. The letting agent didn't mention it."

"It's not a great selling point. Besides, the Fosters are not that bad. They just argue a lot."

"But is Kitty Foster safe?"

"As far as I know. That's an odd question to ask. Why would you think otherwise?"

"Look, have you got a few minutes? I don't want to discuss it outside their house."

"OK," said Brendan. "I can give you five."

He followed me inside, and I didn't wait for him to comment on the smell still lurking in the kitchen, even though the window was now permanently open.

"Drains," I said. "Just ignore it."

He did and followed me through to the living room, expectantly waiting for me to begin.

"I visited the Fosters' flat the other day."

"Lucky you to get an invitation."

"I didn't. The door was open. I'd heard something coming from the flat – a moaning sound. Anyway, I went inside to check it out, and no one was there. Then Kitty Foster came in just as I opened her chest freezer."

Brendan snorted with laughter as if I had just made a joke, but the smile disappeared as he noted the serious expression on my face. "Why would you do that?" he asked.

"Because I couldn't find the source of the noise. I just

thought, well, you know. It was the only place I hadn't looked apart from the bathroom. "

"How did Kitty take your intervention?"

"She completely overreacted. I'd had a domestic violence leaflet delivered that day, and between that and her weird reaction, I wondered if she was OK. She seemed jumpy and very prickly. I thought nothing of it until I saw the leaflet, but then it occurred to me that Kitty would constantly be on edge if their arguments were physical."

"I see what you mean, but I've seen nothing in their behaviour to think it might be true."

Brendan wandered toward the window and peered outside, then turned to face me, looking thoughtful. "I'd never met Lance Foster before he moved here, but my uncle was caretaker at the grammar school and always had plenty of stories to tell. One of his favourites involved a boy called Derek Foster and a bucket full of pigs' guts. A group of boys rigged it up in one of the toilet cubicles, left a trail of coins and slipped a note in Foster's locker telling him to meet a friend there. He fell for it, and when they saw him, the boys pulled a cord and tipped the bucket over, leaving Foster covered in blood and gore."

"What a shitty thing to do."

"Sounds awful, I know. But what if I told you that Foster had pushed one of the boy's brothers into the local pond? The poor kid nearly drowned. And Derek Foster had been stealing his lunch money for months. He'd picked on the boy for no reason, like the big bully he was. And I don't use that word lightly. Uncle Colin said that Foster was a shocking little reprobate who got his just deserts."

"Sounds different when you put it like that."

"Doesn't it just."

"And Derek Foster, is he related to Lance?"

Brendan nodded. "Oh, yes. Derek is, or rather was, his father. He's dead now. And oddly enough, he became a good man in the end. The humiliation of the pig incident had the right effect on him. But you never know, do you?"

"You never do."

"Still, at least he only ended up wearing the pig guts. He didn't marry one," said Brendan bitterly. I chewed my lip, wondering what to say in reply, but Brendan laughed it off. "Sorry, a cheap dig at the soon-to-be ex-wife," he continued.

"Oh, dear. Not amicable?"

"Not fair," he said. "Bloody divorce settlement. The wife gets our house in Charlton Kings, and I have the pleasure of living in a studio flat in the middle of Truscombe."

"Sorry," I said, not knowing the correct etiquette to comfort a perfect stranger publicly airing his dirty laundry.

"Still, you don't want to hear about that," he said perceptively.

"I don't mind," I lied.

"Yeah, thanks. Must go now. Look, I don't think you've got anything to worry about with the Fosters but bang on my door if you hear anything else and you're worried. Alright?"

"I will, and thanks."

"Kitty's a tough old bird," was his parting shot as he left my flat.

I sat quietly for a moment, pondering his words. Derek Foster might be a bully, but it didn't follow that Lance was one, too. And equally, Kitty might be bad-tempered rather than a victim of domestic abuse. But I'd seen more than my fair share of relationship breakdowns while in the RAF, and I didn't like what I'd heard from Flat Four one bit.

The vibrations from a text message received in silent mode interrupted my introspections. I flicked the sound back on and glanced at the screen to see a message from Sean.

*Are you in?*
    Yes, why?
    *Just wondered. How's your head?*
    Fine. Even I can handle two gins, 😊 😊
    *Just came back from the station. I've got nudes.*
    What?!!!!!!
    *FFS, bloody Siri. I've got news.*
    Do you want me to drop by your office?
    *"No need. I'm only a minute or two from yours. I can come over now if you're free.*
    Yep. No worries. I'll put the kettle on.

I zipped back into the kitchen, grabbed a pair of mugs, and spritzed the air freshener around the room. Before long, the buzzer sounded, and I released the door lock. Moments later, it rang again. "What floor are you?" asked Sean.

I told him, opened the front door, and waited while he bounded athletically up the stairs.

"Hey," he said.

"Come in. Through here."

"Nice building," offered Sean.

"Have you been here before?"

"Only to pick up Dhruv. Not very often, though. That reminds me. I'll drop in and see him on the way back. I owe him a fiver, and he wasn't at work this morning."

"I don't suppose he'll miss it," I replied, passing Sean a drink.

"Even so. I hate owing money. More fool me for leaving my wallet at home."

"It's hardly the crime of the century."

"No. But that smell coming from your drains might be."

"Bloody hell, Sean, is it really that bad? What must my neighbours think of me? It's been like Piccadilly junction here for the last few days."

"I bet your visitors didn't stay long."

"I'll have to get the plumber out. I was hoping to avoid the cost."

"I'll take a look if you like. Let me finish my tea first."

"Come through," I said, and Sean reclined on the couch.

"What's the news then?"

"I phoned Kim this morning and told her what you said about Amy Swanson."

"I thought you didn't care. You left rather abruptly last night."

"Did I? I meant nothing by it. Just needed time to process things."

"So, what did Kim say?"

"She swore a lot, then calmed down. But you were right. It sounds like they made assumptions. The neighbour said she'd seen Amy, but nobody bothered showing her a photograph. She'd have known that it was someone else if they had. Kim says they'll send an officer around today to take another statement."

"And after that?"

"It depends what the neighbour reports. But if Amy never turned up at the new flat, they'll need to investigate from the beginning again. It's one thing arriving and taking off, but quite another moving into a new property and never taking possession."

"Fantastic news," I said. "I feel vindicated."

"Hold that thought, but it doesn't resolve matters."

"At least they might start looking, and her poor sister won't feel so helpless."

"Well, I'm impressed, Saskia. It took initiative to discover their mistake. You're hired."

"I thought I was, anyway."

"Well, you're hired again. And this time with a formal contract."

"Where is it?"

"Not written yet, but you'll have it by the end of the week."

"Good. What are we doing next?"

"Nothing for the rest of the day. And you can give me a hand with the admin tomorrow. I know, I know, it's not glamorous. Kim's got something else for us, but not until next week."

"Surveillance?"

"Background checks."

"Oh, good. Much more my thing."

Sean slurped the dregs of his tea. "Let's look at those drains, then."

---

I followed Sean into the kitchen, where he squatted below my sink, removing the few items I had placed below, before examining the u-bend. He stood, ran the tap, looked again, and reported back. "I don't think the drains are your problem," he said.

"Great. I don't know how much longer I can live with the smell."

Sean replaced the items and stood in the middle of the

room, sniffing the air like a bloodhound. "Nah. It's not coming from the sink at all." He spun on his heels and walked toward the kitchen door, then squatting on his haunches, peeled back the cheap linoleum. It came away easily, exposing the floorboards beneath.

"What's that?" I asked, pointing to a discoloured patch about a foot from the door.

"A rotten board," said Sean. "And it's standing proud of the others by a few millimetres. I'm surprised you didn't feel it."

"The floor's bumpy all over," I said. "But beggars can't be choosers. It's a cheap enough rent, so I don't mind the retro feel."

"Have you got a screwdriver?"

"Why?"

"To lever up the board. The smell is coming from below."

"Wait a moment."

I disappeared into my bedroom and rummaged through a bag of bits I hadn't yet found a home for, swiftly locating a large, flat-headed screwdriver. "This should do the trick," I said, handing it to Sean.

"Turn away if you're squeamish," he replied.

"I'm not," I said, but Sean's head was directly in my eye line, and I didn't move away for a better view.

He levered up the floorboard with a grunt.

"Ah, there's the culprit," he said. "A dead rat – must have crawled under the floorboards to die. "Got a plastic bag?"

I pulled one from a drawer and passed it over.

"I'll brew another tea while you're doing that. You deserve it."

"What the...?" Sean sat back on his knees and stared into the hole. "I can't move the bloody thing."

"Do you want me to try?"

"I'm serious, Sass."

"Must be a fair-sized rat."

Sean scowled and tried again.

"Jesus," he said, jumping to his feet and joining me by the kettle, a look of disgust across his face.

"What's wrong?"

"There's a good reason I can't move it. Someone's nailed the bloody thing down."

# Chapter Eleven

I couldn't get out of my flat quickly enough, shocked at the thought that someone had deliberately nailed a dead rat to my kitchen floor. The only saving grace was knowing it couldn't be personal. The smell had been there when I arrived, and whoever nailed the rat must have secured it before I moved in. But why? Who finds a dead rodent and decides that hiding it under the floorboards is the most effective means of disposal?

Sean had asked for a hammer to pry the rat from the board, and I didn't have one. So, I took the opportunity to go downstairs and get out of the way. I knocked on Flat One's door, and Frank Lewis emerged bleary-eyed.

"Hello, my dear," he said.

"Sorry to trouble you, but can I borrow a hammer?"

"What size?"

"Any. I need to remove a nail." I didn't elaborate. It was bad enough that I knew about the rat, but I didn't intend to spread my paranoia elsewhere.

"Of course. Wait here. I loitered on the doorstep as

Frank closed the door, emerging a few moments later with a battered old hammer that had seen better days.

"Thank you. That's perfect." I turned to go back upstairs when Frank stopped me.

"Have you seen Sinbad?" he asked.

"Your cat? No. Not since we last spoke. Why?"

"He's gone missing."

"Oh, no. When did you last see him?"

"Yesterday. I put Sinbad out last night as normal, but he didn't come home. I always leave the kitchen window ajar, whatever the weather, and Sinbad drops in and out as he pleases. But he always comes back for breakfast."

"I'm sure he'll turn up. Do you want me to search outside?"

"That's kind of you, but I'm going out now with a box of his favourite biscuits. If he's around and hears it, Sinbad will come running."

"I'm sure he will. And I'll keep a lookout in the meantime, just in case. I'll bring your hammer back later."

"Leave it by the door, Saskia. I might still be out."

"I will."

I hastened back upstairs and gave the hammer to Sean, who was still looking peaky. Gritting his teeth, he dug in and removed the decaying corpse, dropping it into the carrier bag with a grimace. Then he reached down and faced me, brandishing the nail between his fingers.

"This was right through it."

"No chance it was accidental, then?"

"None at all. It's just weird."

"I don't know what to make of it."

"Nor me. Just forget it, Sass. It's all you can do."

Goosebumps prickled my skin as I tried and failed to dismiss an unwanted vision of someone kneeling in my kitchen hammering a nail into a deceased rodent. "I want to get out of here," I mumbled.

"Me too. I need to see Dhruv. Coming?"

"If you don't mind."

I locked up, and we descended the stairs. Sean knocked on Dhruv's door while I watched Frank Lewis on the front lawn forlornly shaking a box of cat biscuits.

"Perhaps he's not in," said Sean as Dhruv failed to answer.

"Try again."

Sean hammered once more, and this time we heard footsteps and a rattling chain. The door opened a fraction.

"Oh, it's you. Come in."

Dhruv stood in the hallway in boxer shorts and a tee-shirt, his hair tousled and looking as if he hadn't slept for a week.

"Are you OK?" Sean eyed Dhruv quizzically, probably wondering why the usually sharp-dressed man appeared bedraggled and careworn.

"Not really. I've barely slept."

"Why?"

"Mill's in hospital. I was with him most of the night."

"Jesus. I only came to deliver this." Sean withdrew a five-pound note. "Should we go?"

"No. Have a coffee with me. I could do with the company. You too, Sass."

Sean stepped inside, and I followed behind, worried about Dhruv on the one hand but distracted by the condition of his flat. It was different to mine in every way, with a bright, contemporary kitchen, good quality oak flooring and crisply painted walls and architraves. It was hard to believe that we lived in the same building, but now was not the time to enquire about the decor. Dhruv was in bad shape and clearly distressed.

"Take a seat in the lounge. I'll bring your drinks through."

We did as he asked and reclined on a brown leather sofa neatly positioned under the window.

"Looks like you drew the short straw," said Sean, gazing around the immaculate room.

"Is this the first time you've been inside?"

"Yes. Nice, isn't it?"

"I don't understand why this flat is pristine, and the landlord left mine to fester."

"Are you jealous?"

"Of course. Who wouldn't be? But I expect they pay a tonne more rent."

Sean was about to comment further when Dhruv came in bearing a tray of coffee and a biscuit barrel.

"You're lucky. Mill left some chocolate digestives."

"How is he?" I asked as Dhruv sat on a reclining chair in the corner of the room. He pressed a button, and the chair adjusted itself.

"Not good."

"What happened?" Sean leaned forward and gulped from his coffee as if it were his first of the day.

"Sepsis."

"Bloody hell. Will he be alright?"

"I hope so. I love the bloody bones of him."

Dhruv's eyes filled, and he blinked tears away. I didn't know what to say, but Sean took charge.

"He's in the best place. They'll look after him."

"I know. They've pumped Mill full of antibiotics, and he was a much better colour when I left this morning, but the doctor warned it might take a few days to see the full effects.

It kills me when I think of how I found him yesterday, shivering, and delirious. Mill didn't know who I was, and I didn't know what to do for the best. He wanted to stay in bed, and I nearly left him to sleep it off. Mill could have died if I'd listened."

"But you didn't, and he'll be fine," said Sean calmly. "Are you visiting later?"

"Yes." Dhruv checked his watch. "I'll go this evening. He'll have had a full day's rest by then."

"What happened?" asked Sean.

I didn't wait for Dhruv to reply. "Was it his foot?" I asked.

"Yes. He trod on something, and it flared up."

"Poor Mill. I gave him my first aid kit."

"I know. Thank you. I still can't believe how quickly it happened. The infection took hold almost immediately."

"What did he tread on?"

"The doctors asked that, but I don't know. And Mill was too ill to answer."

"We'll leave you to it," said Sean, getting to his feet. "But if you need anything, anything at all, let me know."

"And I'm only a floor away," I offered. "Call in any time."

"Thanks," said Dhruv, following us to the door.

"I mean it," I said, squeezing his hand as we left.

# Chapter Twelve

When I arrived at the office the next day, Sean was shaving in the side room.

"Don't you ever go home?" I asked, walking in to find him shirtless once again.

"Of course. To feed the lizzies."

"Then why not shave there?"

"Old habits die hard. And this way, I get a longer lie in."

"Doesn't your partner mind?"

Sean lowered his razor and grinned. "Stop fishing. If you want to know my relationship status, just ask."

I tried and failed not to blush, frustrated at his arrogance. I didn't give a rat's arse about his dating availability, but the angry red flush on my neck and chest suggested otherwise. "Excuse me for making conversation," I hissed.

Sean smiled smugly. "Not married, no partner, and not currently dating. Probably never will."

"Bad experience?" I asked, hopefully.

His face darkened. I'd hit a nerve.

"Put it this way. I get more pleasure looking after cold-blooded reptiles."

"A bit like my last relationship, then."

"Ah, a fellow cynic. I like it."

Sean passed me a freshly brewed coffee, and I sat at his desk, awaiting further instructions. But instead, he put his feet up and started scrolling through his phone.

"Excuse me. Isn't it an admin day?"

"Yes. But it's only ten to nine."

"I thought you were rushed off your feet."

"I was last week. It's always the same with surveillance when working alone. Sod's law, now that you're here, we've time on our hands and must hang around waiting until Kim sends instructions. Might as well make the most of it."

"Aren't you forgetting something?"

"What?" Sean lowered his phone irritably.

"One, my contract and two, a desk. Perhaps even a phone and if you're feeling particularly generous, a comfy chair."

"All taken care of. I'll bring them up from the basement later."

"The basement? Surely this is the basement. Any lower, and you'd be touching Hell."

"Hilarious. It's over there if you want to look."

Sean pointed to the side room. I walked past the tatty stainless-steel sink, opened a door almost disguised by layers of coats, and descended a couple of steps before finding myself in front of a fire door. Fumbling inside, I located the light switch and entered a surprisingly large and well-organised room. A row of filing cabinets graced the end wall above an array of local maps and whiteboards. Two metal broom cupboards stood next to a pair of matching desks, beside which were a cycle, a moped, and what looked like a metal detector. But for the absence of windows, it would have made a far better office.

"Didn't you believe me?" Sean asked, sidling over.

I ignored him. I hadn't, but it wasn't necessary to say so.

"What do you think?"

"Impressive," I said. "At first glance, your rooms are the poor relations in the building. But this space is useful."

"I thought so too. Come on. Take the end of that desk, and we'll make a start."

"I'm surprised you didn't feel the need for a second desk upstairs, anyway."

"I prefer the space but needs must."

"Charming."

"You're welcome."

I grabbed one side of the nearest desk, and Sean heaved his end off the ground when I heard a sudden knocking.

"Expecting someone?"

Sean frowned. "No. Ignore it, and they'll go away."

"It might be a customer."

"At this time of the morning? Doubtful."

"I'm going to answer it," I said, squeezing past.

"Make up your mind," grumbled Sean as I headed towards the door. He followed, footsteps clumping a few paces behind.

"Wait a moment," I said as someone rapped the door a second time.

"Allow me," said Sean, forging ahead. He arrived before me and wrenched open the door. "How can I help?" he asked.

"Are you open?" A young, brown-haired woman dressed in leathers and carrying a motorcycle helmet stood in the doorway.

"I didn't order anything."

"I'm not a courier."

"I know. It was a joke. Not a very good one, it seems."

"Are you a private detective or a bloody comedian? I can't waste any more time." The woman stood her ground, eyes boring into Sean's, but her downcast eyes and a nervous tic on the side of her mouth belied her apparent self-confidence.

"Sean Tallis, private investigator," said Sean, offering his hand. "This is Saskia."

"Is there somewhere I can put this?" asked the woman, nodding at the helmet.

"Anywhere you can find a space."

She placed it in an alcove by the door, extended her hand and shook Sean's. "I need your help," she said.

"Take a seat."

He showed her to the only spare chair in the office which I had been using. Determined not to stand around looking like a spare part, I darted back to the basement office, grabbed the smartest spiderweb-coated chair, and carried it in. I arrived to find the woman nursing a coffee and preparing to speak and manoeuvred the chair next to Sean, who flashed an intolerant glance.

"First things first. May I ask your name?" he said, taking a printed form and a biro.

"Rachel," said the woman.

"And what can we do for you?"

"Find my sister," she replied.

---

Sean and I glanced at each other, uncertain how to proceed. The next question was obvious, though redundant, but Sean asked it anyway. "Surname?"

"Swanson."

"And your sister?"

"Amy."

"Right." Sean rolled the biro between his hands. It didn't take a mind reader to see that he was deciding whether to mention our current involvement or go in blind. He chose the latter. "And how long has Amy been missing?"

"A while. Amy moved into Marsh House about four months ago and was only there a short time before leaving again. She never returned."

"What makes you think she's missing?"

Rachel Swanson pursed her lips. "She's left all her things."

"How do you know?"

"Because I went to her flat and saw them. Is this necessary? I want to find my sister, and no one seems to care."

"We do," I said, leaning forward and gazing in what I hoped was an empathetic manner. "But it's important to collect all the facts."

"I don't mind that as long as you take me seriously."

"Have you contacted the police?" Sean couldn't look her in the face as he asked, clearly uncomfortable with our deception.

"Yes, for all the good it did. They didn't think Amy was missing at all, and it wasn't until I heard about the rapist living in Marsh House that they started taking me seriously. Now, they're paying lip service, but I'm not stupid. It's only to stop me from making an even bigger fuss."

"Have you spoken to the police lately?" I asked.

"No. I've given up. They said I'd hear something last week, then didn't bother contacting me. My mum is beside herself about Amy. We don't see much of her, and Mum wasn't worried initially. It wouldn't be the first time Amy had moved without saying much about it. But she'd never go off for four months without emailing or texting."

"Has she communicated at all?"

"No. Not a word. Amy's rubbish at keeping in touch, but not to that extent. Mum was so upset when we spoke last night that she said we should go private. You know, hire an investigator. I didn't know where to start, so I switched on the internet late last night and started looking."

"Why me?" asked Sean, uncharacteristically sombre.

"Don't take this the wrong way, but you're the only private investigator in Truscombe. Otherwise, it's Cheltenham or Evesham, and I can't face the journey."

"I don't know," said Sean, considering his options aloud.

"I can pay."

"It's not that."

"Then what? I know Amy wasn't important to anyone else, but we care about her, and she deserves better than this."

"But what do you think we can do that the police can't?" asked Sean.

"I don't know. Whatever you would do if the police weren't involved at all. Do what it says in your literature. Look." Rachel reached into her jacket and jabbed an oily finger into one of Sean's leaflets.

"*Tallis delivered quickly. I dread to think what would have happened without his intervention.* Mr & Mrs J S. What was that? What did you do for them?"

"Do you really want to know?"

"Yes. If you can do it for those people, you can do it for me."

"It was a very different case. They'd hired a nanny and had reason to suspect she was mistreating their child. I carried out some background checks and found nothing sinister. Then, I installed a hidden camera, revealing some disturbing behaviour. Turned out all the nanny's documentation was false. She wasn't who she said she was. More checks revealed her real name, some profound mental health issues, and a list of stalking convictions as long as your arm. If they'd known, the parents wouldn't have left their child with her for a second, much less given her sole charge."

"That's what I mean – background checks and a proper conversation with Amy's employer. Find out what she's been doing for the last year. All the things I asked the police for, but they didn't have the resources to carry out. Or so they said. It's not the first time we've lost someone, and they were useless then. It can't happen to Amy too."

"Rachel. I'll be honest with you. We work with the Truscombe Police Force from time to time."

"So?"

"If we accept your job, there might be a conflict of interest."

"How can that be? Surely you'd both want to find Amy."

"But they may not appreciate our involvement."

"Don't tell them."

"It's not that simple."

"I don't care. How can it be wrong for you to act when the sodding police refuse?"

"Sean?" I'd listened quietly, but I was with Rachel on this. How could it possibly matter?

"I'll do it," he said after a moment's contemplation. But I will tell Kim."

"What if she objects?"

"She shouldn't if we're honest about it. And we can pool information."

"Fine by me." Rachel Swanson retied her hair and slumped back into the chair, looking exhausted. "When can you start?"

"Right away. Sign here," said Sean.

---

"That was unexpected," I said as soon as Rachel left.

"And probably unwise. Kim won't be amused. Especially now she's taking Amy's disappearance more seriously."

"Sorry. No sympathy from me. Kim should have done more in the first place."

"It's not that simple. Not even with the extra information you discovered. We still don't know if Amy is actually missing."

"Come on. Then why did you agree?"

"Because you're probably right," he conceded. "Four months is a long time without contact of any kind. Better to be safe than sorry."

"What now?"

"To the whiteboard, my friend. And some proper policing."

We spent the rest of the day browsing online for information about Amy. Rachel had completed most of the fields on Sean's terms of business, giving us a decent starting point. Amy had dabbled in social media but was not a frequent user. From the little we found, we knew she liked Italian food and open-air concerts and had a small butterfly tattoo on her ankle, which she'd photographed and added to her MyPerfectLife page. Amy didn't own a car but could drive. She was on the electoral roll, though still registered to her old address in Wyegrove Street, and she'd been the subject of a two-star review for chatting on her mobile while leaving a customer waiting. All trivial matters posted before the last sighting of her in February, and none of which helped to locate her.

Next, we drew up a plan of action. One of us would visit Amy's previous employer and talk to the staff, while the other would go to her last known address in Wyegrove Street to see if they'd had any recent contact with her. "Should have already happened," Sean had said. "But let's take a belt and braces approach."

I didn't share his confidence. So far, the Truscombe police had been less than impressive, and it wouldn't surprise me if we already knew more about Amy's life than they did. And what's more, I cared, and they did not. In the end, Sean left an hour before me. It was six thirty before I put the finishing touches to the whiteboard, locked up the office, and headed back to Bosworth House.

# Chapter Thirteen

After several days of hard slog, we'd called it quits on Friday afternoon, ready for the weekend. I had no plans, but Sean was meeting friends for drinks straight from work. His mood had improved as the afternoon went on, obviously keen to socialise after a hard week in the office. But his face hardened following a terse phone call with Kim Robbins, of which I could only hear one side and even then, mostly in grunts.

Sean had finished the call and tossed his mobile carelessly onto the desk.

"She's not amused," he had said.

"Will she work with us?"

"Yes, but reluctantly on the condition that we pool information."

"Will she, though?"

"Time will tell." Sean didn't look convinced, and his mood fell further after receiving a text message. "Bloody hell." He had looked at his watch and sworn again. "Now my delivery is earlier than scheduled. It's not due until tomorrow. I'm supposed to be at Marty's in half an hour."

"I can let them in. I've nothing better to do."

"Really? Would you?"

"Yes, if you give me directions to your house. Oh, and a key."

"How did I manage without you? OK, and we'll call it overtime."

"Fine by me."

Sean had reached into a drawer and retrieved a spare key. "I live at twenty-two Carling Drive. You can't miss the bright blue garage. The door is a little sticky, but you'll be fine if you push it while turning the key. I'll drop by and collect it tomorrow if you're in."

"I will be. Supermarket shopping is the highlight of my weekend, and I can easily put it off until Sunday."

"Sure you don't mind?"

"It's no problem. I'll go now."

I had left the office, glad of something to do but feeling adrift for the first time in a while. The novelty of a new flat and job had started to wane, and loneliness had made another unwelcome appearance. I took stock of my life as I walked past the shops toward the new estate of houses where Sean lived.

After leaving Cyprus, a return to Gloucestershire had felt natural. After all, I had grown up here. But I couldn't face returning to Stroud with all its memories of Mum. Her house was long gone, and my brother Connor had moved to Dublin. My few school friends had moved on with their lives or settled elsewhere, and when the job at Froggatt & Co came up, I had jumped at the chance. Sure, it was in Redditch, a town I didn't know, but it was still close enough to feel familiar. So, I took a flat on the outskirts of Worcester, and after my probationary period, I felt secure enough to move on. I'd cast a wider net looking for rentals, and the flat in Truscombe became unexpectedly available, so I took it and started the referencing process. I hadn't minded the drive from Truscombe to Redditch. It felt good to unwind in the car at the end of a busy day. But just as I started making friends with my colleagues, Curtis Norman made his move, and after the ignominy of my departure, I blocked everyone and refused to answer calls.

So here I was again, uprooted and without friends to drink with on a Friday night. And although it was good to feel useful to Sean, it wasn't nearly as much fun as winding down in The Martingale Arms. I imagined Sean leaning against the bar, quaffing a pint of IPA, and was unprepared for the jolt of envy that followed. I wished he'd invited me, but I didn't know any of his friends, and there was no reason he should feel obliged. Still, it hurt in a way it shouldn't have.

I turned into Carling Drive, a tidy road of modern three and four-bedroom houses, probably only a few years old. Sean wasn't kidding about his garage. The bright blue monstrosity stood out like a cobalt Belisha beacon, and I wondered what the neighbours must think. For a private detective, he sure had a way of making himself stand out. I approached his house, nodded to a dog walker, and meandered up the path, trying to look as if I belonged. Thanks to Sean's instructions, the door opened easily, and I let myself inside.

I squeezed into a small hallway and collected a couple of envelopes lying on the mat. Three doors led off, one to the downstairs loo, which he'd left ajar, another to the kitchen and a closed door, presumably to the lounge. I propped the envelopes against the kitchen counter and examined the room. It was small but tidy, with a breakfast bar along the side wall. The window overlooked a sizeable but bedraggled garden, with a lawn that needed a severe cut and borders running out of control.

I helped myself to a cup of tea, rummaging around the unfamiliar cupboards for a mug, then parked myself in the living room and switched on the television. As Pointless blared in the background, I examined two tanks behind the sofa, containing several very shy geckos peering timidly from the terrarium. Inside the second, were the serpentine features of what appeared to be a corn snake. I grimaced. Sean hadn't mentioned snakes, and I stepped away, repulsed. I couldn't understand the whole caged animal thing generally, but at least birds and hamsters were cute. Lizards and snakes had no redeeming features, and I wondered what Sean got from the strange hobby to which he was clearly dedicated. The tanks were spotless, the occupants healthy, and a row of reptile books dominated the small bookcase by the armchair. And on the wall above the sideboard, someone had painted a watercolour of a lizard family, with intricately displayed markings in shades of fawn and green. But what I saw next to the painting was far more interesting than reptiles. Covered in a faint sheen of dust was a collage of photographs, randomly set into a template. And at the bottom was a wedding picture with a familiar face. Holding hands with his bride, the newlywed groom beamed at the camera. Surrounded by uniformed police colleagues, some very high-ranking, was a smartly dressed Sean Tallis. The same Sean Tallis who claimed he wasn't married. Well, perhaps he wasn't now, but he certainly had been. And I wondered why he'd kept it quiet.

The next day, Sean turned up mid-morning, ringing the door buzzer just as I started washing up. I towelled my hands dry, pressed the door entry system, and he let himself in.

"Any chance of an aspirin?" he asked.

I nodded to a drawer. "Help yourself. I'll make you a coffee when I've finished the dishes. It looks like you need it."

"Thanks. My head's banging."

He quietly stood while I finished my task. Then, grabbing a couple of mugs, I prepared our drinks. "Shall we sit outside? It's too nice to be cooped up in here."

"Whatever," said Sean, following behind and almost walking into Velda as he reached the bottom stair. Velda was hand in hand with a dark-skinned, handsome man who shyly grinned as we passed.

"Morning," I said cheerfully, glad to see that Velda's relationship was going in the right direction and that she'd overcome her embarrassment at living in a studio flat. Her companion beamed. "Good day," he said, flashing a broad smile, then glanced at Velda as if she was the most precious thing in his world.

Sean nodded a greeting, then followed my lead to the rear door, and we sat on one of the garden benches.

"Thanks for last night," he said.

"No trouble. Though you might have told me you'd ordered a tank. The poor delivery guy almost dropped it. Not an easy thing to manoeuvre alone."

"His bad. I booked it for today when I would have been around to help."

"That's the company's fault, not the delivery driver's."

"Whatever."

Sean was taciturn and disagreeable. Temperamentally

unsuited to hangovers, he stared moodily into his tea, and I was relieved when he swigged it back and talked about going home. "Have you got my keys?" he asked.

"Upstairs, in my kitchen. I'll fetch them."

By the time I returned, Sean had disappeared. I checked behind the shed in case he was being nosy and tried the always-locked basement door in case someone had opened it, but it did not budge. Popping my head outside the front door in case Sean had unwisely driven, I checked the road for his car, but it wasn't there, and I couldn't be sure whether he had brought it. I meandered up the short pathway, in case he was waiting further along the road, and spied a pile of cat biscuits at the end of the path. I glanced at Frank's window, but the curtains were drawn, and I hoped he was alright. He would usually be up by now, but Frank hadn't been himself since Sinbad's disappearance and was markedly withdrawn and less cheerful than usual. Making a mental note to ask him if he needed anything from the supermarket before my later visit, I was about to go back inside when a sharp rapping caught me unawares. I glanced towards Dhruv's flat and saw him standing waving. I shrugged my shoulders, and he gestured at me to come inside.

Dhruv was leaning against the wall in the hallway when I entered.

"Sean's over there," he said, jabbing his finger towards his living room.

"Charming. He might have said."

"I saw him waiting in the stairwell and invited him in. Milligan's home."

"Fantastic. How is he?"

"Much better. Come inside, and he'll tell you himself."

I entered the living room to see Sean reclining on the

couch, making polite conversation with Milligan, who was lying down, covered by a blanket. Pale-faced and gaunt, he looked as if he should still be in hospital and was obviously far from well.

"Can I get you anything?" asked Dhruv, sitting beside him.

"For the millionth time, no. I'm fine." Mill flashed a weak smile but looked exhausted.

"When did you get out?" I asked.

"Yesterday evening. The doctor wanted me to stay, but I couldn't face another sleepless night. God, it's awful in there."

"They saved your life," said Dhruv quietly.

"I know. And the nurses were great. It's just not a nice place to be. I'll get better more quickly at home."

"How's your foot?"

"It looks a bloody mess, but I'm not in pain."

"And all that from stubbing your toe," said Sean.

"No, I trod on a nail or something. That reminds me, Dhruv. Have you vacuumed?"

"No. I've been too busy worrying about you. Housework is a low priority. Don't think about it."

"I'm not. I don't care whether the house is tidy, but I couldn't find the nail, and I don't want to step on it again."

"Where did it happen?"

"Somewhere between the bedroom and the bathroom," said Mill as a bleeping sound interrupted him. Dhruv checked his watch and switched off an alarm.

"Time for your drugs," he said.

"I'll look for the nail while you deal with that." Sean rose and walked towards the bedroom, leaving me sitting with Milligan, wondering what to say. But Dhruv returned before the silence became awkward, bearing a glass of water and an egg cup. "Take these."

"We'll leave when Sean's finished," I said, watching Milligan's eyes flutter as he fought to stay awake.

"Don't go on my account. Dhruv will appreciate having someone to talk to. You won't mind if I drop off, though?"

"Of course not."

"Sass. Come here." Sean's voice bellowed from further down the hallway.

"Excuse me," I said as Dhruv passed a magazine to Milligan.

I turned the corner to find Sean kneeling in the hallway opposite the bathroom door.

"What is it?"

"I need your screwdriver."

"Ask Dhruv. He's bound to have one."

"I'd rather not draw his attention to this. At least not until I'm certain."

"What's wrong?" I asked, peering down but seeing nothing except a sizeable, patterned floor runner.

"The screwdriver. Quickly, please."

My hackles rose at his overbearing tone, but the worried frown on his face stopped me from snapping back.

"Give me five."

I quietly left the flat, keeping the door ajar, and climbed the stairs two at a time. The screwdriver was in my kitchen drawer where Sean had put it after the rat incident, and I grabbed it and headed straight back. Dhruv didn't hear as I quietly closed the door and returned to Sean, who reached for the screwdriver.

"Watch," he said. "And don't touch."

Sean peeled back the runner as I knelt to one side and

ran his fingers along the carpet tape. "It's barely sticky," he said. "Someone has taken this up at least once."

"So?"

"There." Sean pointed to a knot in the floorboard. I squatted over to see the glint of something metallic below.

"That's good. The nail must have fallen in the hole. No risk of Mill stepping on it again."

"Look closer."

I peered down but couldn't see what he was getting at. Sighing, Sean dug the flat-headed screwdriver into the floorboard and eased it free until it sat a few millimetres proud of the floor. "Does it look familiar now?"

"Someone's cut the board, just like mine."

"Exactly. It's hard to tell when it's flush to the floor, but there's a small panel in this floorboard, too."

"Why?"

Sean grimaced. "I have my suspicions, but let's find out." He levered the panel until it popped off, and we peered below to see a nail standing vertically beneath the knot hole.

"What on earth?" I reached out to touch it, but Sean roughly knocked my hand away.

"I said, don't touch," he hissed.

"Is everything OK?" yelled Dhruv from the living room as I sat back on my haunches.

"Fine," bellowed Sean. "I think I've found it. Give me a minute longer."

"No worries."

"Hold this," said Sean, handing me the screwdriver. He reached into his pocket, removed a folded handkerchief, then wrapped it around the nail and pulled. His hand jerked up suddenly as his brows creased.

"What is it?"

"A booby trap," said Sean.

"No, seriously."

"I mean it. Watch."

Sliding the handkerchief higher up the nail, Sean pulled it to reveal a simple mechanism below, which clicked upright as he moved it slightly left. Then he replaced the floorboard. The nail now stood several millimetres above the hole, but when Sean rolled back the carpet, it hid the sharp point. "Mill wouldn't have seen this until he trod on it," said Sean.

"You think it was deliberate?"

"Totally. Someone manufactured this, Sass. It's like a home version of Punji sticks. They went to a great deal of trouble."

"To what end? Mill was unlucky to end up in the hospital. He could just as easily have nothing more to show for it than a cut on his foot."

Sean opened his handkerchief and held it towards me. Grime covered the recently laundered white linen. I leaned forward for a better look, but the smell hit me first.

Sean nodded. "Before you ask, yes. It's probably shit and certain to cause an infection."

"Disgusting and deliberate. What the hell has Milligan done to deserve this?"

"Or Dhruv."

"We'd better tell them." I moved to go, but Sean grabbed my arm.

"No," he said before lifting the floorboard again. "We can't talk here. Wait while I disable it."

Sean took the screwdriver and removed the locking device, holding the nail to the floor. Then he returned the floorboard and rug to their original positions, stamping down the corner where the carpet tape had worn away.

"Did you find it?" asked Dhruv as we entered the living room.

"Yep, and binned the little bugger," said Sean. Milligan had fallen asleep, and Dhruv was quietly stroking his hair.

"Thanks, Sean," whispered Dhruv. "Saves me a job."

"Better leave you and Mill to it. Shout if you need anything." I flashed Dhruv a guilty smile as we left the room, still unsure why Sean was being so secretive.

"Why didn't you tell him?" I asked, shutting the door to Dhruv's flat.

"Not here. Walk with me to the end of the road."

Sean waited until we were clear of the building before continuing. "How many keys to the flat?" he asked.

"I don't know. One for Dhruv and Mill and another for the letting agent, I guess."

"And the landlord."

"Probably. But that's it."

"Not good. Anyone could get inside."

"Yes, but why would they?"

"Why is for another time. We should focus on how and who. The letting agency can allow anyone access, including staff and contractors, right?"

"Well, yes. But isn't that all the more reason to tell Dhruv?"

"What if Dhruv laid the trap?"

"Oh, come on. He loves Mill. You can't seriously believe that?"

"I don't. Not at all, but something odd is going on, Sass. Better to keep it to ourselves, for now."

We reached the corner shop, and Sean stopped. "Want anything?" he asked. "I'm starving."

"I'm fine. I'll wait outside." My tone was abrupt. I didn't like Sean's implications about Dhruv. Swallowing my annoyance, I approached a golden retriever waiting patiently for his owner and was still stroking him when Sean emerged moments later with his phone clasped to his head. I stood up, but Sean gestured for me to stay put, and I waited until the dog's owner arrived before catching up with him. Sean was leaning against a tree on the other side of the road and speaking animatedly.

"Yes, but why?" he asked.

I heard a buzz of noise from the other end – no words but the sharp staccato sound of an excitable raised voice.

"It means nothing." Sean was scowling, irritated. "Calm down, Rachel. It may not be worth worrying. He looked at his watch, then up at the sky.

"I hear you. OK, I'll try to catch up with Tom if he's on duty. He'll know more. Yes, yes. I'll call you straight back."

"Who was that?" I asked.

"Rachel Swanson. Have you got to be somewhere?"

"Only the supermarket."

"Then wait for a moment. I need to make a call."

"Why?"

"Because that slimeball reporter has just called Rachel Swanson, asking for her comments about the police presence at Crossways Farm."

"What police presence?"

"Exactly."

## Chapter Fourteen

Tom had not been forthcoming at the start of their conversation. But Sean was persistent, and they had been friends for a long time. Eventually, Tom buckled, giving Sean just enough information to confirm that the reporter was onto something. Kim Robbins and her team had responded to an early morning phone call, and the forensics team was on their way. And without realising it, Tom had accidentally revealed the location, which was not the busy Crossways farm, but a long-abandoned building in the middle of nowhere.

"We played there as kids," said Sean. "Must be the same place they're describing. I don't know any other dilapidated farms around here."

He sped along the winding country lanes, pausing only to cable his phone to Car Play so he could contact Rachel, murmur platitudes, and try to reassure her while knowing little about the incident unfolding ahead of us. But after more promises to keep in touch, he ended the call.

"Careful," I said, as Sean lost concentration and skimmed a verge after dropping the phone in his lap.

"Don't worry. You're perfectly safe."

Sean drove on with his face set determinedly. I couldn't work out what was going through his mind, and he didn't enlighten me. I was still trying to process his earlier comments about the trap in Dhruv's hallway. My stomach clenched with nerves, and I felt sick at the thought. First, the dead rat and now this. It was almost a relief to be outside the flat, driving like a bat out of hell towards something distracting.

The roads became tracks, narrowing as we drove deeper into the countryside, and after a while, Sean pointed ahead.

"Yes, something's definitely going on," he said.

Three marked cars and several civilian vehicles had parked haphazardly further up the lane. Sean immediately pulled over and parked out of sight.

"I'll leave it here. We stand a better chance of getting a closer look if they don't know we're coming."

We exited the car, and I followed Sean into a nearby field, glad I'd thrown on a pair of trainers. We climbed a stile and headed towards the farm before noticing a white tarpaulin in the distance.

"Jesus," said Sean. "Looks like forensics is already there. They must have found something."

"But how did the journalist know?"

"Loose lips," said Sean. "Over-sharing was a problem when I was still serving. We had an uneasy relationship with Miles Savage, especially after Mike Robbins died, but the press can be useful, and some officers don't know where to draw a line. It sounds as if they sent Savage to the wrong location, though. Crossways is on the other side of town."

"A good move then," I agreed as we reached the

outskirts of the farm where police officers, uniformed and otherwise, were waiting outside a newly erected tent. There could only be one reason the reporter reached out to Rachel Swanson, and I hoped it wasn't because Amy was lying dead beneath the tarp.

"Come on then," said Sean, and I followed him towards the farm buildings. Sean swaggered purposefully, and we almost reached the tent before a burly police officer stopped us.

"Stay back," he said curtly.

"Is Kim here?"

"Why? Who are you?"

"Just answer the question."

"I'm telling you to stay where you are," he ordered.

The tent opened, and a slim woman dressed in a white scene suit appeared. Pushing her fringe away with a gloved hand, she shook her head. "What the fuck are you doing here?"

"Acting on behalf of my client."

"Who knows nothing about this."

"And yet she phoned me. Strange old world, isn't it?"

"That's not funny, Sean. Nobody knows we're here."

"Except Miles Savage, who has already asked my client to comment."

"Jesus Christ on a bike."

"What's going on?"

"I can't tell you, and you know it. Now get behind the line and stop contaminating my crime scene."

"Shall I move him along?" The burly police officer fingered a flashlight as if he would like to weaponize it, but Kim ignored him and faced Sean.

"This way," she said, pointing beyond the cordon toward the field. I followed behind.

"Who's under the tarp?" asked Sean.

"You know very well that we can't be sure at this stage."

"Male or female?"

Kim Robbins didn't move a muscle but stared him down.

"Female then?"

"You can keep guessing all day long."

"So much for pooling information."

"You know how it works, Sean."

"I tell you what I know," snapped Sean. "Miles Savage put the fear of God into Rachel Swanson earlier today, and she called me to find out more. The station must be leaking like a sieve if he knows, yet you haven't had the decency to contact Rachel to warn her. I am here as her agent, and it will be a bloody shame if the only way I can get any further information is to tell Savage where the action is and hope he throws a few bones my way. Poor form, Kim. It's a bit of a shit show."

"Alright. Keep it down." Kim glared at Sean as the anger burned in his face. "I don't want the world knowing about the press problem."

"Then shut it down. God knows you've suffered enough by it."

"I don't know where it comes from, and I'm not discussing it now. You know I have an arrangement with Tom, and he stays inside the lines. It's someone else. Look, I'll give you bare bones, and then you can both sod off. I mean it."

"Agreed."

"Female, white, probably young and reasonably well preserved."

"Can't be Amy then," said Sean. A wave of relief washed over me as I watched his face relax. Amy had been gone long enough that any corpse described as well-preserved was unlikely to be hers.

"Not so quick," said Kim. "The girl was in a freezer."

"Shit."

"We've owned the scene, and we'll take her away in the appliance. No point in contaminating the body. But we won't know more until the autopsy."

"Can't be any power out here, though." Kim stared at me as if she had forgotten I was there.

"Of course not."

"Could someone chill the body before dumping it?"

"As I said, we won't know anything until after the post-mortem."

"Then it could be Amy?"

Kim Robbins raised her eyebrow. Then, with a barely perceptible movement, she nodded her head.

## Chapter Fifteen

Sunday came and went without a word from Sean, and I arrived at the office early on Monday morning, half expecting him to be there. Fortunately, he'd cut me a spare key a few days before, and I let myself in, washed the dirty cups and set the coffee machine to percolate. I busied myself tidying, then updated the whiteboard and had lost myself in the filing before realising that it was after nine o'clock and still Sean hadn't appeared. I called him at half-past nine, but the phone rang out. So, increasingly worried and running out of things to do, I called again. This time, he answered.

"It's Sass. Where are you?"

"Sorry, I can't talk now, but I won't be long."

"How long?" An irritating banging noise sounded in the background.

"Say again?"

"I said, how long?"

"An hour or so. Gotta go. See you later."

I sighed, went back to reorganising files, and the

morning slipped away. Sean finally arrived a little after midday, with a sombre expression on his face.

"Here," he said, handing me a pumpkin latte and a doughnut.

"No, thanks."

"Seriously?"

"I appreciate the sentiment, but the thought of either of those items in my mouth makes my teeth curl."

"Shame to waste it," said Sean, swigging the rest of his drink and starting on mine. He put the doughnut beside a packet of biscuits near the coffee machine and sat down, looking apprehensive.

"Where have you been?" I was curious but conscious of sounding like a mistrustful girlfriend.

"Waiting for Kim outside the mortuary. Thought it was the best way of keeping up to date."

"How did you know she'd be there?"

Sean tapped his nose. "I have my sources."

"Did she tell you anything?"

He sighed. "More than she should have. I caught her at a vulnerable moment. That's why I've been longer than I said. We went for a walk."

"Rather informal," I said, shaking my head. I disliked Kim Robbins, and it was hard to hide my feelings.

"You'll understand why in a minute."

Sean emptied his pockets on the table, searching until he located a tiny key that he used to unlock his desk drawer. "Ah, there it is. Good." He tossed another smaller key onto the desk and slammed the drawer shut.

I raised an eyebrow.

"Key to the large filing cabinet," he said. "We'll be busy digging out archives in the basement for the rest of the day."

"What's going on?"

"It's definitely Amy," said Sean.

"Are you sure?"

"Yes. The pathologist confirmed it, and the police contacted Rachel yesterday once they tidied up the corpse. It was in good nick – far too good, in fact. Amy's body had been refrigerated. Rachel came to the station and identified her."

"Damn. Poor girl. She must be devastated."

"I guess so, but I haven't spoken with her since Saturday."

"That must have been a tricky conversation. What did you tell her?"

"To get down to the police station. It's all I could do. Kim took it from there."

"What now?"

"A press conference later today."

"I mean for us?"

"That depends on Rachel. But things have changed, and the police are on fully board, Kim especially."

"Why? She didn't care about Amy before."

"It's just her way, Sass. But she does now, and with good reason. Listen, I'm about to tell you something that is strictly confidential. Understand?"

"Of course. You know my background."

"Sorry. But like I said, Kim was in a bad place. She wouldn't have told me this under any other circumstances, and I know her well enough to be certain she already regrets it."

I waited for Sean to continue, but he opened the latte lid, stirred it, and drained the cup as if biding his time.

"Well?"

"According to the pathologist, Amy suffered a blunt

force wound to her skull before being throttled. The ligature was still around her neck, with petechial haemorrhaging in her eyes. No doubt about the way she died."

"I suppose it reminded Kim of her father," I said, softening a little.

"Possibly, but that wasn't the worst of it. Whoever killed Amy had skinned her leg to the bone."

My stomach clenched as the words hit their mark, and I felt light-headed for a moment. "Are you suggesting…?" I asked, unable to finish the sentence.

"Not me," said Sean. "But it's knocked Kim for six. Far too close to the case that finished her father. After all these years, it can't be the same killer, but it's reignited all the terrible memories of her dad's death."

"What sick pervert strips the flesh from a dead girl? And can I assume she was dead when it happened?"

"I don't know," said Sean. "And neither do they. It must be a copycat killer, but even so. The press will have a field day. You wait until next week. Every headline will scream about the Skin Thief."

# Chapter Sixteen

Sean shut the office at four o'clock, allegedly to clean his lizards but more likely to do some damage to the bottle of whiskey I'd seen on his kitchen counter a few days earlier. He'd vacillated between bouts of silence and poor attempts at humour, with his mind elsewhere, likely on Kim. Theirs was a strange and strained relationship, having been close colleagues and friends, but now necessarily with a gulf between them. He'd known Kim at her most vulnerable, and whatever she had said to him had nested in his thoughts and settled there.

Halfway through the day, Sean telephoned Rachel, and I heard her uncontrollable sobs from the other side of the desk. He'd offered Rachel our condolences but said little else. The worst had happened, and nothing we could do would make it better. Rachel ended the call, saying she would be in touch, perhaps feeling that there was still unfinished business between us. After all, she'd made no secret of her distrust of the police.

I meandered home via the corner store, unable to face

the thought of cooking, where I purchased a microwave meal on special offer. But I wasn't hungry, and, having waited fruitlessly for my appetite to arrive, I gave up, sat in front of the television, and watched an episode of Pointless instead. But I couldn't concentrate. My skin prickled at the thought of Amy's last moments on earth and the horror she must have faced. Only an increasing feeling of nausea from an empty stomach made me rise and blast my meal in the microwave, hoping that it would stop me from feeling sick. But it tasted like cardboard, and I forced myself to finish it. I had just thrown the carton in the bin when I heard a rap at my door. In no mood for visitors, I sighed, tiptoed to the spy hole, and peered through to see Velda standing on my doormat.

"Wait a moment," I said, unlatching the safety chain. Velda stepped inside without being asked, her eyes flitting from side to side mistrustfully.

"Are you OK?" She clearly wasn't, but I didn't know what else to say.

"No, I'm not. I knew it was too good to be true." Velda's face crumpled, and a tear trickled down her cheek.

"What's wrong? Do you want a cup of tea? Or wine?"

"No, nothing," said Velda. "I'm sorry to bother you, but I need company. Mum's at bingo, Angela's just left, and the thought of taking her advice makes me even more miserable."

"Slow down. Come through and tell me all about it."

Velda slumped onto the sofa and put her head in her hands. "I really liked him," she said.

"Your boyfriend?"

"Yes. Ben."

"What has he done?"

"Nothing. He's lovely. Ben couldn't be more attentive. I

know it's only been a week, but I've seen him almost every night. I've been so happy, and I should have known better. Nothing is ever as it seems."

I waited for her to elaborate, and her lip trembled. "I feel so foolish."

"Why?"

"Because I invited Ben into my home when he's little more than a stranger. I haven't met his family and only a few of his friends. I wonder if they know."

"Know what?"

"That he's on a list," Velda whispered, her face reddening with shame.

"What sort of list?"

"I can't say it."

"Please."

"Look. I'll show you." Velda rummaged in her bag and withdrew a crumpled envelope. "Read this," she said.

I took it from her, noting the typewritten envelope addressed to 'The Occupant of Flat Six'. "Looks like a circular," I said.

Velda shook her head.

I unfolded the paper and scanned it, feeling sick at the sight of the words inside. Benjamin Adjaye is on the sex offender's register. Keep your distance. A friend.

"That's terrible."

"I know. I can't believe it."

"I don't believe it. It's unsigned and lacking credibility."

"But that's his name."

"I daresay. But anyone genuinely concerned for your safety wouldn't send an anonymous letter. This is out-and-out troublemaking."

"Why would someone want to hurt me?"

"They're hurting him more. It's a terrible accusation – awful for his reputation. Where does Ben work?"

"At the hospital."

"Poor chap. An accusation like this could cost him his career. What are you going to do about it?"

"Angela says I should walk away."

"Angela?"

"My best friend."

"She believes this accusation, then?"

Velda nodded. "It's more that she doesn't think it's worth the risk. Angela had an awful experience with a stalker. And you know what it's like living alone. I don't want to be worrying about the man I'm dating when I'm on my own late at night."

"Have you spoken to Ben?"

"No. I don't know what to say, and he is bound to deny it."

"I think you should."

"I wouldn't know how to tell him. There must be another way. Where can I see these records?"

"You can't," I said. "The public can't access the sex offender's list online."

"Then, that's it. Oh, God, Saskia. What would you do?"

"It's different for me. I'm a private investigator."

Velda's eyes widened. "Really? You didn't say."

"I've only just taken the job, but I was a military policewoman for a long time. Background checks are right up my street. Leave this with me, and don't take any chances in the meantime."

---

Velda left, and I ushered her to the front door, then walked her upstairs. She didn't invite me in, and I was relieved. I'd been blinking away rainbow auras for the previous five minutes, and a full-on visual migraine was threatening to erupt. But being on her building level gave me a view of the second floor for the first time since I'd moved in. Velda's apartment was opposite Brendan's, but a third door at the end of their small landing came as a surprise. As soon as Velda disappeared, I risked a brief delay in finding the painkillers in my medicine cabinet that ought to see the migraine off. I knew I should take them immediately, but I couldn't resist the opportunity to investigate the door directly in front of me. It would only take a moment.

I pushed the white-painted door, which opened to a tiny inner landing with a narrow wooden staircase rising above. As I climbed the stairs to the loft room, I tried to assess its size and concluded that it must run the entire building's length. From a distance, the door looked inaccessible and did not move when I tried the handle. Someone had firmly locked it. Disappointed, I retreated. I'd been hoping that the loft space contained communal storage to house the packing crates I'd saved in the event of another move. I'd now need to disassemble them unless I could find the key holder and stake my claim to some attic storage. But my temples were throbbing and now was not the time. I headed for home, but as I arrived at my front door, keys jingled in the opposite lock, and I almost ran into Kitty Foster as she emerged from her flat.

"Hello," I said, caught off-guard.

Kitty forced a smile but said nothing and turned towards the stairs.

"Please wait." The words were out before I had considered what to say next.

"Yes. What is it?" Kitty raised a pencilled eyebrow.

"I'm sorry about earlier. It was a genuine mistake."

"I'm sorry too. I was in a bad mood, and you took the brunt of it."

"Good. I mean, not that you were in a bad mood, but that we've cleared the air. Perhaps you'll drop around for a coffee sometime?"

I don't know what possessed me to make the invitation. Chatting with Velda was easy, but I couldn't imagine a conversation with Kitty being anything but strained.

"Perhaps, if time allows, though I usually work during the day."

"Me too. But evening's fine."

"I'll let you know."

"Good. I'll look forward to it."

Kitty smiled, this time showing her teeth, but the smile slid away as she heard an earring tinkle to the floor.

"Let me," I said, reaching for it as Kitty squatted down to search. I got there first and passed the earring to her. But as she stood sliding the gold stud into her ear and clipping the fastener onto the stem, she brushed off a layer of make-up, revealing an angry, livid welt.

My mouth fell open in undisguised horror, and she quickly rearranged her hair to cover the mark before turning to go.

I grabbed her shoulder. "Is everything alright at home, Kitty?"

"None of your business," she said gruffly, and I caught a glimpse of bruising on her knuckles. I gently took her right hand and turned it over to reveal deep gouges on her wrist.

"What happened to you?"

Kitty's mouth set in a firm line. She snatched her hand away, saying nothing.

"I can help. You only need to ask. Is it Lance? Has your husband hurt you?"

Her eyes filled as she turned away, wordlessly descending the stairs with her head bowed. And my heart ached that she should feel ashamed of her wounds. And then, with a shiver of fear, visions of Amy Swanson frozen in death flashed through my head, evoking memories of my ill-fated visit to the Foster's flat. The noises, the groans, opening the wardrobe door to find an incongruously placed chest freezer. The flashing aura pulsed in my eyes as the first stabs of migraine tore through my head. I staggered through my door, put a pillow over my head, and slept.

## Chapter Seventeen

"Bloody hell, you look awful." Sean looked up as I entered the office, swigging from a super green smoothie I'd bought, hoping it would taste better than it looked. It didn't, but a twelve-hour migraine had left me low on energy, and however much it looked like someone had shoved Kermit in a blender, it could only help.

"Are you ill?" Sean tried again, unsuccessfully disguising a glance at his watch.

"Sorry, I'm late," I muttered before he had a chance to mention it.

"Should you even be here?"

"It's only a migraine; the worst of it is over. I'm just tired."

"Go home and sleep it off."

"I already did, and I'm fine."

"Have you eaten?"

"Not sure I could."

"Do it. Or you'll scare the customers." Sean tossed a

half-eaten packet of chocolate digestives onto my desk, and I reluctantly took one and nibbled it half-heartedly.

"You look different."

"No make-up. And no need to go on about it."

"Ah." Sean smiled as if he had just completed the Telegraph Cryptic crossword. I finished the smoothie, scrunched the bottle, and dropped it in the bin. It bounced off an intact file hastily disposed of with little thought.

"GDPR?" I offered.

"I am perfectly au fait with data protection requirements," said Sean. "Open it."

I pulled it onto my lap and looked inside to find a bundle of old newspapers. "Fair enough. But what were you looking for?"

"Some older papers in here," said Sean, pointing to a cardboard box marked porridge oats which he'd shoved by the side of his desk.

"Go on?"

"Coverage of the Skin Thief."

"Interesting. Weren't you still at school when he was at large?"

"College, actually," said Sean. "They're not original newspapers, but archived copies borrowed a few years ago while we worked a cold case."

"Another murder?"

"No. A Misper. Not mine. I was still in uniform then and not directly involved, but I wound up pulling the records from the press archives for reasons that escape me now. Not sure why I kept them. Must have stored them at home, or Callie did. Anyway. I thought I'd take another look."

"Callie?"

Sean scowled and turned away, peeled a newspaper

from the bundle and tossed it towards me. I caught it before it hit the desk.

"Nice move," said Sean.

"What's this in aid of? Are you still sold on the idea of a copycat killer?"

"Perhaps, although it might still be a coincidence."

"Doubtful. How many killers' worldwide skin their victims, let alone in England?"

"I know. But it doesn't do any harm to consider all possibilities."

"Who's Callie?" I wasn't going to let it go.

"It's a long story. I'll tell you about it over a beer sometime."

"I'll hold you to that."

"Now concentrate," said Sean, swiftly changing the subject. "You take one half, and I'll take the other. Read through and tell me what you think. I'd ask Kim for access to the official files, but I can't see her agreeing. Don't take it too seriously, though. Too much journalistic licence."

"OK. Will do. But I'm going to run a quick background check first if you don't mind."

"On whom?"

"A chap called Benjamin Adjaye. Nothing to do with the case. You remember Velda in the top flat?"

"No. Should I?"

"We passed her on the stairs, and her boyfriend said hello."

"Ah yes, a tall chap, friendly."

"And also, a potential pervert." I quickly relayed the gist of the conversation I'd had with Velda the previous night.

"OK. Go ahead. Tap up, Tom. He'll be able to help."

"Really? He doesn't know me."

"Then befriend him. Tom's useful and understands the

grey areas between police confidentiality and sharing information. He might be young, but he gets it. If you're honest with him, he'll tell you as much as you need to know. Here, take this." Sean reached into his drawer, rifled through a large box of business cards, and tossed one onto my desk. "Call his mobile. Don't leave any indiscreet messages."

"Copy that."

Sean took half the newspapers, opened one, and spread it across the desk. Then, leaning over, he ran his index finger down the page, looking for articles about the Skin Thief. Something stopped him in mid-track, and he looked up quizzically.

"Velda, too," he muttered.

"Sorry?"

"Someone nailed a rat to your floor, booby-trapped Dhruv's flat, and now Velda gets a modern-day poison pen letter. Doesn't that worry you?"

"I'm trying not to think about it. The whole thing gives me the creeps."

"No need for that. It isn't sinister, but if I had to take a punt, I'd say someone was trying to get you to leave."

"Don't, Sean. I suffer from nightmares as it is."

"I'm not trying to frighten you. Think about it. That's some weird shit, Sass. And it happened to three of the six Bosworth House occupants within a few days. It can't be a coincidence."

"Four, actually," I said, feeling nauseous.

"What?"

"Sinbad's missing."

"Come again?"

"Frank's cat. He went out a few days ago and hasn't returned."

"See what I mean? How about the other flats?"

"No problems for Brendan, as far as I know. And from what I can tell, Kitty Foster has DV issues. Her husband seems nice enough on the surface, but she was covered in bruises when I saw her last night."

"That's between them," said Sean. "Not really what we're looking for."

"Be honest, Sean. Should I be worried?"

"Not about your safety. Why would anyone deliberately harm you? Nobody knew you until recently. Am I right in saying that the Bosworth House flats are rented rather than owned?"

I nodded.

"Through the same agent?"

"I think so."

"Can they easily evict you?"

"Yes, but it would take time. I've signed a six-month lease, but Dhruv recently renewed for another three years."

"Before or after these incidents?"

"Must be before. A while before."

"Then, the problems might be property related. I'd have a chat with the letting agent if I were you. Perhaps check in with Dhruv first. Sounds like he's been there a while."

"The longest of everyone," I said. "He mentioned it the other day. I will ask them, Sean. But surely you don't think the agent is involved?"

"No. They are professionals. But ask about the landlord. You have a right to know. It should be on your contract. Why don't you pop into the office and tell them you think someone entered the building without authority? See what they have to say."

I nodded, relieved at the thought of a commercial reason for the peculiar recent events. I had just finished setting the alarm on my phone to remind me to visit Bayliss and Finch after work when Sean looked up from his paper and loudly clicked his fingers.

"Irene Paige," he said.

"Who?"

"The Misper. Irene Paige. She disappeared ten years ago, give or take a month or two – simply vanished without a trace. There was no sign that she'd come to any harm, but we went back over all the unsolved local murders, just in case. I can't think why Callie gave credence to the press reports, but she did. Anyway. I'm glad I remembered. I hate a mystery."

"Can I see the article?"

"If you want."

I took the newspaper and read the short report.

*Concerns grow for missing Truscombe woman Irene Gladys Paige, aged 71, from Sunningdale Gardens. Last seen leaving the library over a month ago, Mrs Paige wore black trousers and an olive-green top on the day she disappeared. Described as younger than her years, Mrs Paige, a retired teacher, is physically fit and has a distinctive mole on the left-hand side of her neck. When asked to comment, her daughter, Laura Jones, said her disappearance was completely out of character, and she feared for her safety.*

"You said they never found her?"

"That's right."

"Were there any clues?"

"None. But don't worry about it. The point is, we have the newspapers to hand because of her disappearance."

"It's hard to believe that someone can vanish completely in this day and age."

"Get used to it. I could show you statistics that would make your hair curl. But that's for another time. Read through those papers and tell me what you think."

# Chapter Eighteen

*Schooldays are the best of your life, or so Aunt Dora repeated verbatim on the rare occasions I tried to tell her about my nightmare existence in the hands of adults who should have known better. She wasn't cruel, just stupid – never listening and assuming I didn't understand how the world worked because I was young. Grit your teeth and get on with it was another of her favourite expressions. Oh, if only she knew. But she couldn't see what was in front of her nose. And she didn't care to check when even the most cursory examination would have revealed unexplained bruising, torn clothes, and damaged skin.*

*Miss Devonshire singled me out within days of my arrival, already delayed by two weeks while recovering from glandular fever. An untimely absence in a new school year during which my peers might have accepted me had I been with them from the outset. I arrived to find them settled in pairs, with friendship groups formed, bonds already unbreakable. I turned up, timidly carrying a tartan shopping bag which Aunt Dora had insisted I take – unfashionable, not cool – my cheeks burning as I listened to unsubtle sniggers from the back of · the classroom.*

*The only spare desks were at the front, and I sat alone with an empty chair beside me. In between classes, I read in the playground after trying but failing to find a companion. I never learned why I didn't fit in. I looked the same as the others, spoke the way they did, and lived close to them, yet I was an outcast. Something about me made them recoil – a sixth sense, a fear – a tacit decision to retreat from my attempts at friendship. And when Miss Devonshire suggested I sit in the library after finding me alone, yet again, on the steps by the English room, I thought she was being kind.*

*I did as she suggested and didn't feel so alone, especially when Mr Caldicot took an interest in me. Caldicot was the Science teacher, and I'd overheard the others say that he was Miss Devonshire's much older boyfriend, and I thought, perhaps, that she'd asked him to look after a lonely teenager. She had, and he did. And for a few weeks, I felt special. I didn't have friends, but I wasn't entirely alone.*

*Then one day, Mr Caldicot invited me into his office. And what he did to me there was the stuff of nightmares. Gone was the benign, mild-mannered teacher. It was as if he'd removed his skin and revealed a monster inside. He'd shown me into his room, ostensibly to see a map of the world. I can't remember why – some foolish question I'd asked about geography, I suppose. He pointed to a globe positioned by the side of his desk, and as I stood there, spinning it with my finger, he'd pulled down the blind and locked the door. I looked up, surprised to see him putting a finger to his lips and winking conspiratorially. But as I turned back to the globe, thinking it was all a joke, Mr Caldicot grabbed me from behind and held his hand over my mouth. I'd struggled against him as he hissed in my ear, warning me not to breathe a word or he'd tell the headmaster that he'd caught me trying to steal a wallet from his drawer. Then he shoved my face into the desk and began.*

*I can still smell his odour now. Cheap aftershave and perspiration. The faint whiff of coffee grinds. After the first time, I stopped going to the library, but Miss Devonshire sought me out. I tried to explain, but she cut me short, insisting that Mr Caldicot only wanted to help me.*

*Desperate to please her, I reluctantly agreed, sitting close to the other pupils. Safety in numbers. But Caldicot called me to his office again, and I didn't dare refuse. Trembling and feeling sick to the stomach, I went to my fate. It happened over and over again, sometimes several times a week, and one summer day, emboldened by the misery of my life and the assumption that it couldn't get any worse, I threatened to tell Miss Devonshire what he was doing to me. He laughed in my face, and the next time he called me in, she was there too, and there she stayed throughout my ordeal.*

*Caldicot stopped when I grew too old to intimidate and died the year after I left school. He was a monster who got his just deserts, but Miss Devonshire, the enabler, was yet to face the consequences. But face them, she would. I'd make sure of it.*

## Chapter Nineteen

Sean's concerns about the flats had given me food for thought, and I couldn't concentrate on the newspapers while speculating about it. But Sean enjoyed picking through historical records, updating the office whiteboard, and nodding with satisfaction. "I forgot how different the two cases were," he said.

"In what way?"

"The Skin Thief strangled the fifteen-year-old but stabbed the older girl. One was at school, and the other worked at Gingell's Chemist."

I stared blankly.

"Oh, you wouldn't know. It's long gone. But it was the only chemist in town back in the day."

"Right."

"Sorry if I'm boring you."

"It's not that. I've things on my mind."

"Velda?"

"Not just that."

"Phone Tom. Get some fresh air."

Sean called it right. I needed to get away from the stuffy atmosphere of the basement office and thoughts of home. My flat should have been a haven, but it was giving me the creeps. I dialled Tom's mobile number, and he eventually answered after several futile attempts. Though surprised to hear from me, Tom was affable and accommodating, agreeing to meet for a coffee during his break. I arrived first and sat in the corner feeling self-conscious, but not for long. Tom strode through the door, grinned at the waitress, and beckoned her over.

"Another one?" he offered.

"No thanks. Mine's only just arrived."

"Cake?"

"I'm fine."

"Okay. One coffee and a carrot cake," he said, nodding to the waitress.

Tom scraped back the chair and sat down. "How's it working out?" he asked.

"The job? Interesting. I like it."

"Is Sean behaving?"

"Doesn't he usually?"

"Yes, he's a good guy. But he's not had much luck getting help this year. And not for want of trying. Glad it's working out with you."

"I've arrived in the thick of it, by the sound of things."

"Yes. Finding Amy Swanson was the last thing we expected. You know I can't talk about it, right?"

"That's not why I'm here. Sean suggested we meet."

"He would. I'm a useful idiot."

"That's not how he sees it."

"You don't know him as well as I do. But it doesn't matter. Information gathering goes both ways. Sean's a savvy guy and not bound by as many rules as we are. He finds it easier to turn a blind eye when we can't."

Tom moved his elbow as the waitress returned and placed coffee and a cake in front of him. He speared a large forkful and ate it with gusto. "Sure you don't want some?" he asked, licking butter icing from his lips.

"No. Still not hungry."

"What can I do for you, then?"

I sipped my coffee and marshalled my thoughts. "I have a friend who's just heard that her boyfriend is on the sex offenders list."

"Rotten luck. Has she known him long?"

"No. Velda met him on Conjoined."

"Never heard of it."

"A dating app."

"Ah, swiped right, and the rest was history?"

"Exactly."

"Risky, though, isn't it?"

"Dating?"

Tom laughed. "Not dating but using apps. You don't know what you're getting in this day and age."

"I know. I wouldn't bother, but I understand why people do."

"Are you single?" Tom asked guilelessly, grinning with his hand on his chin while he waited for my answer. The direct approach to my marital status, or lack thereof, would usually bother me, but not this time.

"Yes. I am single now and probably for the rest of my life."

"Ouch. Bad experience, I guess?"

"Yes."

"Me too. Single, I mean, not an unpleasant experience.

I split up with my girlfriend just after Christmas. It was a relief to both of us in the end."

"But you wouldn't use a dating app to find a replacement?"

Tom laughed aloud. "God, no. I enjoy myself far too much with no one to please but me. Anyway, I must stop chatting. You were telling me about your friend."

"Yes. Someone posted a note through Velda's letterbox warning her about the new boyfriend."

"Nasty."

"Spiteful, in my opinion. My first reaction was to ignore it, but as you say, dating is risky."

"And you want me to find out if it's true?"

"Would you?"

"Yes, of course. Your friend could have approached us directly."

"I know. But we've had a few disturbances in the flats, which I won't bore you with. Even if you don't get anywhere with the register, can you run Ben's name through your database?"

Tom drained the rest of his coffee. "I can, but I won't be able to share much."

I passed him a card containing Ben's full name and address. "Enough to give us a steer?"

He nodded. "Always."

# Chapter Twenty

The afternoon passed quickly. No sooner had I returned to the office than Sean took a phone call from Kim Robbins and left for Truscombe police station for a briefing about our next job. I continued working, fielding a couple of promising telephone enquiries, one insurance related and the other a potential employee theft, reducing recent doubts over my long-term job prospects in a seemingly quieter office. After updating the diary, I scribbled notes for Sean about the appointments I'd made and left half an hour earlier than usual to give myself time to speak to my fellow renters before visiting the letting agent later that afternoon.

Frank Lewis was watering the front garden when I arrived, soaking the ground while staring thoughtfully into the distance.

"Any sign of Sinbad?" I asked.

He shook his head. "Nothing. We're missing him awfully."

"He could still turn up."

"I hope so. I've had him from a kitten."

Frank's lip wobbled, and I patted his arm, not knowing what else to say.

"You're a kind young woman," said Frank. "Thank you."

"Take care."

I entered the hallway and knocked on Dhruv's door, hoping he was still on leave. He'd taken time off work to look after Mill, and I wasn't sure when he was going back. Moments later, the door opened to reveal Dhruv dressed in 501s and a tailored shirt, clean and presentable, his appearance back to normal.

"I assume Mill is better?"

"Much. How did you know?"

"Just a wild guess. Can I come in?"

"Of course. But Mill's in the shower."

"It doesn't matter. I need to ask you something, but don't take offence. It's about the rental charges for the flats in this building. You may not realise it, but your apartment is in a different league from the rest of them, and I'd like to know if it's reflected in the rent."

"Why?"

I chewed my lip, uncomfortable with the lie I was about to tell. But Sean had reservations about revealing too much to Dhruv, and I didn't intend to ignore his advice. "I think I'm paying well over the market value for my flat."

"Fair enough. And you want to know what we pay?"

I nodded.

"I don't mind telling you, but if you make a fuss, our rent might go up. We can afford it, of course, but I'd rather not provoke a rent increase."

"I won't use it for that. I can easily estimate the prevailing market rent for a two-bed flat. But for peace of mind, I want to know that the letting agent is treating us equally."

"I see. Are you asking the others?"

"Velda's already helped, and I'll try to see Brendan shortly. I was going to ask Frank, but the timing's wrong. He's still so upset about his missing cat. It's hard to compare rent for a studio against a two-bed, and I dare not ask the Fosters. So, you're my best prospect."

"OK. What are you paying?"

Dhruv parried the question back at me, and I inwardly cringed, knowing my lie would only work if my monthly rent was markedly higher than his. I took the actual amount and added two hundred pounds for good measure. Dhruv sucked in his cheeks with a hiss.

"I see what you mean. That's ridiculous."

"What do you pay?"

The amount he came back with was three hundred and fifty pounds less. My fictitious increase had been unnecessary. Even without it, I was still paying more for my basic flat than they were for a fully upgraded one. It sounded like Sean was onto something.

"Why did you take the apartment?" I asked, assuming Dhruv would say it was because of the low rent.

"We nearly didn't. We viewed the flat but initially turned it down. The location was perfect for my job and Mill's walk to work at the grammar school, but neither of us wanted to live in a shit hole. And that's what it was, Saskia. The flat was clean and recently painted, but the kitchen and bathroom were dated beyond any acceptable level. It was a firm no. But the next day, the agent rang and said the landlord intended to upgrade and we could have a say in the design. They had emphasised the quality of our reference applications and, preferring to rent to professionals, the landlord agreed to reduce the amount if we took it. Well, it was a no-brainer. They completed the work immediately and to our taste. And that's why we've just renewed. It's perfect for us. We'd buy it if we could."

"Is that an option?"

"No. I've already asked."

"Well, my flat is the original shit-hole. And I'm definitely paying more than you are. It's bizarre."

"What are you going to do about it?"

"Speak to the agents, of course. But I won't use the information you've given me. I'll find another comparable."

"Appreciated. Are you going to wait for Mill?"

"No. I'd like to see the agent tonight. Is Brendan in?"

"Should be. He's on nights this week."

"OK. Catch you later."

---

Brendan was in bed when I banged on his door. Tired of waiting, I was halfway back down the stairs when he appeared in his pyjama bottoms, having hastily thrown a tee-shirt over his head. I didn't have the heart to tell him he'd put it on back to front.

"Saskia. What are you doing here?"

"Sorry. Were you sleeping? It can wait."

"No. Just catnapping. I've nothing better to do. Won't you come in? Have a coffee or something. I'm sick of the sight of these four walls."

I hesitated, thoughts of a half-dressed Brendan in a living room doubling as a bedroom almost fuelling a panic attack. Shades of Curtis Newman and the irrational assumption that I'd be asking for it should he make a move flashed through my mind. But Brendan was ahead of me.

"Stay here. Give me two minutes to tidy up and dress, and I'll be right back. That OK?"

I nodded, and he left, reappearing only a short time later with a kettle in his hand.

"Drink?"

"No, thanks."

"OK. Take a seat. Help yourself to crisps."

I relaxed into the black leather sofa and took a crisp from the pot balanced on the drinks caddy in the centre – a typical bachelor set up with his seating facing a monstrous television that dwarfed the room. I fleetingly wondered where the bed was, but a casual glance to my left revealed a hip-height wall partition cleaving the bed from the rest of the room.

Brendan reappeared with a glass of something blue, which he stirred repeatedly and glugged down. As he sat, he discretely kicked an Xbox controller under the couch and shoved a magazine on top of a Call of Duty video game.

"Boy's toys," he said. "At least nobody makes me feel guilty now."

"Ex-wife didn't like it?"

"No. She didn't like me much, either."

I shrugged in manufactured empathy.

"Anyway. What can I do for you?"

"What rent do you pay?" I went straight for it without explanation, hoping that Brendan would be less defensive than Dhruv.

He was and answered without hesitation but with the same follow-up question. "Why?"

I gave the same explanation, and he accepted it. "Have you asked Velda? Only I'd love to know whether we're paying the same."

"No," I lied. Once again, there was a clear disparity in payment, Velda's rent being a hundred pounds less than Brendan's. If it were the other way, I might have said something, but I wasn't about to cause trouble between neighbours.

"She looked like crap earlier," he offered. "Velda, I mean. She shut the door on me when I asked if she was OK."

"Man trouble," I said.

"Too bad. I met him last week. Seemed like a decent guy."

"How long have you lived here?" I asked, diverting his attention.

"About eighteen months."

"You arrived after Dhruv, then?"

"Yes. And Velda. Then Frank and the Fosters arrived in quick succession."

"Weird. Frank seems like part of the furniture."

"I know. It's funny how some people fit right in."

"And others don't?"

"We both know the Fosters are weird fish."

"I'm sure he's abusive. Kitty opened up a little."

"Lucky you. She barely acknowledges me."

"She wouldn't if she fears men."

"Doesn't come across like that."

"You'd be surprised. We had a case in Cyprus – a squadron leader's wife. Always attended social events, ran the officers' wives' club, and taught a conversational Spanish course in the evenings. I've seldom met anyone so together. And then, one day, she had a wardrobe malfunction. The loose top she was wearing slid off her shoulder. That poor woman was covered in bruises. I've never seen anything like it. He'd been using her as a punching bag for years, and but for that chance moment, he'd still be doing it now."

"Bastard! How the other half lives. What happened?"

"She resisted our attempts to help, but her friend

persisted, kept her on the right path, and she eventually left him. They asked him to resign his commission. If it were up to me, he'd be in prison."

"Shouldn't be allowed," muttered Brendan.

"Agreed. But it shows that you don't know what's happening underneath."

"I get it," said Brendan. "What are you going to do about Kitty?"

"Nothing yet. But I'll keep an eye on her and step in if she needs a friend."

"Good for you. I'm impressed. Now, Saskia. I'm on nights for the next few days, but do you fancy a drink later this week?"

Brendan's offer took me aback, and I hadn't seen it coming. But with Sean preoccupied and inundated with friends, there wasn't much chance of a night out any other way. "OK," I said uncertainly.

Brendan laughed. "No strings," he said. "Just a drink."

"Then, absolutely."

---

I arrived at the offices of Barker and Finch just before quarter to six to find a grey-haired man dragging an A-sign into the office.

"Early closing?" I asked, glancing at the signage on the door, which boldly proclaimed opening hours until six o'clock.

He sighed. "Caught in the act," he said.

"Don't worry. My query won't take long." He gestured for me to enter the office, and I sat opposite him, watching as he logged onto a computer system, sighed and steepled his hands.

"What would you like to view?"

"I wouldn't. I'm a tenant."

"Property?"

"Obviously."

"I mean, which property do you live in?" he asked.

"Bosworth House."

"We don't manage that one. Speak to your landlord."

"I would. But I don't know his name."

The letting agent tapped his keyboard and then looked up with a barely perceptible shake of his head.

"Your name?"

"Saskia Denman."

"Ah. Flat Three. Email address?"

I rattled it off.

"OK. Security checks passed. Your landlord is Sentinel Benevolent Properties."

"OK. And how do I reach them?"

"You should have been told."

"Well, I wasn't."

The agent sighed, and I sensed a reluctance to help, then pre-empted a refusal by taking his business card and inspecting it.

"Now, James," I said, tapping the card against the desk. "I really do need your help, and the longer it takes, the more likely you are to miss the appointment you were clearly attempting to shut the office early to reach."

"No need to be like that."

"And no need to stall. How do I contact the landlord?"

James opened the drawer and retrieved a compliment slip. "Just email this address," he said, pointing to a scribbled Gmail account.

"Telephone number?"

"There isn't one."

"Why not?"

"I don't know."

"Alright. How about a contact name?"

"Lindsay."

"Lindsay, what?"

James shrugged. "Sorry."

I leaned back in my chair and surveyed the scant information. "Never mind. I'll look it up on the internet. Should get the landlord's full name from there."

"Unfortunately, not," said James, leaning forward.

"I'm pretty decent at searching the internet."

"I'm sure you are. But Sentinel is a Property Investment Company in the Channel Islands acting on behalf of the landlord. Might be harder than you think."

"Then give me a name."

"I've given you everything I can."

I changed tack. "Why am I paying the most expensive rent in the building?"

James looked away, and I sensed his mind whirring. "How do you know that?"

"Never mind how I know. Just accept that I do. Our rents vary by ludicrous amounts, bearing little resemblance to the size of our flats."

"You'll need to take it up with your landlord. As I said, we don't manage the property."

"That's irrelevant. You let it, don't you?"

"Well, yes."

"And it wouldn't take a genius to challenge the unfair rent using a tribunal."

"You weren't issued with a section 13," James said smugly.

Ignoring my ignorance of lettings jargon, I persevered.

"Still, it's not a good look. Perhaps I'll contact Citizen's Advice, or better still, write a review on your website."

"No need for that," said James quickly. "I can give you an explanation, but Sentinel prefers to keep the matter private. The clue is in the name, you see."

He pointed to his scribblings on the compliment slip. "Sentinel Benevolent Properties is a non-profit making organisation with charitable leanings. All reference applications go straight to the company to approve or deny them based on the potential tenant's personal circumstances. Sentinel might decide to help someone in reduced straits by lowering the rent. Or conversely, by raising it if they think there's a risk."

"I don't buy that for a second. Without revealing sources, I earn considerably less than friends in an upgraded flat, yet my rent is far higher."

"We don't decide who benefits," said James. "That's entirely up to the landlord. They consider each application and tell us how much rent to charge and the length of each contract."

"Understood. But why would they make my rent higher than anyone else's?"

"Because you weren't the intended occupant of Flat Three."

It took a moment for his words to sink in. And my heart skipped a beat at the shock of it. "I don't understand."

"It's simple. Pauline Bateman should have moved into Flat Three. A young professional, keen as mustard, but something happened close to the move-in date, and it didn't happen. Sentinel's landlord was keen on Pauline and pretty unimpressed when she pulled out at the last minute. She'd accepted a job offer in the United States. It was a pity she couldn't have let us know she was applying at the outset."

"So that's why it came back to the market?"

"Yes. Sentinel hoped to change Pauline's mind and offered an upgrade, but she sacrificed the holding deposit and pulled out."

"You're not making me feel very wanted," I said waspishly. "I'm paying Pauline's rent with none of the benefits."

"There wasn't enough time to renegotiate," said James.

"Sounds like an excuse to me. So, let me get this straight. Gretta Smith lived in the flat before I arrived."

"Yes, but she left, and it lay vacant for a while."

"Pauline put down a holding deposit but didn't go any further."

"That's right."

"How long did Gretta stay?"

"Six months. That's all Sentinel offered, and it suited her."

"And someone was there before that?"

"Several someone's. And all with six-month contracts."

"Yet others in the building have renewed for longer."

James nodded.

"Mine's a six-month contract," I said, trying to ratio-nalise the differences. "Why?"

"I know," James replied. "Perhaps something in your background precludes a long contract?"

I didn't answer, hoping the letting agent was ignorant about my redundancy. If not, then bringing it up now would serve no useful purpose.

"Is that everything?" James put his pen and jotter in a drawer, which he closed and locked, before staring pointedly at his watch. He tried again. "I said, is that everything?"

I glanced at the office clock, noting it was a little past the hour – served the sanctimonious git right for trying to bunk off early.

"Yes. I'm done," I said and left, taking the compliment slip with me.

As I walked back to Bosworth House, I considered everything James had said, trying to make sense of it all. I could accept and understand the concept of benevolent letting, but it wasn't working in practice. Higher earners paid less, and certain residents seemed more valued than others. I must have been low in the pecking order as my rent did not match my personal circumstances at all, and Sentinel hadn't offered an upgrade. In context with the letting agent's explanation, it simply didn't fit. Sean's reasoning was better, but still did not account for the situation with Mill and Dhruv. In terms of rent and flat quality, they were the gold standard tenant, yet dirty work was afoot if Sean's theory about the nail trap was correct. Either way, the situation didn't sit well and made me uneasy. Returning straight to my flat was too daunting to contemplate, and without planning it, I found myself inside the Martingale Arms, where I spent half an hour communing with a gin and tonic.

# Chapter Twenty-One

_Imagine looking into a mirror and detesting the person returning your stare, or feeling repulsed by the coward on the other side of the glass. I lived that way for years – hated mirrors, loathed my reflection, a constant reminder of my failure to face up to my tormentors. I could have stopped them, but that would have meant telling someone and articulating the words that would reveal my shame. Instead, I bore it, knowing that my form teacher was complicit. They might have believed me if it was my word against Caldicot's. But not with two of them. I didn't stand a chance._

_I became sullen and withdrawn, a behaviour that encouraged Aunt Dora to greater acts of discipline. And in time, she became the enemy too. I played tricks on her, moved things, hid them, anything to make her life difficult. She hadn't protected me from the horrors of school. Why should she have it easy?_

_After a few years at the hands of Caldicot and his accomplice, something in me profoundly changed. Alone and friendless, I became a collector, seeking insects in the nearby woodlands and spending lonely hours foraging under rocks, in ponds and among the trees. It was an unusual hobby for a teenager when everyone else was playing music or_ *dancing. But it kept me occupied and gave me a focus away from endlessly counting the many ways I would kill Caldicot and Devonshire if the chance came my way.*

*My collection began by accident, as these things often do. I was lying on my belly in a clearing in the wood, reading a nature book I'd taken from home, when a swallowtail butterfly landed near my finger-tips, fanning its wings across the page. I stared transfixed at its lustrous colours, a mosaic of symmetry across paper-thin wings. I coveted the magnificent creature, wanted it for my own. Its body shimmered, wings twitching as it prepared to fly away. But I wasn't willing to let it go and slammed the book shut without a second thought, killing it, of course. The vibrant colours eventually crumbled away until nothing remained but a dusty outline where a living creature once vibrated with new life. I did not regret the act and desired more pretty creatures. But this time, I would do the job properly and have something to look at and admire when school became unbearable.*

*I borrowed a book from the public library and learned how to make a killing jar with plaster of Paris soaked in ethyl acetate. Once mastered, I caught insects in a net, emptied them into the pot, and watched as the chemical did its work. They died quickly at first, and once dead, I would pin them to a board and frame them. Aunt Dora couldn't hide her disgust. She loathed the rows of dead butterflies hanging from my bedroom walls, complaining that it was a cruel, old-fashioned hobby. Well, she didn't know the half of it.*

*I enjoyed pinning the butterflies, stabbing sharp metal through their thorax and onto the spreading board. There's an art to it, and I learned to veer off-centre for the perfect result. But the killing jar soon became more satisfying than my collection, especially when I reduced the ethyl acetate to prolong death. Watching limbs twitch and tremble as life ebbed away brought control into my powerless life. I would have avoided the chemical altogether to lengthen the dying process, but not at the risk of spoiling fragile wings. There was a happy medium, and I took it.*

*My collection grew over time, and in due course, we began studying etymology in science. Mr Rusten, the biology teacher, was everything Caldicot should have been, encouraging learning without malicious intent. I did well in tests and came to his notice. I was quiet in biology lessons, as in every classroom, mainly because of the presence of Slugger, the resident class bully. He'd taken against me like everyone else in my year but singled me out, and I kept a healthy distance, especially after the chewing gum incident. Slugger had been caught with gum, and instead of disposing of it in the bin, he'd squashed it into my hair, not even trying to pass it off as an accident but revelling in his cruelty. I'd tried to walk away, but he rallied the rest of the class to point and bully, even Sarah Suggett, who had befriended me occasionally when she thought no one was looking. And when I didn't react to their taunts, Slugger caught me by the arm, wrestled me to the floor and kneaded the sticky mass further into my scalp. By the time I arrived home, my hair was ruined. Aunt Dora took one look and fetched the kitchen scissors, refusing my pleas for a proper hairdresser. She chopped out the chewing gum, creating a worse mess and bringing further ridicule from my peers.*

*One sunny spring day, Slugger wasn't in class, having been called to the headmaster's office to explain why he had killed the class stick insects. He'd swaggered over, ignorant of the head's intention as, for once, he hadn't committed the crime. I knew more about the incident than he did and gloated inside, knowing I was the perpetrator. My ethyl acetate bottle had become especially useful once I'd sealed the insect tank with a weighty, oversized book on top of homework belonging to Slugger who had left it in the changing room the previous day. I'd been lucky enough to find it and put it to good use by slipping it beneath the heavy book. It didn't take long for the science teacher to find it and draw his conclusions. That day, I was full of schadenfreude and bolder than usual, so I suggested bringing my insect collection to school for the others to see. Mr Rusten was delighted, as much by my newly found confidence as by the offer itself. And he agreed to my suggestion. I would display three frames of butterflies on Tuesday week.*

Seven days later, I woke full of trepidation, a threatening pall of gloom settling over me before I had even left the house. It started with Aunt Dora's sarcastic comments about my strange little hobby, particularly the likelihood of anyone wanting to see my collection of dead insects. I skipped breakfast to avoid her sneers. She couldn't help herself, and though our relationship was marked by arguments or periods of hostile silence, I knew she meant well. She didn't want my peers to single me out. Well, it was too late for that. The damage had already been done, and I still hoped, in some small way, that the sight of the well-organised, pristinely presented butterflies might get admiring stares, or a few well-considered questions. Someone might talk to me and be interested in my life.

I inserted cardboard between the frames and carefully packed them into a sturdy bag. Then I left for school, safely securing my collection in a locker until the science lesson later that afternoon. I had brought my killing jar and a small bottle of ethyl acetate to show the class, and after lunch, I retrieved them and made my way to the science lab to lay them out ready before anyone arrived.

As planned, I was first to the lesson and propped the frames against Mr Rusten's desk using books as supports. Then I stepped back, admiring my display, before waiting for my classmates to arrive. But moments later, a loud voice boomed across the classroom. "What's that shit on Rusten's desk?"

My heart sank. It was Slugger at his obnoxious worst. He swaggered into the room, looked me up and down, and then nodded to Penny Enright, who was tagging along behind. He walked towards her, bent over, and whispered in her ear. I didn't hear what he said, but a sly grin spread over her face, and she left the room, returning minutes later with a brown bottle.

"Good one," said Slugger, taking it from her and staring at me with the same malicious gaze he had worn as he stood silently beside me when she was out of the room. He turned to face me. "I don't like butterflies," he said.

*"Too bad."* The unintentional words slipped out as my heart raced.

*"Feeling brave, are we? Well, let's see what I can do with this."*

Slugger brandished the brown bottle like a cheesy game show host, with the label reading 'Hydrochloric Acid' in my eye-line. Then he opened the lid and gently flicked droplets towards the butterfly frames. Ordinarily, Slugger frightened me, and under other circumstances, I would have cowered away from him. But his gross stupidity was too funny to ignore. He hadn't realised that acid has little effect on glass and he stood perplexed with his mouth hanging open when it did no damage. I couldn't help myself, and my smirk led to an ill-concealed laugh. Penny's hand flew to her mouth. Whatever else she was expecting, it hadn't involved me making a fool of her boyfriend. Slugger's fists balled as his cheeks burned. He stepped towards me and grabbed me in a chokehold with the open bottle of acid, burning trails onto the wooden floor.

*"Stop it,"* hissed Penny, fearing the others would soon arrive.

*"No way."* Slugger's grip tightened around my neck. I was half his size, slim and weak. I took the only possible course of action and sank my teeth into his fleshy arm. He screamed in pain, and the louder he yelled, the harder I bit, tearing flesh from his arm. He tried to move, but I hung on terrier-like. The acid bottle dropped to the floor, spilling onto the boards and pooling with a hiss. One last violent tug and Slugger wrenched his arm free, leaving a mouthful of bloody skin in my mouth. He glanced at the wound and passed out while I spat the bloody mess on the floor. Penny screamed and ran off down the corridor. Still shocked and burning with anger from that day and all the other shitty school days at Truscombe Grammar, I wasn't finished yet. By the time the teacher responded to Penny's frantic wails, I had exacted my revenge. Mr Rusten found me shivering by Slugger's unconscious body, watching the flesh bubble from his lower calf. A few moments earlier, he might have caught me rolling up Slugger's trouser leg, clawing his skin with my fingernails and pressing the gouged mess into the acid pool.

## Chapter Twenty-Two

In hindsight, I wasn't sure which had been worse – Miles Savage turning up at the office or Rachel Swanson finding him there. Sean was late, and I had been nursing a sore head when someone rapped loudly on the door, which was still closed to the public. Washing down an aspirin with a glass of water, I had debated sitting quietly, hoping they would go away. But I didn't like it when Sean ignored potential customers, and I wouldn't fall into that trap just because of a headache brought on by one lousy gin. Sighing, I opened the door to what, at first glance, appeared to be a stranger.

"About time," said the man, sweeping grey hair from his temples as he extended a slender hand. I shook it and, tried to wipe away the hair gel transferred from his palm without him noticing.

"Where is he then?"

"Sean?"

He nodded, hair flopping over his forehead again. The gel, or whatever substance he had used to keep his hair in order, clearly wasn't working. And someone should have told him that a lank-thinning shoulder-length style wasn't a good look. I tried and failed to estimate his age.

"Not here," I said, eventually.

"I can see that. Is your boss coming in today, or am I wasting my time?"

I hadn't liked his hostile tone and, deciding he couldn't be a potential customer, had dropped all pretence at politeness. "How should I know if it's worth your while waiting?"

"Calm down. Don't get your knickers in a knot," he'd said, tossing a notepad on my desk and taking the opposite seat.

My hackles had risen at the misogynistic language. "And you are?"

"Savage. Now, what do you know about Amy Swanson?"

"Why are you asking? What's it got to do with you?"

"I have an arrangement with your boss. We keep each other informed."

"Sean didn't mention it to me."

"It's unofficial."

"Talk to him, then."

The man had stared back with a withering look. "I can't. He isn't here. I'll wait for him. Mind if I use your restroom?"

I could almost hear a series of unvoiced comments about me whirling around his head, none of them complimentary. He obviously saw me as Sean's inferior, and I nearly agreed to his request to get him out of my sight. Savage seemed disingenuous, but I hadn't worked for Sean long enough, to know all his contacts. I'd been on the verge of agreeing when I'd remembered the whiteboard to the side of Sean's desk, which would be visible if the stranger headed that way. And there was something about the man I didn't trust.

"Sorry," I said. "No can do."

He scowled. "Come on. I won't take a moment."

"You just passed a loo in the foyer. Use that."

"I'll use it when I leave if you're going to be fussy," he'd muttered. "Now come on. You must be able to tell me something."

"Wait a moment," I said, lowering my phone onto my lap while quickly texting Sean.

Where are you?

*Corner shop. Why?*

Got a creep by the name of Savage here. Are you expecting him?

*Fucking hell. Get rid of the slimeball.*

He won't go.

*Knee him in the bollocks then. Do whatever it takes. Sod it. Break-fast can wait. With you in 2.*

"He's not expecting you," I said, raising my head.

"So?"

"He'll be here any minute."

Savage flashed an awkward smile. "Deep joy," he said sarcastically.

"I thought that's what you wanted."

He didn't get to reply. The door had swung open, and Sean strode in, red-faced from running.

"What are you doing here? I've told you never to turn up without an appointment."

"You never give me one."

"I'll give you one, alright." Sean turned to me.

"Remember this face, and don't let him in again."

"Who is he?"

"Miles Savage, Chief rat at the Truscombe Gazette. Friend to nobody, and no, we do not swap information, no matter what he claims."

"How did you know he said that?"

"It's what he does. He's a twenty-four-carat shit and, oh, so predictable."

"Oh, come now. You're pleased to see me, really."

Sean flashed a false smile. "You've had your fun. Now, off you fuck."

"Wait, a moment."

"Not even a micro-second."

"I've got something for you. Just need a little information in return."

"Yeah? I've heard it all before from you. Vamoose."

"What information?" I asked.

"Stay out of it." Sean almost bared his teeth. I ignored him.

"I said, what information?"

"*Quid pro quo*," said Savage.

"No chance. I don't trust you." Sean jumped in before I could start negotiating.

"It's about Amy."

"What about her?" I asked.

Savage ignored me and turned to Sean. "First, tell me about the body. They're holding back, and I know you're in with Robbins."

"She doesn't tell me any more than anyone else."

"Crap."

"Not biting, Miles. Close the door on your way out."

"We'll need more. What about Amy?" I glared at Sean, hoping he would let me speak without interruption.

Miles Savage crossed his arms and reclined in his seat.

"Fine. Forget it then," I said, sensing a lost cause.

Savage crossed his hands behind his head and wolfishly grinned. "Tell you what, I'll give you a little clue. Amy Swanson was on her way to make a welfare check the night she died."

"No one knows when she bloody died," snapped Sean.

"I mean, the night she disappeared."

"How do you know?"

"Never you mind."

"Not good enough," I said. "Why would she do that?"

"Apparently, she was worried about someone she once lived with."

"I need more."

"Only if you give me what you've got."

"For that unsubstantiated statement? Not happening," said Sean, firmly.

Miles had opened his mouth to reply just as the door opened and Rachel Swanson walked in.

"Jesus," she said, curling her lip. "I wanted an update, but I don't much like the company you're keeping."

"He's just leaving," said Sean, holding the door open.

"Now, hold on a moment."

Sean raised an eyebrow.

"You owe me information."

"Nope. I don't think so. On you go."

He ushered Miles Savage from the room and slammed the door behind him.

"Sorry about that," he said.

"What did he want?" Rachel sat on the seat Savage had recently vacated, rubbing her eyes with bitten fingernails.

She looked world-weary, with deep frown lines that didn't belong on a young woman.

"Sorry for your loss," I said.

"Me too. I should have done more."

"You couldn't have."

Rachel shrugged. "I suppose."

"Here," said Sean, placing a coffee, teaspoon, and sugar bowl in front of Rachel.

I nearly asked where mine was before realising that the small act was Sean's way of offering his condolences.

"Thanks," she said, spooning sugar into the cup. "Any progress?"

"Not much. We're just getting started."

"Seems the press has plenty to go on."

"They're just fishing. That's why you found the chief rat in my office grubbing around for information."

Rachel raised a weak smile. "The name suits him. What's he after?"

"The usual garbage. Something sensational. Miles Savage isn't getting anything from the police this time. They must have plugged the breach, for now."

"Then why is that cheap rag he's working for pushing lies about connections to the Skin Thief?"

"Because it sells papers," said Sean. "They'll do anything for a story."

"There should be laws against people like him."

"There are. But he keeps just the right side of them."

"You don't think there's anything in it?"

"The Skin Thief? Unlikely, but not impossible. That's why we're making extensive background checks."

"Like the police should be doing."

"They're working harder than it appears," said Sean.

"To give them their due, but policing can be slow. Too much box ticking."

"Tell me about it. All that bureaucracy. Who knows what might have happened if they'd bothered to look for Amy when I told them she was missing?"

"Rachel. For what it's worth, Amy died soon after she disappeared."

"I know. The cops told me that. But all the months of waiting and hoping take their toll."

"I can see that, and I'm sorry."

Rachel sat silently for a moment, and Sean seemed unwilling to pass further comment.

"There's something you can do to help," I said, passing a notebook to Rachel.

"Anything."

"Confirm Amy's last few addresses before she moved, will you?"

Rachel nodded. "I only know the last but one. I'll have to dig out her letters when I get home."

"Can you do that?"

"Yes. I'm travelling back tomorrow. I can't stay here indefinitely. Mum needs me in Cornwall."

"OK. Well, keep in touch and if anything changes, we'll let you know."

We made small talk with Rachel while she finished her coffee, but there was nothing significant to say. It was still too early in the investigation to know what direction to take, and when Rachel finally left, we started planning.

"Need to check out that lead," I said.

"Which one?"

"Savage's clue."

"Don't waste your time."

"You mean you don't believe him?"

"Not at all. And neither would you if you'd known King Rat as long as I have."

"But we need to speak to Amy's previous flatmates?"

"Naturally."

"Then it's the same thing. Look. It's only around the corner."

"If it were as simple as that, the police would have been all over it."

"I know. But it's always good to have a fresh pair of eyes."

"Fine. I haven't eaten yet. We'll go now, and I'll grab something on the way."

# Chapter Twenty-Three

Mulberry House sounded better than it looked. I had visions of a Cotswold stone townhouse with a neat little garden and mullioned windows. But as we approached, ducking down a skinny alleyway more reminiscent of Tewkesbury, we found ourselves outside a dilapidated red brick monstrosity, converted into hen houses that probably broke a few habitation rules.

"Bet a letting agent doesn't manage this dive," I said.

Sean shook his head. "I hope it's better inside. I wouldn't house my dog here."

"Or your lizards."

"Certainly not. Got a few baby geckos going if you want one?"

"No thanks. Accidental or planned?"

"Planned, thank you very much. Carefully nurtured in an incubator."

"Then why are you looking for homes?"

"I'm not really. I have an arrangement with a garden centre."

"Strange."

"Hardly. It's also one of the biggest reptile centres in the county."

"Not that. This."

I pointed to a shabby green communal door with labelled buzzers running down the side from one to four, then a gap, and six to seven.

"Wonder what happened to number five?" asked Sean.

I shrugged, surprised that the narrow building housed that many apartments. It must have been Tardis-like inside.

I knocked on the door and waited.

"You're wasting your time," said Sean after a few seconds.

"Give them a chance."

"Who? Nobody will hear you." He quickly pressed the intercoms one after the other, eventually rousing the occupant of Flat Two.

"What?" snapped a gruff voice.

"Delivery for Number Three."

"Then ring their sodding flat."

"Tried it. They're out."

"Fine."

We heard the drone of the door buzzer, and Sean pushed it open, exposing a dark, unfriendly hallway with two doors leading off and stairs up and down. The metal plate attached to the far wall showed flats three and four below and six and seven upstairs.

"Still no sign of five. What a bizarre numbering arrangement."

It bothered Sean more than me. I just wanted to get down to business and locate Amy's old flat, which, if memory served, was Number Four. I retrieved the compliment slip and scanned Rachel's tidy writing. "Yes, Flat Four."

"Great," said Sean. "Ladies first."

The short flight of stairs took us to an even smaller, darker lobby, and we knocked on the door with low expectations, it being late morning and those people with day jobs settled in their offices. But within seconds of Sean's knock, a voice hollered, "Hold on a mo. I've just got out of the shower."

Sean was explaining how to identify a live lizard egg when the door opened to reveal a young auburn-haired girl with a towel wrapped around her torso. Wet hair dripped onto the lino, and a large tattoo of a centipede rose from her chest and across her left shoulder. Sean stared for a second too long, and she instinctively placed her right arm over the tat, almost freeing the towel in the process. She adjusted herself and scowled.

"What do you want?"

There was no point in beating about the bush with a wardrobe malfunction imminent, so I jumped in. "Did you know Amy Swanson?" I asked quickly.

"Yes. But then you'd know that, wouldn't you?"

"No."

"Aren't you with the police?"

"Not exactly."

"Then who are you, and what do you want? I've said enough about Amy already."

"We're private investigators acting for her sister, Rachel. It's a different matter."

"Rachel? Oh, no problem, then. Amy often talked about her sister. She missed her in her own unique way, considering how bad she was at keeping in touch. Why not step inside while I change?"

The girl darted off, leaving us standing in the cramped hallway. Sean grabbed the handle of the nearest door and turned it.

"Don't do that," I said.

"I'm not hanging around here like a spare part. She won't mind."

"You don't know what's inside."

"The kitchen," said Sean.

He guessed wrongly. It wasn't the kitchen but a decent-sized lounge with a large window overlooking a courtyard with a depressing view of a row of bins.

"Nice," he said.

"It's bigger than I expected."

"Big deal. You couldn't pay me to live here."

"Not everyone can afford a nice new house." His words stung. I hated paying for a rented flat but having always lived in Forces accommodation, I hadn't got a foothold on the housing ladder. No doubt the occupant of Number Four had similar difficulties.

"I know, but it does not harm to save a little for a deposit."

The truth of Sean's statement was like a needle to my heart, and I was sure he'd directed it at me. I swallowed down a barbed retort, knowing full well that I could have drunk fewer brandy sours in the Mess or refrained from splashing money on jaunts around the Cypriot coast. "Whatever," I said.

Sean ignored me and sat on one of the pale blue couches facing each other at a neck-achingly awkward angle to the wall-mounted TV set. He picked up a magazine and flicked straight to the letters page, then snickered periodically, giving no clues to what he found so funny.

Eventually, the living room door opened, and the girl appeared.

"Clem Jones," she said. "Thanks for waiting."

"Thanks for seeing us," said Sean, standing as she came into the room. Clem took the opposite couch, kicked off her shoes and curled her legs beneath her.

"What's this all about, then?"

"You know they found Amy?"

Clem nodded. "So Helen said. The policewoman," she elaborated as I opened my mouth to ask.

"Did you know Amy well?"

"Yes. Not for long, though we were friendly while it lasted. Amy was a good laugh most of the time. Carefree, you know? Didn't stress."

"So, you got along?"

"Sure. We had our moments but never fell out."

"Had your moments?" I stepped in. It seemed important.

"Amy wasn't the tidiest," said Clem, holding out her hands. "I mean, housework isn't top of my agenda either, but I don't leave crap on the floor. I didn't care about Amy's room. It was a mess, and as long as I didn't have to look at it, it didn't matter. But I drew the line at an ironing pile in the front room, and it pissed me off that she never washed up."

"That would bug me too," I said, thanking my lucky stars that I'd secured my own flat. Renting might be undesirable, but at least I had my privacy.

"Are you sharing now?" asked Sean.

"Got to. I can't make the rent alone."

"Is it expensive?"

"Don't be daft. Look at the place." Clem swept her hand in the air as if she was showing off a grand room.

"It's a good size," I said.

"It's damp, and the condensation is awful," said Clem. "Don't use the bathroom if you can avoid it."

"Even so."

"Sure. I've lived in worse. And so had Amy."

"Ah, we were going to ask you that." Sean, who had temporarily zoned out, looked up again. "What do you mean by worse?"

"I don't mean it was a dump," said Clem, "so much as she had problems with her landlord."

"How?"

"A big rent increase not long after she moved in. Far too soon and probably illegal. I told her she should have challenged it. But Amy said that if that's the way it was, she didn't want to live there anyway. And knowing Amy, she'd have been off whatever happened."

"A rolling stone?"

"Exactly. With no financial sense. I mean, I haven't much. God knows I'd be living somewhere better than this if I could practice what I preach. But it's expensive to keep moving. There are holding fees to consider. And it takes ages to get your damages deposit back, if it's returned at all. If the cleaning isn't spot on or there are stains on the carpet, the money's gone forever. I don't know how Amy went from one flat to the next so easily."

"No choice, perhaps."

"Certainly not the last time. But Amy was a free spirit, all the same."

"Did she earn well?"

Clem nodded. "Sure. For a waitress. She worked hard and earned decent tips, but not enough to go flouncing from one place to another."

"Why did she leave here, Clem?" asked Sean.

"She wanted a change. And flats in Marsh Hill House are like gold dust."

"But surely she'd need to give notice."

"Technically. But I was staying, and we didn't tell the landlord until Amy had gone and Suzy moved in. Too late for him to do anything about it."

"Where did Amy live before moving here?"

Clem shrugged. "I don't know. But I'm sure she didn't stay the full six months and was friendly with at least one other renter. She'd go back and visit them from time to time."

"Who was it?"

"No idea."

"Male or female?"

"I couldn't say."

"And you don't know the address or the area she visited?"

"It was in Truscombe, for sure. She was never out for long."

"Do you think Amy had concerns about her friend in the flat?"

Sean looked up and shot me a glare as if annoyed at my reference to Savage's insinuation. But I persevered. He might have doubts, but it rang true for me.

"Funny you should say that. Amy was worried towards the end of her time here, but she didn't go into detail. I know it was over someone she knew, an old friend perhaps. But considering we saw a lot of each other, Amy gave little away. She mostly talked about work colleagues, and for all I know, it was work-related. I wish I'd listened, but I didn't."

"Did it bother you when Amy left?" Sean fired a tactless question into the mix.

"No. Why should it?"

"Because finding another flatmate is inconvenient."

"Not if someone does it for you."

"Did Amy find Suzy?"

Clem nodded.

"Then would Suzy be able to tell us more?"

"No. They didn't know each other. Amy advertised in the Post Office. Suzy rang one night, and that was that."

"Surely you interviewed her together?"

"No. And with all due respect to Amy, bless her, she was leaving. It didn't matter what she thought. Suzy came here while Amy was at work, and they never met, as far as I know. Poor Amy."

"I'm sorry for your loss," I said.

"Thank you. Talking about her seems so matter of fact, but it's been horrible and frightening. I liked Amy, and as far as I was concerned, she left here and happily settled in a new place. The police turning up gave me the shock of my life. Especially when they spoke about Amy's body as if I ought to know she'd died. I didn't. The earlier reports mentioned a young girl, and nobody investigated this address, so I didn't know Amy was missing."

"They didn't believe Rachel," I said.

"The situation was far from clear." Sean snapped back as if he couldn't help it. Old habits died hard, and he instinctively defended his former colleagues.

"So, you've only recently heard?"

"Yes. And now they're here all the time. And if not the police, the reporters."

"Truscombe Gazette?"

Clem nodded.

"A word of advice. Don't speak to reporters; if you absolutely must, then avoid Miles Savage. He's trouble."

"Bugger. Too late. I already have. I didn't say much, but he caught me unawares."

Sean smirked at me in an *at least we know where the rumour came from* kind of way.

"Take my card," I said, handing over one of Sean's with my name hastily scribbled on the reverse. He hadn't ordered my business cards yet, and as far as he was concerned, it was a low priority.

"OK," said Clem uncertainly.

"Call me if you think of anything else. And especially if you remember any of Amy's previous addresses. Right?"

"I will."

We left and turned onto Truscombe High Street after a few yards.

"Thoughts?" Sean, who had been quiet, fired out the question.

"She's genuine," I said.

"Yes. And Savage's source, by the sound of things. I think we can assume she told him about the welfare visit. Can't be certain though."

"But Clem didn't use the term welfare visit," I argued.

"Doesn't matter. She saw Savage."

"I know. But if Savage is ahead of the game, he's probably talked to Amy's other friends. The rumour could have come from elsewhere. Perhaps we should consider..."

I never finished the sentence. Sean stopped outside the bakers, walked towards the entrance, and then turned to face me. "Absolutely not," he said. "Don't even think about it."

# Chapter Twenty-Four

By the time Sean returned to the office, some twenty minutes later, I had already moved on and was working in the basement with a freshly cleaned whiteboard. I had wanted to work alone to see if I could make any progress without the benefit of Sean's opinion and his inevitable natural prejudice following a lifetime spent in Truscombe, where the crimes took place. Ignoring the small pile of newspapers on Sean's desk, I fired up my laptop and wiped down a dusty desk, then searched for online articles without the hyperbole from reporters hustling for a good story. Even a small Cotswold town like Truscombe attracted its fair share of trouble, but it was slim pickings when looking for comparable crimes. I quickly grew bored reading about thefts and vandalism, and my eyes started glazing over. Before I knew it, I'd wasted half an hour.

Aside from the three murders, only Irene Paige's disappearance and an unsolved rape had come to public attention over the last two decades. I quickly discounted the rape, which didn't fit the MO but kept returning to Irene's disappearance. Sean had dismissed it out of hand, but Amy had vanished before she died, and who was to say that the same thing hadn't happened to Irene? But her age troubled me – it was too far adrift from the murdered girls. Still, I scribbled her name on the board before sitting at my laptop to put things into perspective. Sean knew more than I did about the initial police reports, and although he wasn't a serving police officer then, he could place the girls within a family context. I couldn't and would need to accumulate the information myself. Though tempted to ask Sean, I resisted knowing that it would defeat my goal of approaching the crime with a fresh pair of eyes. So, I flipped open the laptop lid and logged onto one of my favourite genealogy sites, quickly sketching out the immediate family trees for each of the three girls.

I was making good progress when I remembered the wedding photograph I'd seen in Sean's house. It had piqued my curiosity, and Sean had retreated when I'd mentioned his marital status, doing everything possible to move the conversation off topic. The opportunity to find out more was too good to miss. I tapped his name into the website, which returned five Sean Tallis within seconds. But when I filtered it by county, only one version remained. Keeping the filter in place, I added a further field, and up popped a 2016 marriage to Callista Partington. As I inwardly basked in the glory of my quick and efficient detective work, a nagging feeling of familiarity took its place. I knew that name, but why? Opening another tab for a Google search, I quickly typed the name again. Only a few entries appeared, the only interesting one to a newspaper report I couldn't reach without a subscription, so I gave it up and keyed in Callista Tallis instead. This time, pages of articles appeared, and I remembered where I knew the name. Callista Tallis had remarried and was now Callista Hart, better known as Callie, and Assistant Chief Constable for the district. I whistled aloud. Sean had married way above his station, and a further check showed that her father was also a high-ranking officer, a situation not unlike Kim's. Callista Hart must be Kim's boss, and I couldn't help wondering how that had worked out when she and Sean were lowly sergeants. Surely there were rules against it? Fraternising between the ranks was frowned upon in the Air Force, so presumably not encouraged by the police. The revelation put me off my stride, and I was still pondering when the door rattled open, and Sean appeared in the doorway. I slammed down the lid of my laptop, hoping he hadn't seen.

"What are you doing down here?"

"Working. Got another whiteboard going."

"Hmmm." He examined the carefully drawn pedigrees and perched on the desk beside me.

"What's this in aid of?"

"Clarity. I was trying to sort through the facts."

"They ruled out family a long time ago. And it's even less relevant in a copycat killing."

"I'm sure they did. But we're not making progress. Let me try it my way."

"Got to start on Kim's brief tomorrow. She's only given us a week."

"What about Rachel?"

"There's plenty of time for that. It's a slow burner."

"I've started now, Sean. Unless you want me to pick up Kim's stuff today?"

"No. Tomorrow's fine. Do your thing. I'll be next door."

He left, and I opened the laptop, deleting my search history in a fit of paranoia. Then I continued with the family trees, taking them back a couple of generations, first

Carla Bryan's and then Debbie Rutt's. Keying their names brought a flurry of public information and a couple of useful sites hosted by unsolved murder aficionados, keen to unmask the Skin Thief with detailed information it would have taken me hours to find. Years of theories hadn't produced a strong contender, and I bookmarked the page for later when I had more time to read it at home. I quickly turned to Amy's family tree, producing it with ease, first identifying Rachel and then her mother, who was born in Gloucestershire and had moved to Cornwall later in life. I almost left it there, as time was pressing, and I didn't want to work late with next week likely busier. But I'd taken the other two girls' trees back a further generation, and it seemed only fitting that I did the same for Amy. By the time I had located her grandmother's birth and subsequent marriage, I was glad I'd made the effort. The police had missed something right under their noses, which might turn the case on its head.

---

"I have something to show you," I said, marching into Sean's office and leaning against the door, still flushed with excitement at my discovery.

"Hang on a moment," he said, fiddling with his mobile.

"It's important."

"So is this. One more line, and I fail."

I sidled behind him.

"Word-up! For fuck's sake. Stop playing on your phone. This is serious."

"Hold your horses. Just wait."

"I can't believe you. I'm not kidding. Really bloody important."

I moved my head close to his, practically shouting into his ear in frustration, but Sean was single-mindedly completing his daily puzzle no matter what. It would have taken an earthquake, or worse, to put him off track.

"Bloody waste of time if you're on line five. Hardly covering yourself with glory," I spat.

"I've had four letters for the last three lines. It's one of those frustrating words that could go either way."

"Hound," I said, leaning over his shoulder.

"Could be wound."

"Fifty-fifty then. Toss a coin."

"No. I'm going with wound. Oh, fuck it."

Sean hurled his phone across the desk and glared at me.

"Don't even consider blaming me for that."

"I don't need to. You know you were a distraction."

"Enough now. Come with me, Sean. This matters."

He picked up his phone and followed behind, positioning himself by the whiteboard as I grabbed a telegraphic pointer. Sean raised an eyebrow, and I could see him swallowing some smart-arse remark before it escaped and upset me.

"Now, look at the board. This is Amy Swanson's tree."

"I know."

"And this is her sister Rachel and mother, Cheryl."

"Nothing new here, Sass."

"Cheryl married Andrew Swanson, but her maiden name was Barker."

"So?"

"So, her mother Irene, formerly Devonshire, married Fred Barker. They had two children, both girls."

I ignored Sean's swift glance at his watch and moved on.

"But they divorced, and she remarried, but only briefly."

"Married, who?"

"Bill Paige."

"Bloody hell."

"Bloody hell is right."

"Are you saying that Amy Swanson is Irene Paige's granddaughter?"

I nodded.

"How the hell did the police miss that?"

"Well, they've only just started taking Amy's disappearance seriously. And they haven't any reason to associate the Swansons with a woman who disappeared a decade before.

"But why didn't Rachel mention it?"

His question triggered a memory. "I think she did the first time she came to see us. Don't you remember? She said they'd lost another family member, and the police were useless then. Neither of us were listening properly, and she didn't embellish."

"Surely she realised the importance?"

"Why? You didn't. Irene Paige vanished ten years ago. She's more likely to think her family has been unlucky than to connect the two disappearances."

"Perhaps she's right, and it's just a horrible coincidence."

"Do you think so?"

"No," said Sean, examining the whiteboard again. "We should look into it. Good work, Sass. It puts us a few steps ahead of the police."

"Will you tell Kim?"

"Absolutely. But I'll give it a day or two first."

# Chapter Twenty-Five

I stifled a yawn as I entered Bosworth House – tired and intending to go straight to my flat. But a sudden appearance on the stairs by Lance Foster caught my attention. I had taken to avoiding him since my conversation with Kitty. And though I hadn't warmed to her and her naturally defensive nature, often spiking barbed comments into our brief conversations, I sympathised with her domestic troubles. I'd seen it too many times before and couldn't condone the idea of aggression towards a woman. Military police training taught us not to pre-judge, but we were only human and formed our own opinions even if we didn't act on them. On duty, I forced myself to remain neutral. But this was different. I might live opposite Lance, but I didn't have to like him. And I certainly didn't want to chat with him, even though he'd attempted it once or twice before.

I sailed past Lance, not expecting him to speak, especially as our last few encounters had resulted in stony silence from me. Still, he tried anyway, nodding hello, and smiling uncertainly through his deep-set, red-rimmed eyes. No doubt the Foster's nightly rows were costing him sleep.

I'd just passed Frank in the hallway, greeting him cheer-ily, and I didn't want him to think badly of me by blanking Foster altogether. So, I stood aside as he trudged downstairs carrying a lumpy cumbersome package in a supermarket bag for life. He said hello, and I grudgingly responded and was about to continue when an overpowering smell stopped me in my tracks. I stood for a second, trying to process the heady combination of something meaty with an underlying fish odour and nearly gagged when I realised it was coming from Lance Foster's bag.

The sight of Foster carrying meat products and Kitty's recent wounds merged seamlessly in my thoughts, resulting in a wild flight of fancy and heart-stopping concern. My first thought was for her safety, and I nearly bolted upstairs to hammer on her door. But I only had seconds to act. Lance Foster had already left the building but might still be in sight if he wasn't driving. As an ex-policewoman with more than enough reason to suspect him of abuse, I moved instinctively towards the door to see where he was going, hoping to glimpse the contents of his bag.

"Everything alright?" asked Frank, who was screwing a post-box back onto the wall.

"Fine. I've left something in the office," I lied, then slipped out quickly before he could continue. Frank liked to talk but now was not the time.

I darted to the bottom of the path, looking left and right, and couldn't see Lance at first. But, glancing up as a car drove past, I noticed him on the other side of the road, striding up an alleyway. I sprinted across, earning myself a blast of a car horn as I shot over, unwilling to wait for the traffic to calm. Not a good start, as everyone on the street, looked my way. Thankfully not Lance, who was already halfway up the alley. I followed behind him, crunching loose gravel as I walked to the top of the short path, locating him easily at the other end as he walked along Drover's way and towards the northern edge of the town. The golden Cotswold stone properties grew further apart, and I hung well back to avoid detection – one glance behind and I'd be fully exposed. After a mile, Lance Foster turned into a field, soon lost behind a high hedgerow. By the time I reached the Truscombe Way post sign, pointing left, disorientation had set in, and I realised I was lost. I cautiously stepped onto the overgrown path, wondering whether to backtrack and go home.

New to the town, I'd never travelled this route, and I'd no idea where it was leading. I'd foolishly set off without a coat, even though the weather had been unsettled all day. And right on cue, the skies darkened and loosed a rain shower. It didn't last long but left me soaked and discouraged. And alone on a narrow bridleway with a man I neither liked nor trusted. The winding path concealed Foster so well that I couldn't tell how far ahead he may have gone, and I walked slowly and quietly, listening for any telltale signs of footsteps in case he had stopped nearby. I couldn't risk running into him. It would be impossible to explain. Whether it was the pollen or the increasingly claustrophobic pathway, my laboured breathing quickly turned into a full-scale asthma attack. Panicking, I patted the pockets of my trousers, finding them empty, and my heart lurched in fear that I might have forgotten my inhaler. But after a second of rational thought, I remembered I was still carrying my handbag when I left the building and rummaged inside. My blue inhaler was there as always, and I sucked deeply on the plastic tube, feeling the hit of soothing chemicals on the back of my throat. Gritting my teeth, I carried on and soon reached the end of the path, emerging onto a minor B road near a signpost marked Caverley.

Relief washed over me. I'd travelled through Caverley before. It was only a few miles from Truscombe, but I hadn't realised there was a shortcut across the fields. And there was no reason I should. It was, at best, a hamlet with a clutch of golden stone properties set around a small green, with no shops or even a pub. I couldn't see Lance Foster as I walked past the sign, keeping close to the verges in case he appeared. And the prospect of him visiting an inhabitant of the village while carrying a large evil-smelling bag seemed unlikely. A dense wood surrounded two sides of Caverley, and I wondered if that might be his destination. If so, I was out. Following him was foolhardy enough, but I wouldn't go full Friday the 13th and take stupid risks.

A short way on, I passed a handmade wooden sign pointing to Caverley cattery, turned a corner and found myself a hundred yards from the village green. In the distance, I glimpsed a bag-carrying figure and ducked into a hedgerow, watching as he opened the gate of the most easterly house and went inside. Though Lance Foster was far away, I could see he hadn't announced himself. He hadn't approached the front door, and no one was outside beckoning him in. Perhaps he was visiting relatives or good friends, and I should have left it there and walked away. But, still worried about Kitty, I pushed on, no longer sure why, given that there was nothing remotely suspicious about a man going into a garden. Yet, the smell of the package had put me on high alert, and I carried on regardless.

The house seemed oddly neglected the nearer I got. But it wasn't until I viewed it from a slightly different angle that

I saw the royal blue square of a Truscombe Estate Agents for sale board. Suddenly, it made sense. The empty property lacked the vitality of an occupied house. Silence reigned with no shrieks of children playing, the grass ever so slightly longer than usual, and the letterbox open where the postman had carelessly shoved mail without pushing it fully inside. But why was Lance Foster poking around in the garden if the house was empty? There was only one way to find out.

Seeing a curtain twitch on the other side of the green, I walked nonchalantly towards the woods as if out hiking, then circled back towards the rear garden of the empty property, hoping to find a gate. After circumnavigating the high wooden fence, I soon realised that the house came with more land than it appeared at first glance. I was heading back towards the green when I noticed an old brick wall running for a few yards between the fence struts. A few feet lower than the surrounding wooden fencing, it was my only possible chance of getting in. Rearranging my handbag from my shoulder to my neck, I reached for the top and hauled myself painfully up the wall, shredding my trouser leg on a nail. Annoyance at the damage to my favourite work trousers replaced my fear of running into Foster. I swore into cupped hands to get it out of my system, then quickly lowered myself down the other side of the wall, landing steadily at the bottom.

Finding myself in a heavily shrubbed area, I crept onto a pathway winding towards a wooden building at the foot of the extensive gardens, then stopped as I heard a familiar sound. I couldn't place it for a moment, but as I came closer, a fine mesh across the structure appeared, and the noises separated into their singular forms of purrs and miaows. I was standing outside Caverley cattery, within the grounds of the building into which Lance Foster had stepped. The cattery abutted a shed, brightly lit, even though it was not yet dusk. Ducking down, I headed towards it, stopping below a large window where I listened as someone clattered around inside. I raised my head and peered through the dusty window. And though I couldn't see his face, I did not doubt that the shadowy figure decanting meaty-looking objects from the bag into an open refrigerator was Lance Foster.

## Chapter Twenty-Six

"Must have been cat meat," said Sean as we discussed the previous night's events over a morning coffee.

"I don't know."

"It stands to reason."

"Perhaps. But why hide it?"

"He wasn't. Carrying something in a bag isn't the same as concealing it. Are you sure it was Foster?"

"Of course. I slipped on the gravel, and Lance turned around, but I saw his face before ducking down and then ran for it."

"Did he see you?"

"I didn't think so, but now I'm not so sure. He knocked on my door earlier. Thank God I checked the spy hole first."

"Must have been early."

"Yes. I was still in my dressing gown, and he was wearing a scarf, on a warm day like this. I don't know what he wants, and it gives me the creeps just thinking about it. And I can't help feeling I ought to speak to someone about Kitty."

"She won't thank you for it. You've offered help, and she's refused."

"They usually do, Sean. It takes a lot of courage to report domestic abuse."

"But is Kitty really in danger?"

I shrugged. "I don't know. The Fosters argue all the time, and it's hard to hear anything else through the shouting."

"Then how do you know he's hitting her?"

"Kitty's hands and knuckles were black with bruises. And it's not the first time I've seen marks of violence on her. It's getting harder to overlook."

"It's up to you, Sass. Personally, I would keep my counsel."

"Then I'll check Lance Foster out. See if he has any form."

"Ask Tom. Has he got back to you about Velda's chap yet?"

"Yes. Just before we left yesterday, I must speak to her later and pass on the good news. She's been avoiding Ben, and it's getting awkward. You can only string out flu for so long."

"Tell her to use a more exotic illness next time."

"Ah, look at this?" I turned my laptop towards Sean. "That's the house with the cattery. I told you it was for sale."

"Nice garden," said Sean. "Call the agent. See if you can find out who it belongs to."

"No need," I said, logging onto the land registry website. Two minutes later and three pounds lighter, I had my answer. "Bloody hell. It's theirs."

"The Fosters?"

"Yes. They're selling the house, yet I know from last

night that the cattery is still in use. There must have been half a dozen moggies."

"Perhaps they're winding it down until they sell."

"Could be. I wonder why the Fosters are moving. Their house is far nicer than these flats."

"Dunno, but we need to crack on. I've promised the first report by the end of the week. Did you hear me, Sass? What are you doing now? We need to make a start on this." Sean chucked a thick buff file my way, which slid across the desk, almost knocking my coffee over.

"Give me five. Cancel that, I don't need it. All becomes clear." I spun the laptop around for a second time, revealing a list of Google search results for Lance Foster. At the top of the page was an entry from The London Gazette.

"You haven't clicked it?"

"I don't need to. Bet it's bankruptcy."

"You think?"

I clicked. "Not quite, but close. A month ago, Foster Grant Limited, trading as Caverley Cattery, entered voluntary administration.

"Nice one," said Sean. "It explains the rows. Nothing like money problems to upset the equilibrium. I guess that's that."

"No way. There's so much more to this. Don't you remember me telling you about the strange noises coming from the flat?"

"Yes, but it could have been anything."

"No. Someone was crying. And neither of the Fosters were there."

"And look at this." I jabbed the laptop screen, scrolled down, and moved the mouse pointer over a picture of a youthful-looking Lance Foster in a sports vest with a medal around his neck.

"He hasn't worn well."

"That's not what I'm getting at."

"So, he can run. Can't we all?"

I expanded the screen and gestured to the caption below the photograph.

"Truscombe Grammar School cross-country team," read Sean. "Sorry, you'll need to enlighten me."

"Milligan works at Truscombe Grammar, Lance went there, and Brendan Marshall's uncle was the school caretaker."

"So?"

"Don't you think it's odd?"

"Hardly. I'm a grammar school boy myself."

"Is Tom?"

"No," laughed Sean. "Stanley comprehensive."

"And Becky?"

"Who?"

"Works at the station. You know, the coffee girl. Gave Tom a mouthful, if I remember."

"Ah, Bex. Yes. Umm... neither. She's from Halifax. Can't you tell from the Northern twang? Educated up north, I should think."

"Right. Three of you were educated in three different schools."

"Hold on, Sass. You're comparing apples with pears. Mill is a teacher, and Brendan is the caretaker's nephew. It's not like they all attended as students."

"We don't know that."

"Sorry. You're reaching. Do you have a connection to the Grammar?"

"No. And I'm sorry I mentioned it now. Fine. It was just an idea."

"Another coffee before we start?"

I nodded and was about to close the lid when a further thought occurred to me as I remembered the name of the girl who should have taken Flat Three. I quickly keyed in 'Pauline Bateman' while Sean poured milk into our coffees, and by the time he put mine on the desk, leaving a wet ring on the surface, I was reading through a job advertisement for a school office administrator. The application instructions were specific – all CVs to pauline.bateman@truscombegrammar.org

---

Sean remained sceptical, but four connections to the grammar school within Bosworth House were two too many for me. I couldn't determine why it mattered, but something sinister was happening in the flats. The sound of weeping, dead rats, rigged traps and poor Sinbad, who was still missing after a week, implied trickery of a disturbing nature. And though it wasn't a matter of life and death, someone was enjoying getting a rise from the tenants. Going against all her natural instincts, Velda was reluctantly hiding from her love interest, and Mill's septic foot could have proved fatal. However trivial the incidents seemed; they had the potential for harm. So far, the only connection, other than our random occupation of Bosworth House, was a tentative link to the grammar school. I was going to investigate, even if only to rule it out, no matter what Sean thought.

My first port of call was Frank's house, and I knocked on the door and waited for him to appear. He was usually prompt to answer, always close by, never letting his frail mother out of sight for long in case she hurt herself. But after a few moments of waiting, I realised he was absent, or perhaps in the bathroom. I was about to give it up and take two flights of stairs to Velda's flat when I heard a faint scratching sound from inside. I dropped to my knees and flipped open the letterbox, hoping against hope that Sinbad had returned. But the soft sounds turned out to be Veronica's wheelchair scraping against the corner of the far wall.

"Only Saskia," I said cheerfully, hoping she could hear me from the other end of the corridor. I didn't want to frighten her, especially as her dementia was well past the point of effective communication. She raised her hand in an almost wave, and my heart lurched at the sight of her heavily bandaged legs and pitifully frail arms. I pushed a few fingers through the post box and attempted a return wave before hearing footsteps behind me and a gentle cough.

"Sorry," I said, brushing dust from my knees. "I thought I heard Sinbad, but it's your mum."

"She's having a rough time of it," said Frank. "Can't get rid of her ulcers, no matter how many antibiotics she takes. The District Nurse will dress her legs again tomorrow. That always makes her a little more comfortable."

"How awful. Poor thing."

"It's her circulation. But I'm going to cheer her up by painting her bedroom. What do you think?"

He brandished a paint container with a splash of yellow on the front.

"Lovely," I said. "Impossible to feel low in a bright yellow room."

Frank grinned. "You didn't come here to talk about paint. What can I do for you?"

"Truscombe Grammar," I said. "Do you know it?"

"Of course."

"You wouldn't have any connection to the school?"

Frank pondered for a moment. "I studied there as a boy and made daily deliveries as a milkman. Does that count?"

"I don't know," I said. "It might."

"Why do you ask?"

I didn't want to bother Frank with my theories and made a lame excuse about researching the history of the grammar school building before making my excuses and heading for the stairs. As Frank closed the door, Dhruv appeared, carrying a loaded bin bag. He called my name.

"Hello, stranger. Too busy to talk?"

I was, but I liked Dhruv and didn't want to offend.

"Not at all. How's Mill?"

"Much better."

"I'm pleased. You must be relieved."

"So much that we're off to Calne Court to celebrate."

"Very nice. Overnight or just a meal?"

"Meal only. And a taxi, so we can both have a drink. Do you want to come?"

"Not really. No offence, but you don't need a gooseberry on your night out."

"Bring Sean along if you like."

"He's got a hot date with his lizards and a bottle of vivarium disinfectant."

Dhruv shuddered. "Sooner him than me."

"Why, Dhruv? He seems so normal in all other ways."

"Don't you know?"

"What? That lizards are good companions? Better to be with a reptile when nursing a broken heart after a nasty divorce?"

"Not where I was going, though it could be true for all I know."

"Then what?"

"Sean wanted a pet, but he's allergic to animal hair. Simple, really."

## Chapter Twenty-Seven

Allergic to pet hair. Shaking my head, I climbed the stairs, annoyed at myself for not considering the obvious. I'd been overthinking, and not for the first time. I'd assumed Sean indulged in his strange hobby for unknown psychological reasons when, all the time, it had come about from a desire for companionship because of a simple allergy. Was I turning into a conspiracy theorist? Perhaps Sean was right, and I needed to stop chasing ideas and follow the facts. After all, in a small town with two schools, it was statistically reasonable for several Bosworth House occupants to have connections to the grammar. Several, but not all, and I made a deal with myself that if Velda had no apparent link, and there shouldn't be one as she'd moved from elsewhere, I would drop it and concentrate on our background checks for Kim.

Velda and Brendan's front doors differed from the others. Ours were older, with brass door furniture and spy glasses. Theirs were more modern, with chrome fittings and a small oblong door light. After a few moments of knocking, I took advantage of the glass and peered inside. Velda's light was on, and an upbeat tune was playing in the background, but she didn't answer. I looked again, this time noticing the edge of an upturned drinks bottle on the mat. Instinctively, I reached for the spare key Velda kept above the door frame with one hand while pushing the handle with the other. The door opened before I grasped the key, and I stepped inside. One pace forward, and I could see Velda's fingers almost within touching distance of the bottle. Shivering, I tentatively walked towards the main room, one baby step at a time, arms wrapped around my elbows in an illusion of protection. Velda lay there, arms outstretched, head lolling to one side, her mouth open, with lipstick smudged across her chin. I knelt beside her, feeling her neck for a pulse. Nothing. So, I took her wrist and checked again. Her skin was cool to my touch. No pulse and probably hadn't been for a while. As I stood, shocked and tearful, my heel touched something smooth, which rolled across the floor. Still shaking, I squatted beside it, careful not to touch. But I didn't need to use my hands to detect the remains of a yellow-tinged liquid in the hypodermic needle. Our tormentor had gone too far this time. Velda had taken an overdose, and it was too late to save her.

---

After phoning the police, I texted Sean with shaking hands, and he called me back almost immediately, promising to come over as soon as he'd safely replaced his geckos in the tank. True to his word, he turned up half an hour later as a pair of uniformed officers ushered me from Velda's flat while they examined the scene. Sean escorted me to my apartment and made a cup of builder's tea, which I drank on autopilot, barely noticing the heat and burning my tongue in the process.

"You OK?" asked Sean as I fanned my scalded mouth.

"Fine. My head is in the wrong space."

"Sorry about Velda."

"It's gone too damn far this time. Pissing around with rats is one thing, but..." My wobbling voice trailed away. I wasn't a public crier, and as much as I felt like a good sob, I wouldn't let it happen in front of Sean.

"I know. What led up to Velda's death seems personal, but it can't be. I still like my theory about a property speculator."

"I don't. Bosworth House is nice enough, but it's no better than anywhere else. And the property market has taken a nosedive recently." I got to my feet and paced towards the window, then leaned out, supporting my chin in my hands. "It all seems connected somehow," I mused. Sean opened his mouth to reply when a sharp knock at the door interrupted his flow.

"I'll go," said Sean.

"No. It's my house. Wait here."

I peered through the spyhole, hoping the caller wasn't Lance Foster again and was quickly reassured by the sight of a pair of blue uniforms.

"Can we come in?" The officer, impatient to move me on from Velda's flat earlier, stood on my doormat next to a short female, clutching a notebook and pen.

"Sure." I opened the door and waved down the corridor. They followed my directions and walked towards the sitting room.

"Oh." The female policewoman glanced at Sean before raising a quizzical eyebrow.

"We're friends," said Sean, with a subtle wink that warned me against mentioning our professional arrangement.

"You're never far from trouble, Mr Tallis."

"Nice to see you too, Mel."

He spoke frostily, and I sensed a history between them. But Velda was lying dead upstairs, and I couldn't care less about their past.

"Mind if we take a seat?" asked the male.

"Go ahead."

"Cup of tea perhaps?" He stared pointedly at Sean, who sighed, but took the hint.

"Milk, no sugar. I like mine strong. She's not fussy."

Sean raised his hand to his forelock, and flashing a sympathetic look my way, he retired to the kitchen.

"Need to take a few details, Ma'am," said the policeman, reaching into his pocket and flashing his warrant card.

I examined it and passed it back. "I know how it works, PC Harding. I'm ex-military police."

"Good. Then you won't mind answering our questions."

"Not if it helps."

After exchanging basic contact details, Harding cleared his throat and dug deeper. "Why were you in Miss Ribiera's flat?"

"I was hoping to pass on some information."

"What?"

"That her boyfriend is not on the sex offenders' list?"

Mel raised an eyebrow. "Why would he be?"

"Someone sent her an anonymous letter. A really nasty one – told her to steer clear of her boyfriend if she wanted to avoid trouble."

"His name?"

I gave it.

"Did you see the letter?"

"Yes."

"Describe it?"

"Typewritten and unsigned."

"Any idea where it came from?"

"None at all. Neither did Velda. But it upset her, and she asked me to check her boyfriend's background."

"I thought you said you were ex-military?"

Mel interrupted again, fixing me with pale blue eyes that didn't miss a trick.

"I still have contacts, not that I need them to check the register."

She frowned and scribbled my response in her notebook with even childlike strokes.

"Would you say the letter upset her?"

"Absolutely. Velda was devastated. She'd only just met her boyfriend and liked him a lot. Thought it could go somewhere."

"Did your checks reveal any information about him?"

"Plenty. He's sporty, has run the London marathon twice, and the closest he's been to the wrong side of the law was a peaceful environmental protest that came to the attention of the press. The Met police hospitalised several demonstrators in the kettling process, and he was one of them. As far as I can tell, Ben is a good bloke without a stain on his character."

"Then why the letter?"

"You tell me. I don't know, but it's not the only spiteful thing that's happened around here lately."

"What do you mean?" asked Mel, tucking a wisp of dirty blonde hair behind her ear.

"That's gossip. It doesn't matter." PC Harding flipped his notebook shut and slid it into his pocket. "I'm sorry about your friend, but as you said, it looks self-inflicted. A sad case of suicide, possibly caused by this unpleasant note. There will be an autopsy, of course. And we'll check the flat to see if we can find the letter, but as much as I would like to punish the sender, it won't be easy to track them down."

"So, that's it?"

"Not entirely. We'll do what we can, but there's no law against anonymous mail."

"Not good enough. You need to hold someone to account."

"We'll do what we can."

"Will you tell me the outcome and whether you find the note?"

"It's easier if you call me. Take this." Harding passed me a card with a printed mobile number and slurped the dregs of his mug. Sean, sitting uncharacteristically quietly in the background, gave a cynical smile. "I'll see you out," he said, following the two police officers.

I remained seated, staring at the card through unfocused eyes until the door slammed, and Sean returned to the room.

"Waste of bloody time," he said, slumping on the couch beside me.

"There's not much more they can do."

"Or want to do. You won't hear from him again. A good thing we've got Tom."

"Do you know them?"

"Mel and I are old enemies for reasons I won't bore you with."

"Ex-girlfriend?"

"Actually, no. A colleague's ex-girlfriend who irrationally blames me for their breakup. Wrongly, I might add."

"You live a complicated life."

"Blimey, it's noisy around here," said Sean, as the sound of raised voices travelled down the hallway.

"Just another night in paradise," I replied. "Welcome to one of the many heated rows between the Fosters."

# Chapter Twenty-Eight

"You weren't kidding," said Sean, as Kitty's voice rose in the background.

"Their rowing does my head in."

"She's rather shrill. Not the diffident victim I was expecting."

I scowled. "Domestic violence comes in many forms."

"I know, but they're usually quieter."

"I don't want to talk about the Fosters when Velda is dead above us."

"She isn't. They were stretchering her downstairs when I showed our police friends out."

"I wonder if the others realise what has happened."

"Who knows? They remove bodies as discreetly as possible. It depends on who was around."

"I can't believe that pair of fools didn't take the letter more seriously."

"Perhaps it seems more relevant to you than it ought. Anything can become the last straw if someone is mentally fragile. Velda could have had a hard day at work, or perhaps someone was unnecessarily unkind. How well did you know her?"

"Hardly at all. But she's been around for coffee a few times, and I've been to hers. Velda helped me to build a flat pack wardrobe last week, and I let the gas engineer into her flat for a boiler check."

"Interesting, but not where I was going. I mean, did Velda have a history of depression?"

"Not that she told me about. Velda was a quiet girl. Anxious, yes, and saddened over the anonymous letter. But she didn't seem depressed. Not in the way you mean."

"But think about the conflict. Velda liked her boyfriend but didn't trust him. She was attracted but fearful at the same time. It can't have been easy."

"It wasn't, and yes. She was gutted. But Velda had family and her religion to turn to. And plenty of friends, for that matter. I can't believe she took her own life. In fact, I don't."

"Perhaps we're looking at a drug overdose?"

"I don't believe that either. Velda wasn't the type. No signs of it at all."

"Druggies seldom fit expectations, Sass. Not unless they're off their heads on crack cocaine."

"If Velda were a regular user, there would be evidence in her flat."

"Maybe. But that's for the police to find."

"If they bother looking, which they won't."

Sean shrugged. "Probably not. Unless the autopsy turns up an unexpected result."

"Then I will."

"Right. By sailing upstairs and breaking the door down?"

"No. By using the key. Coming?"

"Really? How about we grab a curry and watch the TV instead?"

"You do that, Sean. I've better things to think about."

I strode up the hallway, slamming the door behind me and leaving Sean in my flat, to which he didn't have a key. I should have cared more about my security under the circumstances, but only Velda mattered now. My chest tightened in frustration at the thought of all the horrible things that had happened since my arrival at Bosworth House, each tiny incident burgeoning into the moment somebody died. And I couldn't rely on anyone else to get to the bottom of it.

I reached the top of the second flight of stairs, half-expecting to see it covered with yellow-black crime scene tape, but the door stood plain and undecorated. Hardly surprising considering that Velda's death had fallen squarely into the box marked suicide as far as the police were concerned. I reached for the key on the door frame, hoping that some bright spark hadn't thought to check for a spare and removed it, but the key was still there. I seized it and opened the door.

"Wait up." Sean's voice hissed behind me in a poor attempt at a whisper.

"I thought you weren't coming."

"I didn't say that. Just because it's a bad idea doesn't mean I won't help."

"Do as you please."

"Don't be like that. I know you're upset and with good reason. But I'm not the bad guy, Sass."

"Sorry. As you say, I'm upset."

We entered Velda's tiny studio flat and stood in the doorway, looking into her living room.

"Where did you find her?"

I pointed to the rug by the coffee table in front of Velda's two-seater couch. Sean squatted on his haunches and patted the carpet.

"Still wet," he said.

"She'd spilt a drink. The hypodermic was there."

Sean followed the direction of my finger and nodded. "They've taken it away. What's your plan then?"

"To look around for evidence of drug use. The more I think about it, the more unlikely it seems."

"Shouldn't take long," said Sean, casting his eye around the tiny apartment. "Clever layout," he said, nodding towards the low partition wall, neatly delineating the bedroom space.

Sean searched the drawer beneath Velda's television while I did likewise to the small chest of drawers at the end of her single bed.

"Bathroom?"

"No, shower room. Through there," I answered, nodding towards the tiny inner hall. Pausing only to sweep my hand under Velda's mattress, which yielded no surprises, I followed Sean as he opened the bi-fold door while I entered the kitchen space through a narrow archway. The spacious room had surprised me the first time I saw it, being only a fraction smaller than mine and benefitting from a generous side window. Cleverly converted, the builders had made good use of an alcove in the corner, providing a pantry with storage for kitchen appliances in which Velda had squeezed a small chest freezer. I opened it without thinking, finding it half empty and with nothing more sinister than a poorly sealed bag of peas which had spilt across the bottom. The pantry contained nothing of interest, and I quickly began opening and closing kitchen drawers and cupboards in my search for Velda's drug stash.

But Velda led a simple life, and there wasn't so much as a sewing needle, much less a second hypodermic. It didn't stack up.

"Anything?" I asked as Sean entered the kitchen.

"Nope. Nothing in her medicine cabinet but pain killers."

"Same here."

"Any personal docs?"

"This drawer," I said, pulling it out. "I've been through it. Passport, birth certificate, and family photos. The usual stuff. And there's a concertina folder by the freezer in the pantry. Nothing more exciting than insurance docs and bills."

Sean frowned. "It's not right," he said.

"I told you. Someone in authority ought to know."

"It's above Tom's pay grade. Perhaps a word with Kim would be in order."

"I don't care who you ask," I said, feeling my hackles rising at the thought of Kim Robbin's supercilious expression. "As long as they take a proper look. Can you force someone to take an overdose?"

"Of course, but there would be marks – signs of a struggle. Did you see any?"

"No."

"I don't know, then. Best we go. We've done what you wanted."

"Hmmm." I wasn't listening to Sean by then, distracted by a magnetic shopping list attached to Velda's fridge with a pencil clipped to the side. Someone had ripped off the first few pages, leaving a deep indentation behind with a series of easily identifiable exclamation mark imprints. I ran my fingers over the page.

"What's that?" asked Sean.

"I don't know, but it was heavily underlined. Give me a moment."

I placed the list on the kitchen counter, retrieved the pencil, and gently rubbed it over the page. Then I passed the resulting image to Sean, who stared at it with a bemused expression on his face.

"Why is he in the cellar?" he read. "Who?"

"Dunno. But if Velda was curious enough to write it down, then it's a question worth answering."

"Tell me you're not considering it," asked Sean.

"I'm considering it."

"Absolutely not."

"Then I'll do it alone."

"Fine. I'll join you, but we can't go now." Sean eyed me warily as I locked Velda's door, returning the key to the door frame.

"Why not?"

He glanced at his watch. "Because it's quarter to ten, and I'm going home. There's no way you're rummaging around the basement alone."

"Don't tell me what to do."

"Bloody hell, Sass. Do you ever wonder why you don't have any friends?"

"You bastard."

"Come on."

"Fuck off, Sean. Leave me alone."

"Calm down. We've got to work together."

His careless remark had wounded me in a way he probably didn't intend, and my usually slow-burning temper was at Mach 1.0 and climbing. I swallowed the urge to tell him to fuck off again and bit my lip, seething with hurt and resentment.

"You're right. It's been a long night. Go home, and I'll go to bed."

"Sure?" Sean raised a half-smile while glancing at me with a look somewhere between sympathy and pity.

"Positive."

He walked me downstairs to my flat. "See you tomorrow," he said as I entered, resisting the urge to slam the door behind me.

I grunted and went in, not caring if I ever saw Sean again. Flinging myself on the couch, I turned on the television, flicking pointlessly through Freeview channels and finding nothing of interest. Then, burning with curiosity and determined to do as I pleased whether or not Sean approved, I dug out my old police issue torch, changed the batteries and went downstairs.

Ten thirty on a weekday should have been quiet, but the front door was open, and Frank and a shadowy figure that looked like Brendan were talking on the doorstep in hushed voices. I ducked back up the stairs, not wanting to be seen, sat down, and waited quietly, hoping that Brendan was not on his way to his flat. But he was heading out rather than in. And five minutes and a numb bum later, Frank went inside, shutting the door behind him and leaving the hallway free of people. Taking advantage, I tiptoed towards the door by the stairwell and fumbled for a light. The switch clicked, a bulb fizzed, and the basement stairs remained dark. But I was prepared and switched my torch to low before closing the door behind me. Once inside, I changed the setting to bright and crept down.

The cellar door, like the attic room, was usually locked, and it wasn't until I descended the rough-hewn steps, I realised I hadn't been this far before. An overpowering odour of urine and underlying dampness assailed my senses, and I paused for a moment, wondering if rough sleepers could access the basement another way. The longer I lingered, listening for sounds of movement, of other human life, the more my pulse throbbed as fear stole through me like a fox in a henhouse. My heart fluttered, and an adrenaline rush left me paralysed into inaction, torn between whether to carry on or return to the light. For a moment, I did neither, briefly wishing that Sean was with me. But I didn't need a man, and certainly not a lizard-loving, low-life insensitive bastard like Sean. And the surge of rage gave me the impetus to move. I took a deep breath and strode downstairs as if walking to the corner shop.

But it was a short-lived sense of empowerment. My flashlight revealed two low-height doors, both locked and secured by chains. I fingered the padlock to assess the security and whether I could pick it. But the padlock was sturdy and built to contain whatever was inside. Instead, I dropped to my knees, searching for a keyhole with my torch. The doors were solid. I waited for a second, considering what to do next, when a soft thud heralded the clatter of something falling that rolled across the stone floor of the locked room with a rumble loud enough to alert the floor above. Something or someone was in the right-hand room and I wasn't hanging around to find out who. I tore up the stairs and, knowing I couldn't reach the front door of my flat without detection, I slunk through the rear door into the back garden, crouched below the bin storage area and waited.

## Chapter Twenty-Nine

I phoned in sick the next day, not just because I was fed up, nor because my nose was dripping like a dodgy kitchen tap, but because I had spent one hour, fourteen minutes and a bunch of tedious seconds hiding behind the rubbish bins in the rear garden. Frank and Mill heard the commotion in the cellar, though presumably neither realised what it was and debated the issue in loud voices until everyone else heard and arrived in the foyer. They stood there, speculating about the police presence in the building, not connecting it with the fact that Velda wasn't among them. And though I was only a few yards away and close enough to hear most of what they were saying, I couldn't enlighten them without revealing myself, so I sat in the drizzle instead. I waited another five minutes before Dhruv finally announced that he was going to bed. More time passed before I dared go back inside, and I stood on the rear doormat wringing water from my cardigan before giving it up as a bad job. I removed the wet woollen garment and hung it on the chunky metal radiator by the back door, hoping it wouldn't shrink in the night. Back at the flat, I disrobed, showered, and crawled into bed without setting my alarm.

Seven o'clock arrived, and I snoozed my clock and continued snoozing it until seven forty-five, by which time I had already decided not to go in. And, still burning from Sean's friendless jibe from the previous night, I texted him rather than calling. He responded with a one-word answer – *fine*.

I rose at noon and emptied the washing machine. Then put stale cheese on an oatcake, moodily chewing the unappetising mess while watching an unconvincing police procedural on the television. My nose still running, I hunted through my kitchen drawer, finally finding an old menthol stick which temporarily did the trick. Wondering whether to go into the office for a few hours, I first checked my phone to see a message from Sean.

*I hope you're feeling better*, to which I replied, *not particularly. By the way, there WAS something in the cellar*. I went to the kitchen to make a coffee, and by the time I returned, Sean had answered.

*Please tell me you didn't go down on your own.*
     I'd be lying.
     *Seriously?*
     Yep.
     *What did you find?*
     No idea. But it made a lot of noise.

The phone flashed to indicate that Sean was typing, then stopped and blinked again before fading away. I watched it for a few moments more, but Sean must have erased whatever he was texting and given up. Shivering, I grabbed a woolly blanket from the back of the couch and draped it over my shoulders as if it were December and not mid-July. I raised a hand to my forehead and wiped my sweaty brow, still feeling cold and fevery. Curling into the couch, I started dropping off when my security alarm buzzed. I ignored it, assuming delivery of a cheap air freshener multipack I'd ordered online to cut through the lingering smell of rat, but I didn't care enough to rouse myself and let the driver in. It buzzed again, and I put my head under the blanket and squeezed my eyes shut. The vibration of an incoming text followed the third buzz, and I opened an eye and glanced at the screen. It was Sean.

*Open the sodding door, will you?*
Go away. I'm ill.
*I've brought cold powders and a box of chocolates. Let me in. You won't regret it.*

Sighing, I wrapped the blanket around my shoulders, trudged to the door and wordlessly pressed the buzzer, then leaving my door on the catch, I returned to the couch.

Moments later, Sean bounded inside, the picture of health. I sniffed, blew my nose, and stared, bleary-eyed, at the soggy tissue.

"So, you weren't pulling a sickie?"
"Go away, Sean."
"Only joking."
"Jokes are funny. This wasn't."
"Point taken. And I'm sorry."
"So, you should be. I feel like shit."

"Not about your cold, although I am, I guess. I mean, I'm sorry for what I said last night. I feel bad. And anyway, it's not true."

"Yes, it is. All my friends are sunning it up in Cyprus. I've made none over here and don't care enough to try."

"You will when the time is right."

"If you say so. Why are you here?"

"I was worried about you. What happened last night?"

I explained, alluding to my wait outside afterwards but omitting the time spent crouching near rotting waste matter.

"What do you think it was?" asked Sean, grilling me about the noises inside the cellar.

"I don't know, but the sound came from a living thing. I could hear it."

"Surely not a person?"

I shrugged. "I don't know, and I wasn't waiting around to find out. It spooked the hell out of me."

"You shouldn't have been there."

"Alright. I know."

"Did they speak?"

"No. Just moved."

"Then it could have been an animal."

"I suppose. Like what?"

"A rat?"

"Maybe. Yes. That would explain the soft footfall. On that basis, it couldn't have been human."

"Good. Then time is on our side."

"What do you suggest?"

"Bolt cutters."

"Ah. I saw some at the office. Good plan. When do you want to go down because now is not an option?"

"Tomorrow, when you're feeling better. But only if you are. No coming in if you're still rough."

I opened my mouth to thank him but flinched at the sound of loud rapping at the door.

"Oh, God. I could do without visitors."

"Shall I see who it is?"

"Yes. But only answer if you absolutely must. I'm not in the mood."

Sean tiptoed down the hallway, and I watched him crouch by the door and peer through the spyhole. He was grinning when he returned. "It's your friend," he whispered.

"Who?"

"One half of the noisy Fosters."

"God, not Lance?"

"'Fraid so."

"Keep your voice down, then."

We sat silently, almost ready to speak, when Lance hammered on the door again. Sean raised his finger to his lips while I covered my mouth with the blanket, unsuccessfully trying to suppress a giggle. But after a moment, Sean's benign expression changed. He narrowed his eyes, cocked his head, and stood in the middle of the living room.

"What it is?" I whispered.

"Ssshhh."

Sean listened and walked towards the living room door, examined the light fitting, shook his head, and made his way towards the bookcase, running his fingers along the rear. I watched, half bemused and half wishing he would leave me to die in peace and go home. Then he rechecked the spy hole before pouring himself a glass of water and swigging it down as he entered the room.

"Your visitor has gone. Why not stay at my house tonight?" he asked suddenly.

"No. I feel like death warmed up. You'd have a better conversation with your lizards."

"Not for me, for you. I'll make you dinner, and you can have an early night."

"Do what?"

"That sounds wrong. I didn't mean it like that. You need a friend, and I can look after you."

"Not necessary. I'm sick, and you're being weird."

"Come with me, and don't argue." Sean pressed his lips close to my ear and whispered. "You need to leave, Sass. Right away."

"Are you threatening me?"

Rolling his eyes, he tried again, whispering urgently into my ear. "Please trust me. I'll ask you again in a moment, and you'll say yes, right?"

I pulled a face, but Sean patted the back of my hand repeatedly, and after a moment, I recognised the pattern. Three short taps, three long taps, three short taps. SOS.

"Go on, Sass. Come to mine for tea," he said brightly. "Promise I'll treat you like a princess."

"OK," I replied.

---

"What the actual fuck was that about?" I asked, manhandling a sports bag into the boot of Sean's car.

"Wait," he said, slamming the passenger door behind me. He jumped in, revved up the engine and sped down the street.

"Are we really going to yours?"

"Too right. Let's keep your germs away from the office."

"What's going on?"

"Hold on. I'm only five minutes away."

Sean sat stony-faced until we pulled up in his driveway,

where he took my bag. I followed him into the house, feeling slightly surreal.

"Sit down," said Sean. "Want a cup of tea?"

"No. Just tell me why I'm here?"

"Have you ever noticed a noise in your flat?"

"Often. And it's usually the Fosters rowing."

"I mean a buzzing sound."

"You mean my door security system? Is this a quiz?"

"Seriously."

"I don't know. Sometimes, I suppose. But then I suffer from bouts of tinnitus, so it's hard to tell."

"Well, I don't. And I sure as hell heard something in your flat."

"Like what?"

"A soft buzzing, intermittent clicks."

"Another rat?"

"More like a bug. An unsophisticated one at that."

"You mean a listening device?" I sat on the edge of Sean's sofa, eyes as wide as the corn snakes in the tank beside me.

Sean nodded. "I think so. We'll test it tomorrow. I have a radiofrequency detector back at the office."

"I can't believe it."

"Hold that thought. I may be wrong, but it's better to be safe than sorry."

"Why would anybody bug my flat?"

"I don't know, Sass. But then, why would they hammer a dead rat to your floor?"

"I feel sick."

"I know. It's a horrible business."

"I mean, I really feel sick."

Sean looked at my face, which had turned a shade paler, as salty saliva rose in my mouth.

"Bathroom's that way."

I got there in the nick of time, clutching the toilet bowl and vomiting masticated oatcakes across a blue cistern block. Tired, cold, and sick at the thought of being spied on, my stomach heaved until nothing, but bile remained. By the time I crept back into his living room, Sean had made us both a cup of tea. I snuggled inside the blanket I had brought and tried to force down a mouthful of the dark brown liquid, but one sip was enough.

"You're not going to manage a meal, are you?"

I shook my head.

"Then I'll show you to your room."

I staggered up the stairs and into bed, not expecting to sleep. But by the time I'd set the thirty-second shutdown on my audiobook, my eyes were growing heavy and I heard nothing past the first few lines.

# Chapter Thirty

I stayed in bed the next day, drifting between sleep and trying to eat the snacks that Sean insisted would be good for me. And I felt a little better by the evening and watched television with Sean for a few hours before returning upstairs for an early night.

Seven o'clock dawned, and I woke to the familiar sound of my alarm thrumming, but it took a few moments to remember where I was. I pulled back the covers and stared at the white walls of the bedroom, but it wasn't until I spied a book about reptile husbandry that everything made sense. I stood gingerly to my feet, walked towards the window, and looked out over Sean's porch and towards his car. A mellow early morning sun bathed the front garden in warm hues, and birds chirped quietly in the trees. It was a perfect summer's morning, and my temperature was back to normal, all traces of nausea gone. I reached for my sports bag, slung it over my shoulder and made for the bathroom, hoping it was free, then jumped into Sean's shower, enjoying a satisfying soak under a large showerhead, more powerful than my own. After applying light make-up and brushing my teeth, I felt a million times better than the night before and was raring to go. Sean's mood matched my own, and I heard him singing discordantly to the sound of the kitchen radio. He must have heard me showering and was fully prepared to offer breakfast when I came downstairs. As I entered the door, he passed me a mug of tea and a plate of toasted scotch pancakes.

"Perfect. I'm starving," I said, sitting down and sipping my drink.

"Thought you might be. How are you feeling?"

"Like a woman who hasn't been bugged and didn't have the living crap scared out of her in a grotty old cellar."

"Amazing what a good night's sleep can do."

"Isn't it?"

"Tuck in," said Sean. "Ah. That's the postie. Good."

"How the hell do you get your mail this early? Mine's midday if I'm lucky."

"The luck of the draw," said Sean, mock gloating. By the time he returned, his smile was gone, replaced by an angry frown. "For fuck's sake," he said.

"What's wrong?"

"Callie."

I raised an eyebrow as if I didn't know who she was.

"Ex-wife," he said. "Sticking the knife in again."

"How? You don't work for the force anymore."

"So, you know about her then? I won't ask who's been gossiping."

"Only a little. What's she done?"

"Threatened to withdraw our funding."

"Does Kim know?"

"Not yet. It's a threat, Sass. It doesn't mean she'll follow through."

"Then why worry?"

"Because she wants something, and this is ammunition."

"What does she want?"

"Me."

I raised an eyebrow, lost for something sensible to say.

"I'm not bragging. Callie's second marriage is falling apart. It has been for a while, and she's made it clear that she regrets our split. Callie's an intelligent woman and capable, but she's volatile and likes to get her own way. So now and then, she rattles my cage."

"What will happen if she goes through with it?"

"No police work for a few months like last time."

"I guess you won't be needing me, then?"

"Don't worry. I'll find something for you to do. Police work is only part of my business."

"Good," I said nonchalantly, not letting him see the momentary spark of fear that left me wondering what I'd do if I had to return to the grind of a nine-to-five office job. Not that we'd worked much outside recently. But it was far more interesting than shuffling requisition orders from tray to tray at Froggatt & Co.

Sean's phone buzzed on the work surface. He dropped a couple more pancakes in the toaster before checking his message.

"Ah, young Tom. I wonder what he wants."

Sean scanned the phone, his eyes darting across the screen.

"Hmmm. Change of plan. He wants to see us."

"Why?"

"He hasn't said, which means he probably knows something he shouldn't be telling us. He's asked to meet at Fat Vi's at ten o'clock."

"Where?"

"Same place you went last time."

"That wasn't the name of the cafe."

"It's a private joke. Don't worry about it."

"Do you mind if I go back to my place first? I've left my charger behind, and my phone is as flat as one of those." I pointed to the newly buttered pancake Sean had removed from the toaster.

"Sure. Be careful, though."

"I'll just be in and out. Will we have time to run the bug checker today?"

"I already did. I borrowed your keys and checked it out while you slept."

"You might have asked."

"I didn't want to wake you."

"Did you find anything?"

Sean nodded. "Oh, yes. One in the kitchen and another in the hallway."

"Shit. Why?"

"I don't know. I found this in your kitchen." Sean reached into his trouser pocket and pulled out a small, flat device. "The other is inside the smoke detector in your hall-way. I haven't tried to move it. Better not draw too much attention to my visit. With a bit of luck, whoever left it will think one has malfunctioned and that you're still none the wiser that somebody's listening."

I examined the black plastic square, sick to my stomach at the invasion of my privacy. "Which way was it facing?" I asked.

"Which device?"

"The one in the hallway."

"Towards the living room."

"Thank God. At least this creep wasn't watching me get undressed."

"Yeah. Which rules out a pervert."

I shuddered. "That would be bad enough, but not knowing their intention puts the fear of God in me."

"You can stay here for as long as you like."

"Thanks, but I can't. I need my own space. I should report this to someone."

"You could mention it to the letting agency. They have keys, right? Could be an agent or one of their contractors."

"They're hardly going to admit it."

"No. I'd keep it to yourself for now."

"Or tell the police?"

"We're seeing Tom shortly. He'll know what to do."

"OK. I'll pop home and see you at Fat Vi's."

---

Home didn't feel like home anymore, and I crept towards my bedroom, feeling as if the hidden eye in the smoke alarm was boring into my back. I tried not to stare, so it wasn't obvious to whoever had my flat under surveillance. But the effort of not looking was too much to take, and I allowed myself a few subtle glances to see if the camera was completely concealed from view. It was too high to be sure and standing on a chair for a better look would be counter-productive. Instead, I unpacked my bag, grabbed my charger, and took the largest bath towel I could find, hanging it over the shower door to remind myself never to risk an uncovered shower again.

That done, I sifted through my post, chucked a decaying lettuce into the bin, and left the property, wishing I hadn't signed a six-month contract. As I walked out, I saw Brendan Marshall sorting through a bundle of complimentary newspapers in the hallway. He held one out as I passed by. "Saves me a job," he said. "Where have you been? I haven't seen you for a few days."

"I was staying with a friend."

"Then you won't have heard."

"About Velda?"

"Oh, you know."

I nodded. "I found her, and I'm so sorry."

"Me too. Velda was a good kid, though quiet. I wish I'd tried harder to get to know her. Is it true? Did she kill herself?"

"It looked that way, but I can't be sure."

"What did you see?"

The neighbourly part of me wanted to answer frankly, but years of police training left me reluctant to speak openly. I settled for a balance between the two.

"Velda was lying on the floor, near an empty glass," I said, avoiding mention of the hypodermic syringe.

"Overdose then?"

"Perhaps?"

"Why were you there?"

Brendan's question confused me momentarily as I tried to remember the reason for my visit. Then clarity struck.

"I wanted to ask her about Truscombe Grammar."

"Why? Velda wasn't a student."

"I know. But I wondered if she'd ever been to the school. I found some records about one of the old teachers, Irene Paige."

"Now there's a blast from the past. Uncle Colin could tell you a thing or two about that one. Though she was Irene Devonshire when he worked there."

"He knew her?"

"Of course. Col knew most of the teachers, and the students, too. Uncle Col was the school caretaker for a long time. Joined straight from the classroom and never left. Col retired long after he should have – couldn't stay away from the place. It broke his heart when they made him leave, until he started breeding racing pigeons, that is. He was happier after that."

"I suppose you know that Irene Paige disappeared?"

"Yes. Got fed up with the old man and legged it, I shouldn't wonder."

"They were divorced by then."

"Were they? Col would know more."

"Would he speak to me about the school?"

"He'd speak to anyone about anything. Uncle Colin can talk for England, he's a chatterbox through and through."

"Will you call your uncle and ask him if I can pop by?"

"No need. He's always there. Hold on a moment." Brendan removed a pen from his top pocket, took the free paper from my hand, and scribbled a message over an advert.

*Uncle Colin, I've told Sass you'll help her. Talk nicely, and I'll see you on Sunday. No swearing, mind. Brendan.*

---

Sean was propping up the counter when I arrived at Truscombe tea rooms, otherwise known for reasons that escaped me as Fat Vi's.

"There you are," he said, sorting through his pockets for change. "Tom's not here yet. What do you want to drink?" He plucked a couple of coins from his palm and fed them into a collecting tin for The Dogs Trust.

"A cup of tea and a granola bar," I said. "And I thought you only liked things with scales."

"I love dogs," Sean replied. "I'd have one if they didn't bring me out in hives."

"I bumped into Brendan earlier."

"Who?"

"The chap in Flat Five. They've heard about Velda."

"Not surprised. Did Brendan know her well?"

"I guess. They were near neighbours. Anyway, I've got a hot date with his Uncle Colin."

"Why?"

"To talk about the school. He knew Irene Paige."

"You're supposed to be helping me with background checks."

"I will. I can see Colin later. Want to come?"

"No. You go, and I'll concentrate on proper police work while we've still got a contract. Ah, here comes Tom."

They greeted each other with man hugs, followed by a series of fist bumps, which made me feel like an outsider. The young server had taken Sean's order and started setting out mugs of tea on a tray. I took mine and sat at a four-seater table by the window, waiting for Sean and Tom to finish their love-in. Five minutes later, Sean appeared carrying a tray with Tom trailing behind.

"Not in full view – over there," said Tom, nodding to a table at the rear.

I stood and relocated to a chair near the toilet, close enough to smell the faint whiff of urine. I grimaced, but Sean ignored me.

"What's this all about then?" he asked, getting to the point.

Tom offered me a plate of cakes, none of which resembled what I'd asked for, and I took the least calorific option.

"I didn't tell you this," he said, depositing the empty

plate on the table. "But they've finished Velda Ribeira's autopsy."

Sean tapped his nose. "Of course not. And thanks. I appreciate it. What did they find?"

"It looks like a self-administered drug overdose," said Tom.

"I don't believe it." Anger welled inside me at the thought of Velda's life, now inevitably judged by the manner of her death. She didn't use drugs. I was sure of it.

"But there's room for doubt," he continued. "A couple of bruise marks on her upper arm are consistent with someone holding her forcibly."

"You mean someone might have injected her?"

"I didn't say that. But the bruises are there with no reasonable explanation. And Miss Ribeira had taken a strong sedative, a sleeping draught."

"Good information, Tom," said Sean. "But we've been in the flat. No drugs or drug paraphernalia in sight."

"We didn't find any either. There were no suspicious substances to remove, and the young woman didn't leave a note. But under the circumstances, they'll send someone round later for a second check. Hopefully, everything is as we left it. I won't ask how you accessed the property."

"A key on top of the door frame. You're welcome."

"Do her parents know?" I asked, ignoring Sean's inappropriate smugness.

"Yes."

"And her boyfriend?"

"I don't know about that. What's his name?"

"Ben Adjaye."

Tom raised an eyebrow. "I ran checks on him recently. Good grief. Were they the same checks you requested?"

I nodded.

"Then Velda received the anonymous note?"

"Exactly."

"That puts a different light on things."

"Does it?"

"More than you know. The medical examiner found something else. And this is in the strictest confidence. I mean it, Sean. They are not releasing this detail to anyone."

"What is it?"

"An injury on the dead girl's foot. It looked like a cut, and they thought she'd injured herself until they cleaned it up and discovered clean edges. Someone had excised a small square of skin with a knife."

I glanced at Sean, too queasy to take another bite.

"The Skin Thief?" he asked.

Tom nodded. "It could be."

## Chapter Thirty-One

Sean and I went in separate directions after leaving Fat Vi's, him back to the office and me to find Brendan's Uncle Colin in Grosvenor Street. Though Sean had reluctantly agreed to the visit, his set jaw and clipped tones indicated a growing resentment at my lack of involvement in the mundane police background checks with which Kim Robbins had tasked him. And it was a fair point. Sean had employed me to help reduce his workload, and so far, I'd done nothing but add to it. He couldn't have foreseen the number of problems I'd arrive with. Nor could I have anticipated finding myself the subject of covert surveillance. And as I strode up the High Street towards my destination, I promised myself I'd work harder and be invaluable to Sean.

Thirteen Grosvenor Street was a shabby terraced Cotswold stone property which had leeched all the attractiveness of the mellow golden stone with which it was built. The cottage, facing directly onto the pavement, stood lifeless and unbalanced. Tan curtains hanging haphazardly as if most of the hooks were missing, framed a solitary window in need of a good clean. The painted door was scratched and peeling, with a tiny letterbox positioned only inches from the floor, which would undoubtedly have frustrated the postman. I knocked, uncertainly wondering if Colin would be in, despite Brendan's reassurances that he never left home. But after a few moments of waiting, the door opened to reveal a slight, clean-shaven man with sticking-out ears sporting a bemused expression not dissimilar to the late Stan Laurel. "Hello, young lady," he said. "What can I do for you?"

I handed him the newspaper, and he reached into his top pocket and removed a pair of glasses, peering at the page before smiling back at me.

"So, you know, young Brendan, do you?"

"Yes. We live in the same block of flats."

"And what can I help you with?"

"Truscombe Grammar School. I'd like to ask some questions about a teacher who worked there some time ago."

"Truscombe Grammar, you say? Well, you'd better come inside."

I peered past him and down the dark hallway, wondering why I'd come alone. Brendan's uncle was an ordinary-looking man, slight and elderly, yet something about him made the hairs on the back of my arms stand to attention. I felt in my handbag for the personal attack alarm I habitually carried, its smooth surface reassuring me as I ventured inside. With the door shut, the inner gloom felt even more oppressive, and as I walked past a narrow table containing several unopened letters addressed to Colin Marshall, I glanced into the front room. Two high-back chairs curiously arranged near the door impaired my view beyond, but I could hear the steady tones of a wall clock. I followed Colin into the rear of the house into a much lighter room with a sofa and low coffee table set beneath a wide rear window and immediately felt safer away from the gloom.

"Would you like a drink?" he asked.

"Just a glass of water, if you don't mind."

I watched as he shuffled towards the sink, took a glass from the draining board, and filled it with tap water. His hand shook as he held it, and I realised he was frailer than his appearance initially belied. He came towards me, clutching the glass in both hands, putting it on the table with relatively few drips, and slumped on the opposite end of the sofa.

"Thank you," I said.

"You're welcome. Now, what can I tell you about the old school?"

Colin Marshall leaned forwards, his worn body exhibiting signs of interest in the conversation we were about to undertake.

"A little about Irene Paige, I hope."

"Irene Paige?" He raised his brows. "Goodness me. That's going back a bit."

"I know, but her name keeps coming up. And oddly enough, four people in our tiny block of flats have strong connections to the grammar school."

"Oh, yes. Brendan said he'd bumped into an old school friend recently. I nearly fell over when I heard it was Lance Foster."

"Why? Didn't they get on?"

"Yes, well enough, though they were in different years. But I was thinking of Lance's father. Old Derek Foster, otherwise known as Slugger. He was a nasty piece of work who got his comeuppance."

"Really?"

"Yes. And although he thoroughly deserved it, I wouldn't wish his injuries on my worst enemy. Slugger persuaded one of his girlfriends to steal a bottle of acid from the lab to destroy another pupil's work. But something went wrong. He tripped and fell over, knocking himself unconscious and sending the bottle flying. Well, the acid pooled on the floor, and by the time he came round, it had eaten away half his leg. The leg became infected, and he lost it. To cap it all, the headmaster expelled Slugger from school. I was surprised that he let Lance sit the eleven plus. But Derek didn't seem to mind Lance attending Truscombe Grammar, despite his chequered past. It seems he mellowed with age."

"I wonder if Lance has his father's temperament."

"I saw no signs of it, quite the opposite. Lance was a quiet boy, diffident. I stepped in more than once to stop his classmates from picking on him."

"That doesn't sound like the man I know," I said, thinking of Kitty and her poor, bruised hands.

"I'm sure you know best, dear." Colin Marshall leaned against the cushion and smiled, an insincere smirk that didn't reach his eyes. Brendan had spoken of him as a chatty, ebullient man, but he seemed sinister to me. A keeper of secrets, perhaps. Or a pot stirrer.

"Tell me about Irene Paige," I asked.

Colin leaned forwards and rubbed his hands together in undisguised enthusiasm.

"Now, she was another who improved with age," he said.

"How do you mean?"

"I knew Irene as Miss Devonshire, and she seemed like a nice young woman. Had little time for me, but most teachers set themselves above humble caretakers, don't they? Them and us, at least that's what Mr Pratchett used to say, God bless his soul."

I opened my mouth to ask who Mr Pratchett was, but Colin kept talking.

"Yes. Miss Devonshire, your Mrs Paige, was friendly with a chap called Caldicot – he taught science if I remember rightly. My God, he was a handsome young devil, and half the female staff would have dated him in a heartbeat, but he favoured Irene Devonshire, and she seemed to worship the ground he walked on. He died young, though. A sudden heart attack, I think."

Colin turned rheumy eyes towards the window with a faraway look as he spoke. He was silent for a moment, then cleared his throat and continued. "There were other rumours about Caldicot," he said, "that I won't discuss. After all, you're interested in Miss Devonshire, and I don't like to speak ill of the dead."

I resisted asking for details. Colin Marshall was right, and salacious gossip was none of my business. I waited for him to speak again, and he did, the words rushing out like water from an unblocked drain.

"I thought Miss Devonshire was kind to the children in the early days. She favoured the quiet ones, sought them out and befriended them, especially if they were lonely. You know what kids are. But as time went on, I saw a different side to her. She'd belittle them in class or draw attention to their faults in front of their peers. It was as if she didn't like children at all. She saved the worst of it for the weaker ones. And I know that because a few of the children talked to me. At first, only one or two, but then more when they realised, they could trust us; me and Mr Pratchett, that is. And it was Charlie Pratchett who went to the head teacher in the end. I wasn't in her confidence and never found out what they said, but Miss Devonshire walked into the Head's office one day with a shadow hanging over her and out the other side, a different person. She married a few years later and had her own children. Being a mother changed her, and she doted on those girls."

"Was she really that bad? I mean, wasn't it just a youthful error of judgement?"

"No. Someone heavily influenced Irene Devonshire. It stands to reason – she changed overnight. Now whether it was something the Head said or whether it's because Steven Caldicot had recently died, I don't know. But I think she regretted the way she had behaved. When she returned to the school after the girls were a little older, she couldn't have been more friendly and treated her pupils with respect. Like I said, a different woman."

"Do you know what happened to her?"

Colin shook his head. "No. I've no more idea than the police. But she doted on her girls, and I half expected to hear that she'd turned up in Cornwall. One of them lived there, you know. But Irene vanished into the ether. I don't suppose we will ever know. Rumour has it that she's dead."

"Thanks for telling me about her. It's been useful."

"Who are the others?"

"Others?"

"You said four of you were linked to the school."

"Oh, yes. Frank obviously and Pauline Bateman who should have taken my flat. She worked in the school office."

"Can't recall her. The only Bateman I knew was Harry, who married Penny Enright, one of Slugger's friends."

"And I don't know about Velda, but I can't see how she'd be familiar with the school. Velda came from up north, poor girl. Such an awful thing to happen. Did Brendan tell you?"

Colin shook his head. "Tell me what? I haven't seen him this week."

"She died – took her own life, they say. A couple of nights ago."

"Sorry to hear that. What was her name again?"

"Velda Ribeira."

"Doesn't ring a bell. Hang on. It might be a long shot, but there was a school nurse with a similar surname."

I couldn't hold back a sharp intake of breath at his words. One thing I hadn't expected was Velda's possible connection to the school.

Colin hadn't noticed my discomfort and was cogitating. He suddenly clicked his fingers, making me jump. "Not Ribeira, Garcia," he said. "The nurse's name was Imelda Garcia."

I swallowed down my disappointment and mentally ticked Velda off the list of Truscombe connections.

Colin Marshall pressed ahead, determined to find out more. "Who were your other candidates?" he asked.

"Mill Carthy. He's currently teaching at the school."

"Ah yes, Mr Milligan."

"Do you know him?"

"No. He arrived way after my time, but Brendan speaks highly of him. And I knew his mother. She was a pupil here."

"Surely not? He's Irish."

"Irish father, English mother. That's why the young man returned to Gloucestershire. Family roots."

"God," I exclaimed, with a shiver of realisation that Mill's connection to the Grammar was far deeper than it first appeared.

"Well, thank you," I said, rising to go, my mind preoccupied with the latest piece of information.

Colin nodded and slowly followed me up the corridor as I returned to the front of the house.

I turned to thank him one more time, but as I opened my mouth, he spoke again.

"You've forgotten someone," he said.

"Who?"

"Milligan's flatmate."

"Dhruv? He's not a grammar schoolboy. He would have said."

"No. But his father was. Quite unusual for the time. He did very well. A doctor now, I believe."

## Chapter Thirty-Two

"Well, that painful interview reminded me of the many reasons I left the chuffing police force." Sean thundered through the office door, strode to his desk, and tossed his leather-bound clipboard onto the desk. "Idiots."

"Anyone in particular?"

"All of them. Every bloody one."

"Tom?"

"Except Tom."

"I'll make you a coffee, and you can tell me what happened."

Sean grunted, which I took as a yes and scrolled through his phone while I emptied the filter jug dregs into the sink and filled it with fresh, clean water. It bubbled away as I sat opposite Sean, expectantly waiting for him to speak. "Callie?" I asked after a few moments of silence.

"No. She's stuck her oar in, but Kim's up to her ears in it and gave Callie short shrift. And that's about the only productive thing she's done over the last few days."

"Kim's pissed you off?"

"Too right, she has.

"Why?"

"Poor judgement, moving too slowly, making the same mistakes her father did. Take your pick."

"But do we still have the contract?"

"Yes, for now."

"Good. I'll devote the rest of the week to your checks. No distractions, I promise."

Sean cleared his throat. "No, you won't."

"Sorry?"

"I've still got the contract, but only if you're not involved."

"What?" Adrenaline coursed through me, and not in a good way.

"Kim says you're too closely involved with Velda. She insisted I keep my distance from you if I want to keep hold of the contract.

"Sean, no." I blurted the words out, feeling utterly betrayed.

"Don't worry. I have no intention of doing it. But we need to be discrete. You must steer clear of the background checks for now. I've got a few other cases on ice. You can work them from home."

"God, no. I can't face being there twenty-four seven with a spy camera in my hallway."

"Take your laptop to Fat Vi's, then. You can't come back here until this dies down."

"But what about Velda? What about the Skin Thief?"

"That's just it. Kim is finally taking it seriously. She's going after the gas safety engineer and any other contractor granted access to the flats. They're up at Bayliss and Finch now trying to learn more about the landlord, hoping to find due cause to serve a search warrant on the property."

"Why?"

"She wants to get into the locked rooms."

"Locked room. The basement was half open when I went in. Did you mention that?"

"I haven't. Tom might have. Anyway, they have little to go on. The only evidence linking Velda to the Skin Thief is that tiny, excised wound on her foot. And that could be anything. They're pulling medical records to see if there's another reason for it."

"But what's that got to do with me? I know Kim doesn't like me, but wow."

"It's nothing personal, Sass. But if Velda's death wasn't natural, and can't be attributed to a greedy corporate land-lord, or an unscrupulous agent, then the rest of you become suspects."

"Fantastic. What a perfect end to a shitty day."

"Why? Didn't Colin spill the goods?"

"Yes. Creepy Colin was odd but helpful. It turns out that everyone apart from me, Velda, and Kitty had strong connections to the grammar school. Even Dhruv."

Sean whistled. "You're kidding."

I pulled a face. "Think so?"

"No. I mean, I thought you were exaggerating, when you said everyone."

"Yes. Every bloody one."

"Makes my theory look more likely, then."

"Less likely. Why would someone amass a collection of people with grammar school connections only to hound them out of their flats? It makes no sense at all."

"You're right." Sean pondered for a moment while I stirred my coffee with all the enthusiasm of someone about to eat their last supper.

"Gonna use the bolt cutters," he said.

"Now?"

"Of course not. But there's not much time, and Kim isn't covering herself in glory over this. I have serious concerns about her tactics. And timescales. They are planning to question the residents today, which is why you must go back now. All that police activity will put the cat among the pigeons."

"Great. As if I wasn't worried enough."

"You'll be safe with plod all over the building. And I'll be back with my bolt cutters at nine o'clock. Maybe something else if I can call in a favour."

Too preoccupied to ask for details, I left the rest of my coffee, packed away my laptop and reluctantly headed home.

---

The first thing I saw when I walked through the door was the normally mild-mannered Frank, red in the face and barking angrily at a young, uniformed police officer.

"How dare you?" he yelled.

"I'm sorry. I didn't think."

"No, you didn't. I'll have your guts for garters."

"What's wrong?" I asked, placing my laptop against my leg as I watched Frank blinking away tears.

"He tried to barge inside. Frightened Mother to death. She's shaking like a leaf."

I glanced at his front door, still ajar, and glimpsed Veronica Lewis, ashen grey, wringing her hands in her lap at the end of the corridor.

"Shall I go to her?" I asked.

"No. She doesn't know you. Better if I do."

"I haven't finished with you, Sir," said the PC.

Frank ignored him and strode back inside, making soothing noises to his ailing mother.

"Good work," I said, unable to bite down the sarcasm.

"I misjudged it," said the PC. "Do you know them?"

"A little."

"What's wrong with the old girl?"

"Give it a rest. What do they teach you about customer relations at Police Training college these days? Certainly not respect."

"Point taken. What's up with Mrs Lewis?"

"Dementia. And before you ask, she can't talk at all, so it's no use grilling her for information."

"I'll need to speak to Mr Lewis again."

"And I'm sure he'll be delighted to help when he's taken care of his mum. Try someone else for now."

"They're both out," said the PC, pointing to Dhruv's flat. Nobody upstairs either."

"Are you sure? Brendan works shifts. He might be in bed. Knock harder. Is this about Velda?"

"Miss Ribeira? Yes."

"Then you won't want me either. I found the body, and your colleagues already have a detailed account."

The PC extracted a notebook and peered at it while I hooked my laptop bag over my shoulder.

"'I'm afraid I do. They didn't note your movements that day."

"One moment." I tapped my mobile and checked my diary, then my email client, before showing it to the policeman who jotted the information down.

"Did you go anywhere else?"

I racked my brains. "The corner store for milk?" I offered uncertainly.

"Sure?"

"I think so."

"Ring back and confirm when you're certain."

"I'm certain. Will that be all?"

"For now."

As I headed upstairs, I heard Dhruv's excitable voice in the hallway and turned to see him carrying a briefcase. Mill walked beside him with a large pizza box stowed under his arm.

"Not now. Our supper will go cold," said Dhruv as the police officer approached them.

I imagined how much nicer it would be to join them rather than return to my lonely flat with the intrusive listening device. But Colin Marshall had left me suspicious of everyone, including his nephew. Bosworth House was not a place of refuge if it ever had been. I didn't belong. Truscombe Grammar meant nothing to me. Then, with a jolt of horror, I realised that I couldn't be sure of that either.

## Chapter Thirty-Three

I spent the next two hours poring over my family tree as far as I knew it and was relieved to find nothing connecting me to the grammar school. But I only had part of the picture. I knew nothing about my background, and it wasn't inconceivable that my birth parents could have held important positions within the school structure. I was still mithering over things when Sean appeared at my door just before nine. I opened it, about to embark on an explanation of my recent thinking, but he greeted me with his finger to his lips and hastily shoved a sports bag through the door, which clunked onto the tiles.

"Any chance of a coffee?" he asked.

"Sure," I said, reaching for the kettle.

Sean leaned closer to me and whispered in my ear. "Turn the TV up and run the shower while you're at it."

I did as he asked, trying to ignore the potential cost to my heating bill. Sean clearly had something to say and didn't want anyone listening.

When I returned, he was helping himself to a drink and

taking a chunk out of a piece of bread he'd found in a bag on my work surface.

"Help yourself," I said sarcastically.

Sean grinned and devoured the rest of the slice in a few short bites.

"Bloody starving," he said. "I haven't been home yet."

"Poor lizards."

"Don't worry. Gary's got a key now. I don't know why I didn't think of it sooner."

"Gary?"

"My next-door neighbour. He knows what to do in a crisis. Which this isn't, you'll be glad to hear."

I didn't know what shape a lizard-related crisis took and was too distracted to ask. "What's this all about?" I whispered instead, pointing towards the back of my flat.

"I've brought my lock cutters for the basement, but they won't do for the attic room."

"I know. We'll need to leave that to the police if they get that far."

"Ah. Did Kim's lot turn up?"

"One of them did. An officious little shite who scared the living daylights out of Frank's poor mum."

Sean frowned. "I thought Kim was taking this seriously."

"More likely hedging her bets. She doesn't want to go all out with it in case she's wrong while covering her arse at the same time."

"I'm disappointed," said Sean. "But not altogether surprised."

"I am. You were her flag-waving greatest admirer until a few days ago. What's changed?"

"She's gone off the boil, and I think you're right. Kim must be feeling the effects of her father's failure. And think about it, Sass. Kim doesn't know if the Skin Thief is back or if it's the son of Skin Thief or nothing at all. Even Miles Savage has quietened down. Nobody wants to look stupid."

"Well, they can afford to wait it out, but I can't. Something is going on right here in the flats, and I don't want anyone else to end up like Velda or Amy Swanson."

"Connecting their deaths is still a stretch."

"Then why are you here?"

"Better safe than sorry. And we'll know a bit more when Dave's done his thing."

"Dave? What thing?"

"A friend of mine. Dave is a locksmith."

"Right."

"He's meeting us here at midnight to drill out the upstairs lock. Unless we find what I'm looking for in the basement."

"Bloody hell, Sean. That's risky. You'll be in every kind of shit when Kim finds out."

"She won't."

"Unless you get caught. Brendan will hear drilling, even if the others don't."

"Have you got a better idea?"

"I don't know what you're looking for."

"A central point to view the cameras."

"Cameras? You disabled the second one, didn't you?"

"I saw one in Velda's flat, too."

"Oh, my God. Why didn't you say?"

"No point in worrying you."

"Do you think there's a camera in every flat?"

"That's what I'm hoping to find out."

I waited for a moment, taking in Sean's words, and trying to calm the throbbing pulse in my neck. I needed to stop thinking about a hidden voyeur and concentrate on other problems.

"Before we go, I need to tell you something."

"What?"

"I've always assumed that I don't have a connection with the grammar school. And now I'm wondering if I might do, after all."

"Don't you know?"

"I'm adopted, so no."

"Sorry. I forgot. But I don't think that's it."

"Why?"

"Because they never intended Flat Three for you. You're one of a steady stream of six-month lets."

"That's true. The occupier should have been Pauline Bateman, but she dropped out. Gretta had it before I arrived and another girl before her."

"A girl?"

"Yes. I'm sure someone said a girl. I might be wrong. It doesn't matter, anyway."

"Ready then?"

"If the policeman has gone."

"I think so. Everything's quiet."

"Perhaps we should leave it for a while, just in case."

"No. Kim will do her nut if she finds out what we're doing, and I need to get on with it before I change my mind."

# Chapter Thirty-Four

*She saw me enter. I knew I was taking a chance visiting her flat during daylight hours, but I couldn't help myself. I needed to know.*

*I'd harboured suspicions since the second camera stopped working. And that friend of hers was always hanging around like a bad smell. Typical police type, shifty – and her friend looked tech savvy, so I knew there would be trouble.*

*The girls in Flat Three have always caused me problems. I don't know what it is about the damned place, but they cannot settle down and look pretty in their boxes. What's the point of collecting something so flighty and unruly? The first, well, we don't talk about her. She was such a disappointment and nosy too. Nearly ruined everything, that one – until I took care of things. Gretta was a stopgap. Then, my perfect replacement didn't make it across the threshold of Bosworth House. I have seldom been so disappointed. I'd arranged everything, but the exhibit fluttered off to unexpected pastures new in the United States. She'd lost her holding deposit but didn't care. Some people have far too much money. I inherited the Denman creature. Not part of my collection at all. I didn't want her and had no need for her. She didn't tick a* single box and was, quite frankly, getting in the way of other, more valuable items.

*Bayliss* and bloody *Finch*. What a joke. They misunderstood my instructions. Well, those that filtered through the limited company I'd used in the Channel Islands. Wheels within wheels. Not money laundering, exactly. I wouldn't do that. But a carefully constructed paper trail to hide my identity within the bounds of a corporate entity. Nobody knows me. Nobody cares what I own and how I conduct myself through my business assets. I am anonymous. I can do as I please, and I do. Often playing games with my carefully hand-picked collectables, each a nod to my past. My playthings. I can hurt them, heal them, and indulge in cat and mouse strategies until they are half-mad, wondering if they have imagined the sights, sounds, and smells. They are not. It is I, their owner, their controller.

But I digress. The young girl in the top flat was an unusual choice. She wasn't a product of my tormentors, nor did she recently work in the hellhole I attended during my junior years. As far as I know, and unlike the others, she had never been near Truscombe Grammar School. Ordinarily, I wouldn't have bothered with her. But when I received her application, I conducted my usual social media checks, including a quick search on *MyPerfectLife*. I was on the verge of saying no to this young girl from Yorkshire. She didn't suit my purposes at all. But a casual post on her *MyPerfectLife* blog offered an interesting comment, which she later deleted, but not before I had clicked on the poster's name and jumped to her page. An hour later, I learned that the pretty, mild-mannered girl who had placed a holding deposit on flat five and wouldn't say boo to a goose was a serious class bully at school. Not physically, but in the underhand, insidious way of a social media stalker, preying on the vulnerable and weak. I learned through her old classmates of hidden allegations, implied but unsaid, serious but unprovable, swirling, unstoppable, endless rumours with no substance. *Becky747killerqueen* told a tale of the suicide of a young girl. A *teenage life snuffed out too young, cancelled by her peers because of unsubstantiated gossip that she couldn't stop any other way than by taking control and shutting them out forever. And I thought – that could have been me. Alone and reviled by my classmates, an easy victim for the Veldas of this world. And that's when I decided to let her in, to give her a place in my collection.*

*She enjoyed an extended occupancy before I set my plans in motion. I hadn't known what to do with her. Velda was so dull that there were no obvious activities to take advantage of until I listened in on the conversation with the girl in Flat Three. It soon transpired that Flat Five was romancing a young man – a very nice young man, wholesome and smart, and sharing her religion. Odd, isn't it, how the godly can be so uncaring? A bully yet devoted to an invisible being. I soon learned her boyfriend's name, which was rare enough for me to unearth a little about him without trying too hard. A salt of the earth type who did a bit of charity work. Nothing wrong with him at all, so I created a little note and made him a paedophile. Oh, I enjoyed her reaction when she opened the envelope. I'd hopped into her flat the day before while she was at work and added a few extra cameras, so I'd see her reaction wherever she was. Velda didn't disappoint and literally howled in anguish as she read the words, dropping the letter to the floor as if it was burning her hands. She sobbed solidly for a good hour, didn't speak to anyone, and dashed off a quick text, probably throwing a sickie. She was dressed for work but didn't leave the flat for the rest of the day, poor dear.*

*I enjoyed giving her a taste of her own medicine and doubled down on the enjoyment the following day while replaying the camera from Flat Three. They were becoming friends, Flats Three and Five, not something I usually encouraged. Fear magnifies when faced alone. But in this case, she confided in the Denman girl, so I heard her terror in stereo. And days later, I received a warning about Denman's background. It turned out she was a policewoman turned private eye. Who* would have thought it? But a timely reminder that I would need to row back on the little treats I had planned for her and everyone else in the block. In fact, I'd need to go a step further. Hold back on all my planned fun until her lease ended. Thank God, we'd put her on a six-month tenancy. Quiet times ahead for a few months, or so I thought.

But then, I did something foolish and checked Velda's movements during the day. God knows why. I'd always waited until the dead of night, never running into anyone, not once in all these years. Knowing her work pattern, I thought she was out. She shouldn't have been there, but the silly girl was, and she saw me leaving the upstairs room. I met her on the landing, and she was friendly enough, making nothing of it at the time. But when I next checked the cameras, my worst fears were realised. She'd doubled back and checked the door handle, which meant she was suspicious, and it was only a matter of time until she spoke of it to someone. I hadn't a moment to lose. I took her key, entered her flat and placed a sedative in the drinks bottle she habitually kept on her coffee table.

Once she was asleep, I slipped back inside, taking a syringe I had prepared earlier and shooting it deep into her veins. Oh, so satisfying. Pity about the gloves, though. These things are much better flesh on flesh, but there's no point in taking silly chances except I did. Old habits die hard, old pleasures even more so. There she was, dying on the floor, the only trouble coming when she briefly woke, arms flailing as I pumped cocaine into her vein. She lashed out, and I held her arms until she flopped back to the floor, mouth gaping like a dying fish. I tried to stop myself and left the room, my hand resting on the front doorknob as I fought the urge. Fought and lost. Just one sip. Just one tiny sip. One tiny cut. It needn't be much. No one would ever know. Not from the sole of a foot. Oh, the ecstasy as I slipped the knife in, blood welling around the wound. Less than an inch. Nothing really, but I scored a tiny rectangle and flopped the piece of excised skin onto Velda's thigh where it sat, pulsing as if it had a life of its own. I watched it, gloried in the vision, then took it and held it under my tongue for safe passage to its *new home with all the others. Velda was finished, dead to me. An unfortunate piece of collateral damage too close to home. But I had been careful, and there was no reason for anyone to suspect me. After all, I was nothing, no one. Taking one last look at the bully in Flat Five, I left, disappearing into the ether as if I had never been there.*

## Chapter Thirty-Five

"What if someone sees us?" I asked as we tiptoed downstairs towards the basement.

"We can't let that happen. Only Frank and Dhruv live on the ground floor, and why would they be out and about at this time of night? Brendan won't trouble us as we passed him on the stairs earlier and the bickering from Flat Four is still loud and clear."

I could think of many reasons why Dhruv and Mill might socialise beyond the heady hour of nine o'clock, but if I argued with Sean, I risked unnerving him, and he might change his mind about the whole operation. And that's how I viewed it – an officially sanctioned military covert surveillance op. And as long as I kept my head in that space, I could ignore the nervous gripes inside me that spoke of illegal breaking and entering, with all the consequences that might follow. *Focus, Sass. Focus.*

The foyer was quiet save for the soft burr of Frank's television, always with the volume set louder than necessary, probably to compensate for his mother's impaired hearing.

Dhruv's flat was silent, and I couldn't tell if they were home. But we ducked through the first basement door quickly and without being seen, and I was relieved that it was still light, and I had company this time.

"Ready?" asked Sean, who had retrieved the bolt cutters from his sports bag and was brandishing them near the padlock.

"Wait," I said, cocking my head, sure I had heard a faint noise again.

Sean listened before dropping to his haunches and putting his ear to the door. Then he nodded, jaw set firmly, eyes glistening in anticipation of action. His fingers trembled, but not with nerves. Sean was enjoying himself. Never a natural desk jockey, he wanted to be in the thick of it, and who knew what was beyond the door?

Sean stood, closed the bolt cutter jaws over the thin brass padlock, and then firmly snipped. The broken padlock clunked onto the concrete floor. We waited, hearts pounding, ready to flee at the sound of an opening door. But silence reigned. No one had heard us, and we were safe for now.

Sean cleared the padlock away and slowly opened the door, feeling around the edges for a light switch. I followed behind, almost blinded as the light flashed overhead, then quickly died as the bulb popped.

"Damn it," he said. "Just our luck. Get inside quickly."

I pushed past him, and he shut the door, feeling inside his sports bag for a light source. I was one step ahead, having jammed my trusty flashlight into my back pocket. But as I reached for it, something soft weaved against my lower leg, exposed from my three-quarter chinos, and I dropped the torch on the floor in panic.

"What the fuck was that?" I said, flinching from the fur-like intruder and careering into Sean, who fell against the wall and held himself there momentarily, trying to regain his balance.

"What?" he hissed testily.

"There's something in here."

"I know."

My fingers inched along the grainy concrete floor, searching for the torch in the pitch-black cellar. Then, they alighted on something smooth and metallic, a bowl or receptacle placed incongruously on the floor. I ran my fingers into a pulpy mess. Snatching them out, I raised soggy digits to my nose, and a disgusting fishy odour assailed my nostrils, making me gag.

"What's wrong, Sass?" asked Sean, puzzled by the sudden noise

"Not sure," I replied, wiping the sticky mess onto my hoodie.

Sean was still fumbling in his sports bag, and I struck out in the other direction, hoping for no more surprises. Finally, my hands closed over the missing torch.

"Got it," I said and switched it on to reveal a low ceilinged, windowless room with a concrete floor in the middle of which stood a pair of shiny chrome bowls, one containing water and the other a pulpy brown mass. I looked at Sean, puzzled, and he returned my stare. Then, a rustle of cardboard sounded from the far end of the room, heralding the arrival of a black mass which bounded towards us and weaved itself around my ankles.

"It's Sinbad," I said. "He's alive."

"Sinbad?"

"Frank's missing cat. Thank God. At least whoever has been playing these spiteful games with us isn't cruel enough to hurt an animal."

Sean and I climbed the stairs, blinking at the bright light in the foyer. We were in two minds about whether to leave Sinbad in my flat until the following day, but Frank had been so worried about his missing pet that we decided to return him that night, even though it was, by now, after ten. Sean had thoughtfully brought along a second padlock, similar to the one we had destroyed, and fixed it before we left. Though not identical, it was close enough that whoever had hidden Sinbad might not notice the difference, though they would have fun and games trying to access the room. For obvious reasons, we wanted to keep our basement visit covert. And we didn't want to alarm Frank by telling him his cat had been imprisoned in the basement. He'd suffered enough worry. Instead, we slipped out the front and made a big show of returning inside loudly enough to rouse Mill, who opened his door at the commotion.

"Look who we found?" I said as Mill stared bemusedly from his hallway.

"Is that...?"

"Yes. It's Sinbad. I can't wait to take him to Frank."

"Good work," said Mill. "Poor Frank has been out of his mind with worry."

"Who is it?" A shrill female voice with an Irish lilt came from inside the flat.

"Don't worry, Mum. I'll only be a moment. Ask Dhruv if you need anything." Mill smiled ruefully. "It's my mother," he explained. "Dhruv must have convinced her I was at death's door, and she's flown in from Ireland to look after me."

"Sorry I intruded. I won't keep you then. Tell Dhruv

about Sinbad, won't you? He helped me look a few nights ago."

"I will. He's fond of the little chap. Best you go before he escapes again," Mill continued, watching Sinbad struggle in my arms.

"OK. I'll leave you to it."

I knocked on Frank's door while clutching Sinbad to my chest while Sean waited quietly near the stairwell.

It took a while for the door to open, and I wondered if Frank had gone to bed, but he appeared fully dressed with his glasses in his top pocket and blinked several times at the sight before him. Slowly, he focused on Sinbad and his eyes filled with tears.

"Oh, my boy," he said in a quavering voice as he reached for his cat.

Sinbad purred and burrowed into his master's arms, making snuffling noises.

"Where did you find him?" asked Frank, raising his nose from Sinbad's soft fur.

"Outside," I lied. "He must have been coming home."

"I don't know what to say. Thank you. I love this cat. No children, you see. He's everything to me."

I nodded, unable to speak, as I choked back tears of my own. At least Frank had a cat. I had nothing to care for, not even a tank of lizards.

Frank reached into his pocket and withdrew a dog-eared wallet. "Get yourself something nice," he mumbled, pulling out a note.

"Thank you, but absolutely not. It's been my pleasure. I'll see you around, Frank."

I made for the stairs, Sean trailing behind me, and heard Frank's door shut as he took his precious pet inside.

"That was a good night's work," I said as we approached my flat.

"All very heart-warming, but not what I was hoping for," said Sean. "Means we'll need to proceed with Plan B."

"Ah, yes. I suppose so. I wish I weren't so tired, and we've got a good few hours to kill until then."

"Exactly. Let's put on a film and have a bit of supper while we wait. You can snooze for a while if you want to."

## Chapter Thirty-Six

Sean's idea of a good night's television was a documentary about the life and times of the Sumatran gliding lizard. I made it through the first ten minutes, then must have fallen asleep on the couch. Sean roused me with a solid elbow to the midriff just before midnight.

"Wakey, wakey," he said cheerfully, then in a lower voice, "Skeleton Dave's due any moment."

"What? Oh, yes," I murmured, rubbing sleep from my eyes, and trying to remember why Sean was in my flat.

"Shoes on." Sean nodded to the trainers I'd kicked off in my sleep. I slipped them back on, too tired to undo the laces, and noticed my charm bracelet lying beside them on the floor. I fastened it around my wrist and squeezed the metal clasp tight while making another mental note to get it repaired. Then I thought about Sean's friend. "Skinny, is he?" I asked.

"Who?"

"Your mate Dave."

"Not skeleton as in thin, skeleton, as in key," he whispered. "If it's possible to break into a place, Dave's your man."

"Then why is he bringing a drill?"

"Worst-case scenario. Buzz down, and I'll collect him."

I did as he asked, and Sean bounded from the flat like an excitable police dog. I was still half asleep and waited by my open front door as if in a daze. The soft tread of someone walking up the stairs broke my reverie, and Sean put his finger to his lips, then waved his companion onwards. I followed behind. On arriving on the top landing, Sean pointed to Brendan's flat and made a hand signal to indicate one occupant, then a further gesture to come. Dave, wearing a cap and a dark scarf over his mouth, crouched by the side of the door, flicked a switch on his hat, and a bright beam of light appeared by the lock. He peered at the mechanism, ran his fingers over the metal and removed his rucksack, unzipping a small compartment to reveal a folded cloth. Dave examined the tools and rechecked the lock."

"Problem?" whispered Sean.

"Shouldn't be," said Dave. "Be patient, now." His lilting Welsh accent somehow filled me with confidence, and my heart stilled, relieved that we wouldn't be risking the whine of a drill at this ungodly hour. "Eeny-meeny," he said, his hand hovering over the middle tool.

My heart sank, confidence ebbing away.

"He's joking," whispered Sean. "Don't fret. Those are the tools of his trade, a tension wrench, a pick, and a rake. A gin and tonic says we'll be inside within five minutes.

I glanced at my phone, checking the time. Not that an alcoholic drink was that important, but it took my mind off the immediate peril of standing in full view of Brendan's flat should he choose to emerge.

I didn't see which of the three tools Dave selected, and by the time I looked up from my timer, Dave was puffing the nozzle end of a bottle of graphite into the lock. Moments later, he tried the door, pushed it, and then scowled. A jiggle with one of the other tools, and the door quietly popped open.

"Great stuff," said Sean. "I owe you one."

"We'll settle tomorrow," said Dave.

"Make that Saturday, and I'll take you for a beer."

"You're on."

"Front door is on the latch," said Sean.

"Right you are. Catch you later."

Dave disappeared down the stairwell, and Sean pushed the door open, immediately finding a switch.

"Come on then, we haven't got all night," he said.

---

The long desk with its six state-of-the-art monitors reminded me of a military command-and-control centre and could not have looked more incongruous in an unkempt block of flats if it tried. I stared, open-mouthed, and Sean did likewise before a slow grin spread over his face.

"I bloody knew it," he said.

"Impossible."

"Had to be, to account for the cameras."

"But why?"

"That's what we're here to find out." I followed Sean's gaze as he stood next to the desk, making a sweep of the room while a satisfied smile played across his face.

"No need to be so damned smug."

"Ah, come on. You're just jealous because you didn't think of it."

"Not the time or place," I said, approaching a corkboard on the left-hand side of the door. Six yale keys swung from six hooks, with a further two tagged together on a seventh hook located randomly at the bottom of the board. I picked up the first key and checked the label. "Flat One," I said.

"Every flat key will be there," Sean replied. I looked. They were.

"What about these two?" The remaining keys were unlabelled.

"Basement and front door, I should think."

"So, whoever set this up can access any room whenever they like?"

"That's about the size of it."

"God." My flesh crawled at the thought of an unknown stalker able to gain access whenever he wanted, and I decided that if I returned to the flat tonight, I'd be sleeping with something heavy wedged against the front door.

"You okay?" Sean put his arm around my shoulder in an unexpected gesture of camaraderie.

I nodded. "I've had time to get used to it."

"Good. Because this is the nerve centre, take a look."

Sean pulled out a chair and sat in front of the first set of monitors while I stood behind him. All were on the split screens showing snatched glimpses of objects rendered barely visible in the darkened rooms.

"Can't see much at this time of night. Screen one equates to Flat One. Check out the first camera. There's a lump in the bed."

"Too small to be Frank," I said. "Ah, yes. There's a wheelchair in the corner. The camera must be trained on his mum. What sort of low-life spies on someone with dementia? Bastard."

"Agreed. Look at the second half. I can just make out a night light. It seems like the other camera is in the hallway."

"I don't know what to say."

"Nothing. Just look. This must be Dhruv's apartment. Too dark to see anything on that camera. Oh, hello. Perhaps not. Something just flashed outside. Maybe a car passing by. The camera might be in the living room. The second is definitely in the hallway."

"How can you tell?"

"I can't. But that's where we found the trap, and I guarantee whoever set it will have wanted to know if it worked."

"We'll check another time."

"Too right. Now see below the screen – someone has written a number down on a sticky label. Don't know what it means, but jot it down, will you?"

I opened a drawer under the desk, rummaged for pen and paper, found both, and scribbled until my eyes were drawn to the shadow of a logo underneath. I turned the page. "Bayliss and bloody Finch," I said.

"Hold that thought. It's looking more like corporate sleaze. There's nothing remotely benevolent about Sentinel."

I turned my gaze to the first split screen on monitor three, relieved to find nothing but black space where Sean had disabled the camera. The right-hand side of the screen was a different matter, the camera pointing from the hall to the living room and taking in a good eyeful of a late show where I'd forgotten to turn off the television. At least I now knew how much the unknown surveiller could see of my activities, and memories of my earlier conversations set my teeth on edge.

"Jesus. He must have heard everything I said to Velda?"

"He? What makes you think it's a man?"

"I just assumed."

"I wouldn't. Which of us is better with a PC, you or me?"

"Obviously me, no contest."

"Quite. How many staff at Bayliss and Finch?"

"I've met two. One male and one female."

"There you go then. It could be either. Still not sure how our spy listens, though."

I glanced at the wires coming from the screens and tracked them towards Sean's left-hand side, then reached over and picked up a set of headphones. "Try these."

Sean placed them on his head, and moments later, he grinned. "You're right. Loud and clear, but all I can hear is snoring," he said. "I'll put them back. Doubt there's anything worth listening to at this time of night."

Sean stood and then moved to the second chair in front of the other screens. "Flat Four," he said, pointing to another grey mound in bed. The second monitor revealed the same.

"Odd. Must be two cameras set at different angles."

"No. Look at the size of the windows. Completely different."

We looked again. "Ha," said Sean. I should have guessed. The Fosters sleep in different bedrooms."

"Good," I said, relieved that Kitty had some space away from her violent husband.

"Hello, hello. Lance is on manoeuvres."

I followed Sean's finger to see Lance fumbling bleary-eyed towards his bedside lamp before leaving the room.

"If he lays a finger on her, I'll kill him," I said.

"Steady on. We shouldn't be here."

"I don't care. I won't watch Lance lashing out at Kitty and bugger the consequences."

"Kitty's fine. Her room's still dark. Hold on. I'll get the headphones and listen in."

Sean shoved them over his ears and stared blankly. I grabbed the mouse and slid it across the screen, switching between audio outputs. "Got it," he said. "Lance is in the bathroom. I can hear the flush."

"Good thing. I wouldn't want to stage an intervention. It might get bloody."

"Give over, Sass. Look. He's back in his room. It must be hot. He's taken off his tee-shirt. Blimey. Is he a rugby player?"

"How should I know? He gives me the creeps. Why?"

"Check out his back?"

I did. Even in the dim light cast from the side lamp, there was no disguising a mass of bruises on Lance's shoulders. "Looks like she gave as good as she got," I said as the light dimmed and Lance slid under the duvet.

"They need therapy," said Sean, then his hand suddenly snaked towards the fifth monitor, and he shut it down.

"What did you do that for?"

"You don't want to know?"

"Except that I do."

"What I mean is, you don't want to see."

"For God's sake Sean. I'm not a child."

"Then I'll turn it on again, but you'll never think of Brendan Marshall in the same way."

"What's he doing?" My stomach sank as I imagined the possibilities, not because I was a prude but because I'd be watching with Sean, which would undoubtedly feel awkward.

"Sure you want to see?"

"Just tell me already."

"Your friend is entertaining a lady of the night."

"What?"

"Brendan is shagging a Tom."

"Oh, please. You sound like a reject from the 1980s."

"Good times, they were."

"I think we've moved on."

"Didn't have you down as the sensitive type."

"I'm not. But never mind. I can't be bothered to argue. How do you know Brendan's friend is a sex worker?"

"Money changed hands, and not in the usual way."

I tried not to blush and failed. "I don't want to know."

"Didn't think you would. Anyway, the screen now matches Flat Six."

I'd already noticed that Screen Six was off, requiring no further monitoring as the occupant of the apartment was dead. A shiver traversed my spine at the thought of poor Velda lying cold and alone in a drawer in the morgue. "Let's finish up," I said.

Sean nodded and started opening drawers while I walked over to a whiteboard at the end of the room, neatly boxed with magnetic tape into a three-by-two grid. Someone had filled boxes three and six with red marker pen crosses. I puzzled over it for a moment, and then terror clawed at my chest as the implication hit me. Velda was dead, which explained the cross in box six, but why was there a cross in box three that, by rational deduction, must correspond to my apartment?

"Sean. Come here," I said, my voice trembling as I struggled to contain my fear. "Look at this. What's this cross for?" I stabbed a finger into the red text, smudging it into the magnetic strip.

Sean's eyes rested on the grid; jaw set as he marshalled his words.

"I think this is the reason," said Sean, handing me a bundle of letters.

Bile rose in my throat as I read the address. "Amy Swanson, Flat Three, Bosworth House."

## Chapter Thirty-Seven

"This is one for Kim, not me. Way past my pay grade." Tom Manning looked anxiously towards the window as he stirred his coffee and took a sip, flinching as the dark liquid burned his lips. Sighing, he pushed the cup away.

"I know. I was on my way to tell her. We can't wait much longer." Sean broke a flapjack in half and offered a piece to Tom, who waved it away.

"Then why am I here?" asked Tom.

"Because we have a problem and need to buy time."

"What could be more important than informing the investigating police officer that a murder victim once lived in a block of apartments with a state-of-the-art surveillance system?"

"Callie's on the warpath, and I need to keep on the right side of Kim Robbins. Financial budgets and all that."

"That's all very well, but it doesn't explain why you need more time."

"Tell him, Sass."

"Sorry to put you in this position, Tom," I said, going all

out to appease him. Tom had always struck me as mild-mannered and largely unflappable, but his usually benign expression had turned into an irritated scowl.

"What position?" he asked abruptly.

"I was wearing a bracelet when we first entered the attic room."

"Broke into the attic room," snapped Tom.

"That too. Sean was leaving for the police station when I noticed it was missing."

"The bracelet? Good grief. Have you checked your flat?"

"Of course. It's the first thing I did. And I retraced my route from home to the corner store, but it wasn't there. And the catch was faulty. I remember adjusting it as I left last night."

"Pity you didn't think to take it off and put it somewhere safe until you fixed it."

"Hindsight, and all that…" I muttered lamely.

"So, we need to get back inside," said Sean.

"And I'm supposed to turn a blind eye after what you've just told me?"

"Just for half an hour, possibly less."

"Then why bother me at all? I'd be a darn sight happier in blissful ignorance."

"Because you answered your phone," quipped Sean.

"Won't be doing that again so readily."

"OK. I didn't mean to be flippant. Cards on the table. We've reason to think that Sentinel Benevolent monitors its tenants. God knows why. This building can't be worth much unless it's sitting on a previously unknown supply of shale gas."

"Is that a thing?" asked Tom, momentarily confused.

"Of course not. The point is, I don't know why Sentinel

needs to spy on their tenants, but Sass found a letter sent to them by their letting agent, so their hands are dirty."

"What did it say?"

"The letter? I didn't read it. Remind me, Sass?"

"It wasn't a letter. Just a statement of account for works."

"That's proof of nothing, let alone a serious crime. What exactly do you want from me?" Tom retrieved his coffee and tentatively sipped.

"Have you found more information about the beneficial owners yet?"

"No. It's a complex trail. But our team is on it, and we'll soon know more."

"Damn. I'd love to hear that information before involving Kim."

"Involving Kim? It's her sodding investigation. I don't mind our little arrangement. Kim's tipped me the nod that she expects some cooperation outside normal protocol, but you take the biscuit, Sean. And she'll send me to traffic if you push me any harder."

"I know, Tom. Half an hour. That's all. Wait thirty minutes, then call Kim and tell her anything you like."

"Oh, no, you don't. You can telephone Kim at precisely eleven-thirty when I'll be back at the station and not implicated in any more of your nonsense."

"Deal." Sean grinned. "And you'll let me know as soon as you hear about Sentinel?"

"No promises."

"Come on, Tom. Just this once. It's important."

"You don't give up, do you?"

"Nope."

Tom scowled, knocked back the rest of his drink and strode from the cafe without a backward glance.

"What have you done to him?" An impossibly slim woman appeared beside us and regarded Sean sternly. "Don't you go upsetting my best customer."

"I thought I was your best customer," said Sean, flashing a charming smile.

"In your dreams." The woman scowled, narrowing her eyes, as she collected Tom's empty cup before thrusting a blotchy veined hand towards the unfinished flapjack.

"Hands off the goodies, Miss Violet," said Sean, holding the plate to his chest in a dramatically protective gesture.

"Give over," she said, took my cup and disappeared into the back.

"Who in the world was that?" I asked.

"Can't you guess?"

"No."

"Fat Vi."

"Come again?"

"It's ironic. I've seen more meat on a butcher's pencil."

"Child."

"Whatever. Come on. Duty calls, and the clock's ticking."

---

Sean and I returned to the flat, hoping that the picked lock we'd left open hadn't been secured by Sentinel or one of their agents while we'd been away. Time being of the essence, we raced straight up to the second-floor landing and spent a nervous few seconds gaining access while a clattering in Brendan's hallway implied he was about to emerge from his flat. Fortunately, we made it inside and shut the door before a cheerful whistle heralded the thud of footsteps going downstairs.

"Nicely dodged," said Sean. "Let's crack on. Tom's at the end of his rope, and if he gets any more upset, he might tell Kim."

"Will she really cut our funding?"

"It's not up to her. But if Kim's offside, Callie will do as she pleases. But that's by the by. Funding is inconvenient. Breaking and entering is unlawful."

"Noted. We'll be quick. Take this half of the room, and I'll take the other."

I walked to the rear, patting the beige carpet to feel for the tiny gold bracelet I'd worn every day since Mum died. It held no monetary value but had belonged to the woman who'd loved and cared for me, with no genetic obligation and who I missed more than words could say. But Sean didn't need to know about the sentimental value, only that if the police found a bracelet that shouldn't be there, they would undoubtedly start asking awkward questions. And if it led back to me, it would also expose Sean.

"This it?" whispered Sean from across the room. A fragile gold chain glistened in his hand.

"Oh, well done." I thrust the bracelet into my jeans pocket, determined not to make the same mistake twice. "Where was it?"

"Under the desk," said Sean. "Beneath monitor three. Guess that held your attention more than the others."

"Well, it would, wouldn't it? Imagine if you had a spy camera in your house."

"They'd be bored stupid."

"Whatever. Wow. The screens are a lot clearer in daylight." I peered at the monitor with the camera pointing toward my living room. "Unbelievable. I can read the title of my book."

"Only because you know what it says."

"No. Look."

"I see what you mean – amazing clarity. Unsurprising as this is a state-of-the-art system. Hello. The Fosters are at home." Sean had turned his attention to monitor four.

"Is Lance on Kitty's case again?" I sat beside Sean, peering at the screen as he jammed the headphones over his head.

"Yep. Once again, the Fosters are arguing for England. I don't know why they're together. They don't get on at all."

"What are they rowing about?"

"Cat food."

"Don't be silly."

"I kid you not. And it's getting heated."

"Hold on. I want to listen."

I pulled the cord from the PC, changed the audio settings, and quickly lowered the volume as Kitty's shrill voice screeched through the monitor speakers.

"I'm not spending another fucking night with cat food in the freezer, you useless idiot. I told you to get rid of it. Do it, or I'll get rid of you."

"Don't start, Kitty. Please don't start."

Lance Foster held out his hands in a gesture of supplication.

"Oh, stop it, will you? Don't make this my fault. You never listen, and I wouldn't need to raise my voice if you did as I asked."

"I'll move the rest of it soon. You know I've already started, but it's tricky with the cats still there. I know the cattery must close, or the house won't sell. The estate agent says…"

"Don't tell me what the sodding agent says. We've been over this umpteen times. Do I need to call them again?" Kitty Foster's face twisted into an angry scowl.

"No. Please don't do that. I'll sort it."

"When?"

"When I can find homes for the cats."

"Turn them out. Put the smelly creatures down. I don't care."

"Come on, Kitty. We're down to the last three, and you know I need to wait until the owners are back in the country. I'll close it down for good in ten days if you're patient a little longer."

"Not good enough." Kitty strode purposefully towards her husband.

Sean and I exchanged glances. "That's one angry lady," he said.

"No, Kitty." Lance Foster dropped to his haunches in the corner of the room, arms crossed in front of his face.

"You're pathetic." Kitty stood over her partner, hands on hips, watching him cower like an animal. Suddenly, her stilettoed foot shot out and connected between his legs. He fell to the floor, hands on his genitals, face silently contorted in pain.

"You-have-one-more-sodding-day-and-that-is-all," she hissed, pounding the middle of his back with her fist in time with the words. Lance closed his eyes, lowered his head, and lay curled up in a foetal position.

Sean stared at me, mouth agape, face as pale as I'd ever seen it. "You called that wrong," he said. "I've never witnessed domestic abuse towards a man before, but this sure as hell is it."

# Chapter Thirty-Eight

"What now?" Sean was still staring at the monitor, ashen faced.

"I don't know. Kitty's gone. It's over."

"Then why isn't Lance moving?"

I shook my head. "I don't know. He can't be that badly injured."

"Exactly. He ought to be up and about."

"Perhaps he's exhausted."

"I don't doubt it, but it's more than that. Look carefully."

I opened the software and zoomed in closer. Lance was visibly shaking. "He's terrified," I said.

"Yet she's left the room."

"Oh, shit."

"What?"

"He must be expecting her back. God, how long has this been going on for?"

"And how much worse does it get?"

"Sean, look. I think we're about to find out."

Kitty Foster flew through the door and walked towards the left-hand side of the room. I tried and failed to rotate the camera, and for a moment, she disappeared from sight. Seconds later, she reappeared, carrying a wooden object. I zoomed in again to see the curved edge of a hockey stick. Lance remained motionless on the floor, his forehead on top of his arms as if hiding his face would make it all go away. Kitty paced towards him, her fists clenched around the stick, then retreated to the other end of the room. She strode backwards and forwards, narrowly avoiding the bed and clutching the weapon to her chest as if she was fighting with inner emotions, her face an ugly mask of unsuppressed anger.

"She's waiting for him to do something, anything that gives her an excuse to hurt him," I said, my heart thumping at the tinderbox scene before me.

"Stay still, mate," whispered Sean. "Don't rise to it."

Still pacing, Kitty's eyes flashed maniacally from side to side. Lance Foster jerked his foot a quarter of an inch to the left, a tiny involuntary movement that changed Kitty's whole demeanour. A cruel smirk played across her face as she lowered the stick, approached the bedside table, and flicked a switch. A radio burst into life, playing a high-tempo jazz song. Kitty pressed again, and the volume increased once, twice, and once more for luck. Then she shouldered the hockey stick as if it were a rifle and walked toward her husband.

Sean and I exchanged glances. "Shall I?" he asked. But suddenly the music stopped. Kitty turned to the bedside table and muted the radio, staring towards the doorway with a heavy frown on her face.

"What's happened?" I whispered. Then the shrill buzz of the doorbell sounded through the monitor speakers.

"Someone's at the door."

"Thank goodness. I wonder if the caller heard anything."

"I doubt it. Will Kitty answer?"

"God, I hope so."

Kitty didn't move but remained still, scowling at the irritant noise. The buzzer sounded again.

"Fuck off," she mouthed, but whoever was at her door wasn't getting the message, and the noise continued in three short bursts.

"Damn it." Kitty hurled the hockey stick onto the bed and strode from the room.

I watched Sean, chewing his lip and concentrating hard on the prone body of Lance Foster in the corner of the room. He remained face down until he heard the click of the front door opening, then raised his head, seemingly gulping for air, his expression hidden and only the back of his head in view.

Muffled sounds came from the hallway, too distant for the surveillance equipment to detect fully. But after a few moments, Kitty raised her voice, and we heard her telling her visitor that Lance was at home but in the bath.

"Who is it?" I whispered unnecessarily.

"Dunno. Hold on."

Sean moved towards the other monitors. "Mill's at home. Can't see anyone else."

"OK. Never mind."

The door slammed shut. Sean grimaced and returned to sit beside me in front of monitor four just as Kitty Foster strode through the bedroom door. Lance lowered his head, but not before she saw him looking up.

"I suppose you'd have preferred speaking to that nosy old fool? Well, you can't. Guess what he wanted?"

Lance remained silent.

"I said, guess what he wanted?"

"Who was at the door?"

"Don't you do that, Lance. Don't wind me up. How many nosy old fools do you know?"

"Do you mean Frank?"

"Of course, I mean Frank. Jesus, Lance. Why do you provoke me like this? Why must you make me so bloody angry all the time? I only wanted you to answer the sodding question? You say you love me, and then you deliberately bait me. Do you enjoy arguing?"

"No, Kitty. I do not enjoy it."

"Do you love me?"

"You know I do."

"Then why, why, why must you taunt me?"

"I'm sorry, dear."

"Don't fucking call me dear. It makes me sound like a little old lady."

Kitty's voice, which had softened, was becoming shrill again. "Get up," she commanded.

Lance raised his head again and pushed himself to his knees, his back towards Kitty.

"Turn around."

He shifted one hundred and eighty degrees and tilted his head upward.

"Pathetic." Kitty's lip curled as she stared into her husband's face. He raised his hand and wiped below his eyes, then dried his fingers on his shirt.

She reached for the hockey stick and raised it over her head.

"Don't, Kitty."

"Then take the stick away from me, and I won't be able to. Go on."

"No."

"Be a man for once in your life. Fight back. Take the stick away."

"I won't hurt you."

"Coward."

"You need help, Kitty. We can do this together."

"I need a real man, not a fucking counsellor. Take this stick, or you'll know about it."

"I won't raise my hand to you, no matter how much you goad me."

"Fuck you, then." Kitty lunged to one side, raising the stick above her husband's back.

She slammed it down, crunching wood against his shoulder blades and sending him flying into the side table. His head bounced off the corner, leaving a bloody mark.

"That's it. I'm not standing by and watching this any longer. Stay here."

Sean flew through the door, stomping down the stairs towards flat four. I stared open-mouthed, watching through the monitor as Kitty raised the stick again, willing Sean to hurry. But she stopped mid-swing before he ever got there at the sight of blood on the furniture.

Throwing the hockey stick to the floor, she lunged towards Lance, cradling him in her arms as she examined his head.

"Oh, you poor thing," she cooed, making butterfly kisses over the wound. "You shouldn't have made me do it. Don't worry. I'll make it better, I promise. Don't wind me up next time, and everything will be alright." Lance stared blankly ahead as if he had heard it all before.

"I mean it. I'll even get rid of the stick. You'll be alright now. Kitty burrowed her head into his shoulder, leaning into him as if they had just finished making love. And by the time Sean arrived and hammered on the door so loudly that she had no choice but to let him in, Kitty's face was covered in her husband's blood.

# Chapter Thirty-Nine

*Leaving Truscombe was the best thing I ever did, giving me a clean start and time away from my peers and the teachers who had made my life miserable. Time away from old habits, temptations, and the increasing risk of being caught was cleansing. I set a precedent. Something that conventional psychiatry deemed impossible. I stopped killing. Simply cut it from my life as if lancing a boil. Gone, but not forgotten. I fought my demons like a recovering addict and, for a while, used alcohol to quell my urges, drowning them in lethargy. I replaced one bad habit with another. And as time went by, I rose above my urges, conquering my dark side and overcoming my unique challenges. I excelled at work and having no one to care for, lived frugally and saved my money. As I grew in confidence, I invested a little here and there in stocks and shares and then in property. Time passed, and I lived in quiet contentment, never intending to return to my old ways. And but for a random meeting at Paddington station, I would have happily stayed where I was. But fate stepped in and turned my life on its head.*

*I'd been in London on business, hawking an antique salver around carefully chosen contacts, none of them too fussy about the provenance of my wares. Things had gone well, and I had arrived at Paddington station fifteen hundred pounds richer, carrying an empty bag and in excellent spirits. So much so that I decided to reward myself with a snack and a drink – non-alcoholic, of course. Those days were over. I headed towards the nearest coffee shop when a feeling of exhaustion suddenly came over me with hunger pangs out of kilter with what I'd eaten during the day. And I recognised the symptoms at once and remembered the words Aunt Dora would say. "Little and often, dear. It will stop the dizzy spells." And she was right. It did. And I always tried to keep a biscuit or a piece of chocolate on me, especially when travelling. But inevitably, I'd eat them and forget to replace them, or they'd get lost. So, I sat on the nearest bench and patted my pockets, searching in vain for something to take the edge off my dizziness until I finally found a half-wrapped humbug at the bottom of my shopping bag. I picked away the fluff and popped it in my mouth, immediately feeling much better, and I passed five minutes on the bench before deciding to stand up and carry on with my plans. But the wrapper I thought I'd carefully placed in my pocket fell to the floor as I stood, and a sudden gust of wind carried it away. I was oblivious to its escape, but a nearby woman had seen the litter and started yelling. It took a few seconds before I realised she was directing her anger my way, and I remember standing there with a bemused expression on my face feeling a gut-wrenching déjà vu before she tapped me on the shoulder.*

*"I believe this is yours," she had said, handing over the wrapper.*

*I murmured my apologies, eyes lowered in humiliation and held out my hand for the offending object, which she dropped in my palm.*

*"Put it in the bin next time," she hissed before moving off, striding briskly ahead, hips swaying in an all too familiar way. The train tannoy sounded, but it was just an echo in the background. Everything around me slowed, stalled, and started again in slow motion. Voices drawled, lagging as if set to half speed. I felt otherworldly as if being dragged back to the past. And then the penny dropped, and I under-*

stood. *The slow strutting walk, sharp tone of voice, thinner lips, and pinned hair had aged her, but were not that different from the woman I had known from school. By pure coincidence, I had run into Irene Devonshire again. And at that moment, all the years of good work and hard-won progress came undone. Hurling the sweet paper onto the platform, I headed for the nearest pub.*

# Chapter Forty

It took a good five minutes for Kitty to unwrap herself from Lance and answer the door to Sean, who had been hammering impatiently and was undoubtedly close to the point of shouldering it open. But I didn't have time to examine the scene properly. I had spotted a movement from screen one out of the corner of my eye and momentarily broken away from the drama in Flat Four to take a closer look. At first, I wasn't sure what to make of it. Frank must have left his mother alone in her bedroom, and judging by the dim screen, her curtains were drawn. But a glint of metal had caught my attention, and I could now see that something was awry. Scrabbling for the speaker controls, I increased the volume, listening to the sound of laboured breathing competing with Kitty's excitable tones. But I still couldn't hear properly and shoved the headphones on, volume up again, concentrating properly on Frank's mother. As my eyes grew accustomed to the darkened room, I could see Veronica wasn't in bed. Gone was the familiar sleeping body, and the wheelchair wasn't in its usual place. I listened hard, eyes focused on the room, watching intently, and as I zoned away from all the other distractions, I heard a faint moaning, a barely audible cry of someone in distress. Then my eyes were drawn to a small white object protruding from the side of the bed. It moved slightly, just a fraction, a clench of toes. Poor Veronica had fallen on the floor and was lying on her side in the corner of the room.

I leapt up, glancing at monitor four for signs of Sean, but I couldn't see him, and the sound of multiple voices told me he was mid-discussion with one or other of the Fosters. There was no time to lose. Veronica was in trouble, I couldn't see Frank, and she needed my immediate help. Darting towards the door, I almost left the room but stopped mid-pace as I remembered that the hooks on the side wall contained keys to every property. I grabbed the first and checked the orange tag. Flat One. Correct. Clutching the key, I pulled the door to, leaving it on the catch for Sean, and tore down the stairs, two steps at a time, towards the closed door of Flat Four, knowing Sean must be inside. But just as I approached, I heard footsteps coming from below. Unsure who they might belong to, I instinc- tively ducked into my flat and waited inside, crouching close to the floor as a shadow passed by. The door to Flat Four clicked open and closed again just as quickly, although nobody appeared to enter or leave. But I couldn't waste time speculating. Casting fate to the winds, I left my apart- ment, glancing up and down as I moved, but the landing was empty although I could still hear faint voices coming from Flat Four. I ran downstairs, breathless by the time I reached the bottom, and glanced around. Nobody down- stairs either. I knocked firmly on Frank's door, waited momentarily, and knocked once again for luck. Silence. Predictable silence, so I used the yale key and went inside.

Frank's hallway was like mine, with a kitchen on the opposite side, a lounge door to the right and a dogleg leading to two bedrooms and a bathroom. I ignored the faint smell of lavender competing with something meaty and hurtled towards the second bedroom, feeling sure that's where I'd find Veronica. I pushed open the door and shouted her name. But as soon as I went inside, I knew I'd called it wrong. Sure enough, the room was like my second bedroom, bordering on a box room. But this room was bigger, with a different configuration, but no doubt the smaller of the two. Frank must have sacrificed his comfort for that of his mother. The room contained a double bed, but not much else, with double doors, likely leading to a built-in wardrobe. I didn't stay around to investigate. Veronica needed my urgent help, and I disregarded the rest of the room, heading back up the corridor to the larger bedroom.

I flung open the door to relative darkness. Grabbing the nearest curtain, I hauled it back, letting daylight seep into the space. The situation was as I feared. Veronica Lewis lay sprawled down the side of the bed, which had moved away from the wall, leaving her wedged into a small gap, unable to move and as trapped as a beached whale.

"Oh, you poor thing." I rushed towards her, arms outstretched, trying to work out how I could manoeuvre her into a more comfortable position. She lay on the ground, tossing her head from left to right.

"It's OK. It's Saskia. I'm here to help."

Veronica raised her head, opening and closing her mouth like a guppy. Her maw looked odd, alien somehow, in a way I couldn't account for. I reached toward her, pushing the bed away with my hand and kneeling on the floor. Then, grasping her chest and putting both arms around her frail body, I heaved her free of the confined space and onto her feet. She moaned pitifully.

"Good girl. Well done," I said. "Sit here."

I lowered her to the bed and waited for a second to ensure she was strong enough to sit. She wobbled a little and rocked back and forth, keening from the back of her throat with a sound that sent shivers up my spine. I grabbed the upended wheelchair, which she must have tried to use to steady herself and turned it the right way up. Then I wheeled it towards her, pulled her to her feet and gently settled her in the chair before peeling back the second curtain, allowing more light into the room.

Veronica stared at me through distant eyes, still rocking, still moaning with her arms crossed over her body like a mummified corpse. And then I noticed a dark stain on her poor bandaged legs.

"Have you hurt yourself?" I asked.

She looked past me, towards the window – thoughts in another place, another time.

"Don't worry. I know you can't answer. Frank said you were poorly, and you can't remember things. It's OK. But I'll look at those legs, perhaps change your bandages. Let me see. Ah. There's a first aid box on the side."

I unclipped the green box, expecting bandages but finding only syringes, ampoules, and a scalpel. But the drawer below contained a ready supply of bandages, plasters, ointments, and creams.

"There we go," I said. "Let's have a little look at you."

Veronica flinched as I approached.

"Don't worry. I'm a first aider. Ex-military. I know what I'm doing, I promise."

She moaned again, and her breath came in heavy, ragged movements.

"I could leave it to Frank, I suppose," I mused as she shrank away, moving tiny, clenched fists over her face. But another look at the bandages told me otherwise. She must have knocked one of her leg ulcers, and it was bleeding copiously.

"Just stay still."

I grasped the top of the bandage and started peeling it away, recoiling at the terrible smell as the stained fabric unravelled. Then, the crepe stopped coming away easily, meeting resistance as if stuck to something below. I eased it down and then stared in puzzlement at the red pulpy mass beneath, my brain making no sense of what my eyes were seeing. I'd only peeled the uppermost part of the bandage, but if the rest of it covered the same level of damage, Veronica must be missing most of the skin on her legs. How had it happened from leg ulcers? This woman was seriously damaged and needed hospitalisation. Anything else would have been negligent beyond any acceptable level. Why had Frank failed to do more for his ailing mother?

The bandage slipped from my hands, and I jumped back, my eyes meeting Veronica's. She blinked back tears, and her eyes momentarily came alive. And in a supreme act of concentration, she lifted a shaking hand and pointed towards the built-in wardrobe to the side of the room.

"You want me to open it?"

She nodded, her mouth agape and drooling. And at that moment, I realised what looked so wrong. Her tongue wasn't there. It was absent – missing. She couldn't speak because she lacked the means to do so.

Sick with fear, I stood paralysed, numb at the horror of Veronica's broken body. She pointed again, this time struggling to move her pale, veiny hand much higher than her waist, her energy sapped. Somehow, I moved one shaking leg in front of the other, taking baby steps, and then reached my trembling hand towards the doors. Clutching one of the battered wooden handles, I pulled it open and peered inside.

---

The cupboard was not a cupboard in the conventional sense of the word. Like the second bedroom, it had been recon-figured and was at least double the depth. Almost a walk-in wardrobe without the clothes. In its place stood a large computer server, two screens, several keyboards, and a state-of-the-art gaming chair with a small drink fridge to the side. An array of speakers and intercoms across the upper sides and ceiling peppered the inside of the cupboard. Both monitors pointed to the empty attic room. I stared, trans-fixed, trying to understand how Veronica Lewis managed to use computer equipment while in an advanced state of dementia. Wheeling around, I turned to face her, wondering for a moment if she was faking it and might spring forward at any moment and attack me. But my medical training told me otherwise. Veronica's legs were ruined. She must be in every kind of pain, and walking would be nigh on impossible. Veronica stared at me, head lolling to one side, her mouth flecked with drool as if she was a moment away from passing out. But as I met her gaze again, I knew I wasn't looking into the rheumy eyes of a half-crazed woman, one step away from the grave. Veronica was a victim, trapped in a mutilated body, but with keen intelligence behind her pain. She was aware, alive, and more alert than any of us had realised.

"Was it Frank?" I asked, kneeling on the floor, and clutching her hand.

She gave a gentle squeeze and moved her head a fraction, loudly exhaling, as if relieved to communicate, however feebly. Then suddenly, her whole body jerked. Her eyes widened as she flinched and dropped my hand.

I turned towards the monitor. The room was no longer empty. Sean had returned and was just visible, sitting behind screen four. I could only see half his face, but he wore a puzzled frown, and I guessed he had finished with the Fosters and was looking for me. I grabbed the gaming mouse to the side of the screen, cursing at the unfamiliar shape and irritated by unnecessary buttons which might slow me down. The cursor pinged on the monitor, and I searched for the audio to establish a connection to Sean, to let him know where I was and tell him about Veronica. I opened the control panel, clicked to expand, hit an unfamiliar wheel on the mouse, and closed the screen by accident. Swearing under my breath, I slammed the mouse down, and the cover flew from the battery compartment and skittered across the desk as one battery popped out and the other lost connection with the cradle. I ducked beneath the desk, recovered it, and shoved it back inside with shaking hands. The red light glowed, and I re-opened the screen and stared in shock at the sight before me. Sean had moved to screen one and had noticed me just as the monitor flickered back to life. He cocked his head in puzzlement, then grinned and waved. But his smile faltered as I gaped in horror, staring at a shadowy figure behind him.

"Sean. Oh, my God. Turn around. Turn around," I screamed, but Sean just shook his head and frowned, unable to read my lips. There was no time to open the audio again, so I started pressing buttons, flicking intercom switches, anything to establish a connection. A faint moaning sound came from the second screen, pointing to one of the Foster's bedrooms, now empty. Somehow, the audio was working again. And the sound evoked a memory of waking in the early morning hours during my first week at Bosworth House to groans and moans from the building. The same cries that had lured me into the Foster's flat and a confrontation with Kitty. I clicked the intercom again, and the noise stopped.

The figure was advancing on Sean, an arm raised towards him, brandishing a sharp object. My heart lurched as I saw a syringe. With no time to spare, I abandoned all attempts at using the unfamiliar equipment and reached for my phone. I held it towards Sean and started pressing buttons. He half stood and stretched a hand towards his back pocket, but the figure lunged forwards. Sean's phone rattled to the ground, and the computer screen went black.

*Dear God, no.* Panicking, I dialled Tom's number. I should have called 999, but I knew the call operative's compulsory set questions might cost vital seconds. Tom could get help more quickly if only he were there, if he was still prepared to respond after our earlier confrontation. I jumped to my feet as the phone rang and ran through the flat. It buzzed once, twice, and then Tom answered.

"What do you want now?" he snapped.

"Sean's in trouble. Come quickly."

"Where are you?"

"Bosworth House. He's in the attic room. And get an ambulance, someone's badly injured."

"Your exact location, Saskia?"

"Downstairs in Flat One. Send the ambulance there. I'm going upstairs."

"Stay where you are. I'm five minutes away in the car. Wait for me."

"You don't understand. There's no time."

"Stay where you are."

"Hurry."

I scrambled upstairs, tripping over my feet in my haste to reach Sean. "Help me," I screamed as I climbed the stairs. The Foster's door opened, and Kitty emerged. She took one look and slammed it shut. I carried on yelling as I ran, hoping that I would attract the right attention. I tore towards the attic door and wrenched the handle, which turned but did not budge.

"Sean," I screamed, shouldering the door. A sickening wall of pain shot through me as my bones met solid wood. I reeled, almost vomited, and then recovered enough to start hammering on the door. Where the fuck was Brendan? Why couldn't anyone hear me?

I tried once more, this time slamming my foot into the door. The wood gave with a slight indentation. I tried again, making little progress. It would take hours at this rate, and an ominous silence had descended inside.

I roared in frustration and prepared for another go before hearing the faint click of a lock. But that was all. The door didn't open, and nobody moved. Cautiously, I tried the handle and pushed, meeting no resistance. Sweeping the damp hair from my forehead, I ignored my thumping heart and went inside.

Frank Lewis was standing behind Sean's unconscious body with a scalpel held to Sean's throat.

"Over there, dear," he said softly, nodding towards the whiteboard.

"Oh, no. What have you done to him?"

"You should be more concerned with what I'll do to him if you don't follow instructions. Move along, there's a good girl."

Frank's voice was icy, emotionless, bearing no resemblance to the friendly neighbourhood uncle-to-all he'd appeared to be up to now.

"Do it," he said, narrowing his eyes as I tried to think of all the ways I could help Sean and still stay close to the door.

"Oops," said Frank, as he plunged the tip of the scalpel into Sean's neck. A bead of crimson blood swelled from the wound and trickled into Sean's collar.

"Okay," I said, raising my hands. "Just stop, will you?"

"Then lock the door behind you first," said Frank affably.

I did as he asked and stood beneath the whiteboard, feeling more exposed than ever before in my life.

"Take a seat."

"On the floor?"

"Yes, dear, unless you have a better idea."

I squatted on my haunches and stared defiantly, but Frank glanced purposefully at the scalpel, and I knew I must cooperate. I dropped to the floor and sat cross-legged, waiting for him to speak. But he just watched me with a satisfied grin.

"Why are you doing this?" I asked. "And what have you given Sean?"

"A good question," said Frank, nodding as if I had pleased him. "Just a dose of succinylcholine, which should wear off in a quarter of an hour. He glanced at his watch. "I can give you ten minutes of my time if you wish to know more. You may as well hear why you're going to die before we move things on."

"The police are on their way. You don't have ten minutes."

"Then I may as well kill your friend now. You're not afraid of blood, are you?"

"Alright. You've got me. It was worth a try."

"Toss your phone over here, my dear. Let's not take any chances."

I slid it over, knowing that the game was up if Frank asked for my pin and checked my call history. But he wasn't interested and kicked it under the desk, far from my reach. "Now, you wanted to know why I'm doing this, by which I assume you mean sedating your friend. It's because you are a pair of interfering fools. You don't belong here, I didn't invite you, and neither of you is interesting enough for my collection. Did I mention that? I'm a collector," he said. "A collector of people. I purchased this building to house my exhibits."

# Chapter Forty-One

"No, you didn't. Sentinel own it."

"Sentinel is an offshore holding company. An umbrella organisation if you like. The property belongs to me."

"Why bother to hide it?"

"Because I didn't want anyone knowing it was mine. I had plans, and still do if you haven't ruined them with all that shrieking. Let's take a look."

Frank grabbed the mouse and clicked. All the monitors had been blank, but number four fizzed to life, showing two empty bedrooms on each side of the screen. Frank scowled, moved the mouse again, and the faint sound of voices from the speakers grew louder as he turned up the volume.

Kitty and Lance Foster were bickering again in another room, Kitty speculating about Sean's intentions and Lance reassuring her that all would be well.

Frank smirked. "Good. Good. I'm not surprised they didn't come to your aid. Kitty detests you. I made sure of it weeks ago. She wouldn't help you, and her stupid husband wouldn't dare. Exhibit number four is safe and sound. No thanks to you."

"How can you watch her treat him like that? She's vile."

"Because he deserves it. Sins of the fathers and all that."

"I don't know what you are talking about. Nobody deserves that level of abuse."

"What about me? I didn't either, but it didn't stop Slugger from making my life a misery, although I made him pay for it in the end."

"Slugger?"

"Slugger Foster, the school bully. Lance Foster's father. My tormentor."

"Oh, my God. Slugger lost a leg at school in an accident."

Frank raised an eyebrow. "It was no accident, my dear."

"You didn't… I mean, how could you?"

"Use your imagination. Slugger was out cold, and I was alone with a pool of acid on the floor. What would you have done?"

"Fetched help, obviously."

"But I hated him. He made my life miserable."

"So, you got your revenge. Then why take it out on Lance?"

"Because I can. I'm a collector, my dear, I always have been. Back in the day, it was insects, and now it's people. Those who have wronged me."

"You mean you've hand-picked everyone in the building?"

"Absolutely. I've carefully chosen them all."

"Except for me."

"Yes. And wasn't that a mistake? The agent talked me into taking you on instead of leaving the flat empty while I selected a more suitable exhibit. I should never have listened."

"Then why plant the dead rat in my kitchen?"

"Oh, you found it. A nice housewarming gift. Only it was meant for Pauline Bateman, not you. Still, I'm glad you enjoyed it."

"What about Dhruv and Mill? How did they hurt you? Surely you can't destroy Mill just because he teaches at the Grammar?"

"No. That was a bonus. I was after the other one."

"Dhruv?"

"Yes, filthy little animal."

"Shut up."

"Watch your mouth. You're in no position to lecture me with your friend lying so close to the end of my blade."

"What's Dhruv ever done to you?"

"He carries his father's traitorous genes."

"God, you're sick. He's not his father."

"Sadly not. And if Satish Patel were not living in India, I would be looking for ways to lure him into my collection, too. But this is the next best thing."

"Did you set the trap in their apartment?"

Frank grinned. "Of course. I didn't dream it would go so well, almost killing his flatmate. I only intended toying with Dhruv, but his friend's death would have been equally satisfying."

"Why?"

"Because it would have broken his heart like his father broke mine."

"Were you in love with his father?"

I regretted the words as soon as they left my mouth. Frank's face darkened, his mouth twisting in fury as he spat a denial. "Don't be disgusting. I would never do that. Just because that man – that excuse for a teacher – did what he did. I hated every moment."

"Did what?" I asked gently.

"Never you mind. Just know this. I helped Satish Patel when Slugger picked on him. You can imagine what it was like to be different at school. I spoke to Patel when the others ignored him and walked with him to lessons the first term he arrived. But he disowned me when he found favour with Slugger, just abandoned me, disloyal, fence-sitting traitor."

"And that's enough reason to ruin his son's life?"

"More than enough."

"What about the others?"

"Who?"

"Velda and Brendan Marshall."

"Your friend Velda was a disgusting bully."

"No way. She wasn't like that."

"Oh yes, she was. And if you don't believe me, have a look at MyPerfectLife. I know you use it, I've seen your page. I hate bullies, and she was the worst kind. Insidious, cunning and deadly."

"Oh, my God. You killed her."

"I didn't intend to, but she saw me. I'd barely started with Miss Ribeira and had so much planned for her. It could have lasted for years. And now I need to replace her – you too. It's extremely inconvenient."

My skin crawled at the thought of Velda's last hours at the hands of the monster before me. Frank was sick, evil. A bitter narcissist who couldn't see right from wrong. He had no boundaries, killing came naturally. And no matter what Velda had done in her past, she'd been nice to me. Perhaps she'd changed, seen the error of her ways.

"You sent the anonymous letter," I said.

"Of course, I did. Her boyfriend seemed such a nice chap, and I had no intention of letting her keep him."

"And Brendan?"

"Ah, yes. He's far too interested in the ladies since his divorce – ladies of the night, that is. I'm saving him till last. Haven't thought of a way to get even with him yet."

"Why would you?"

"Because Marshall's uncle was the school caretaker's assistant in my day. I asked him for help once when Simon Caldicot hurt me so badly that I could barely walk. I tried to tell Marshall without using the words, the actual words. You can't imagine the shame and embarrassment; I did my best and said as much as possible. But he didn't believe me. Said I shouldn't tell lies. I never forgave him, and I never will."

"But Colin Marshall only lives a few streets away. Why take it out on Brendan?"

"I told you, I haven't yet. Colin Marshall is in poor health. He may yet end up as one of my exhibits. I will certainly suggest it to Brendan before long. Ah, your friend is waking up. You're out of time."

Sean moved his head and let out a gentle moan. I glanced at the door. Where the hell was Tom? He should have been here five minutes before, yet the building was eerily quiet.

Frank brandished the scalpel and gazed fixedly at the blade. His eyes darkened, and a smile played on the edges of his mouth as blood lust rose within him.

"Your mother's poorly," I blurted out, remembering Veronica alone and in pain downstairs. "She needs help."

"Why?"

"Her ulcers have burst. Her leg's in a terrible mess. Why haven't you taken her to the hospital?"

"Oh, my dear. Your naivety is touching. Haven't you guessed?"

"That you're the Skin Thief?" I said the words confidently, as if I had always known, even though the full horror of his identity had only just dawned on me.

"It's such a silly name," said Frank. "The skin is incidental. Just a little token, if you like. A reminder of Slugger, and quite possibly the most satisfying moment of my life."

"But your mother – her legs. You didn't. Surely, you couldn't?"

"I could, and I did. Not all at once. It must have taken the best part of a decade."

Bile rose in my throat, and I visibly gagged.

"Sorry if you find it upsetting," said Frank. "Indulging little and often has kept me from far worse. I'm sure I'd be in prison by now, but for my little hobby."

"You killed Carla Bryan and Debbie Rutt."

"Correct."

"And Amy Swanson. Why?"

"Why do you think?"

"Because she lived here. She was the girl in Flat Three. Before Gretta, before me."

"Well done. Amy was the first of my exhibits – always risky to have around, but with distinct advantages."

"I don't know what you mean."

Frank smiled, a loathsome, sickening grin as if he concealed a secret too terrible for words. And as he faced me, I could see the door handle move in the distance. I tore my eyes away so he couldn't follow my gaze as Sean pushed his hand towards his face and scratched silently in his sleep.

"Enough now," said Frank. "Your friend is waking."

"Tell me about Amy."

"No."

"Why not? Or are you angry that you made such a mess of it?"

"What mess?"

"Putting her rent up. Driving her out."

"She lied. I would have let her have the flat free of charge to keep her here. She was the most important of all my exhibits."

"Then why did she leave?"

"The stupid flighty little thing couldn't stay anywhere for long. And Amy knew – deep down, she knew. She didn't understand who she was helping or why. The bonds of family run deep."

Frank was distracted now, his eyes glinting with an evil lust born of dearly held memories. He watched me intently, not noticing Sean's eyes open drowsily, before fixing on me. I heard a faint shuffle from outside the room. Frank cocked his head, and I coughed loudly to hide the noise. But it wasn't good enough. Frank stood and reached for the monitors, flicking on the rest of the screens. Downstairs and visible on monitor one, a paramedic crouched in front of Veronica while administering painkillers.

"You bitch," said Frank, spittle flying from his mouth. I flinched at the words. Frank had kept his temper even amid his smug confession. Glancing towards Sean, still feigning sleep, he lunged towards me, knife outstretched. I jumped to my feet, not quickly enough, and a welt of blood spilt as the blade snaked across my collarbone. I screamed, and Tom hammered on the door. It thudded once, twice as he tried to gain entry.

"Hold on," he shouted. "We're coming in."

Clasping my hand over my wound, I tried to stem the blood as I sidestepped Frank and ran towards the door.

"No, you don't," he said, striking towards me, agile, wiry

and nothing like the ageing man he had pretended to be. Tom still battered the door, which bowed and buckled but refused to budge.

"Give it up, Frank," I said as he advanced toward me.

"Why? It's over. I'll have my last treat."

He lunged again and caught my arm: another slash, another welt of blood.

I raised my hands defensively as Sean moved groggily towards Frank, teetering forwards unsteadily as he tried to recover from the drug. He half lunged, half fell into Frank, sending him reeling towards me. I moved away just in time to see Sean fall to the floor, unbalanced and unable to stand. Frank recovered his footing and grinned wolfishly.

"Got you now," he said.

I flattened myself to the wall, feeling faint-headed from the blood loss. Frank raised his knife, his eyes black with bloodlust, holding it directly over my head. The blade plunged towards me, its trajectory over my heart. Then the door splintered open, and everything went dark.

## Chapter Forty-Two

I'd only been admitted to Cheltenham General Hospital once before for an emergency appendectomy as a young girl. And I awoke with the same nervous trepidation I had then, not knowing where I was or how I'd got there. It took a moment for the memories to come rushing back, and when they did, I sat up with a start, my heart beating in terror.

"It's okay." Sean Tallis was sitting beside me and reached for my hand.

"You're alright. Thank God."

"Never mind me. You're the one with the war wounds."

"How long have I been here?"

"A couple of days."

"That long? Oh, my goodness. Where is he? Where's Frank?"

"Dead."

"How? What happened?"

"Tom broke the door down with the help of the ambulance man. Frank realised the game was up and turned the knife on himself. Cut his throat and bled out before they could save him."

"Damn it. He deserved so much worse. Did you see the state of his mother? He skinned her alive." I wretched again, unable to stand the memory of her poor, bloodied legs.

"Veronica wasn't his mother," said Sean. "She's in hospital now and needs a couple of amputations. She can't talk, but they gave her a pen, and she can write. We now know that Veronica Lewis is really Irene Paige. Frank kidnapped her a decade ago and took her with the express purpose of harming her. How she lived with it, I'll never know."

"But why? How could he do that to another human being?"

"Kim Robbins saw Colin Marshall this morning. I didn't hear everything that happened between you and Frank, but I remembered Colin's name through the fug of the injection and passed it on. Colin knew Frank from school and said that he'd made a serious accusation against a teacher. He wouldn't say what it was but implied sexual abuse. Colin knew the man - a chap called Simon Caldicot. His girlfriend was Irene – Irene Devonshire. Rumour had it that Caldicot abused some children, and Irene turned a blind eye. You worked out Amy Swanson's genealogy, so you know the rest."

"Oh, my God. Amy Swanson was her granddaughter. She returned to Bosworth House because she knew some- thing was wrong with Veronica. Knew it yet didn't realise she was helping her own grandmother."

"Understandably. Irene had been missing for a decade,

and Amy would have been young when she left. Frank kept his mother away from everyone, and you all thought she had dementia."

"Her tongue was missing. Frank wasn't involved, was he?

Sean nodded. "Frank didn't do it himself. It was a clean operation, according to Tom. Frank had money and somehow persuaded a surgeon to remove her tongue. God knows how, but unscrupulous people will do anything for money. Kim's team is tearing his flat apart, searching for evidence. I don't know if they'll ever find it."

"There's one thing I don't understand, though. Who put Sinbad in the cellar?"

"Frank, of course. I should have realised the moment we found him. Frank was devoted to that cat, but he couldn't appear to be the only person in the building unaffected by the trickery. Frank would never hurt Sinbad, so he put him in the cellar with all the food and water he needed and told everyone he was missing. That way, he gained victim status too."

"What will happen to us now? To the building? Frank owns it. He was Sentinel."

"Not exactly. Sentinel was a cover for his company, but it amounts to the same thing. Honestly, I don't know. But do you want to stay there under the circumstances?"

I considered the hidden cameras and the lack of privacy. I could never settle there now. "No, I don't think so," I said, trying to ignore the wave of adrenaline-fuelled uncertainty over my future. "But I can't afford another move."

"Don't worry about that," said Sean. "Callie's backed off, and Kim's onside again. There's enough work for two if you still want to work for the firm, that is."

I gazed at Sean, sitting where my mother would be if she hadn't died. I barely had any family left, no friends in

England, and an unresolved genealogy. Sean owed me nothing, yet he'd been willing to give me a chance and was watching over me now. He was all I had, and I took his offer gratefully.

"Don't mind if I do," I said.

# Next in the Denman & Tallis Cotswold Crime Thriller Series

vinci-books.com/never-escape

**Will they escape the killer's grip?**

When a twisted killer leaves shackled bodies in peaceful towns,
two seasoned detectives must confront their own demons to
unravel the mystery.

Turn the page for a free preview…

# You'll Never Escape Me: Prologue

## September 2019

The boy stood, hands on hips, with a steely glint in his eyes.

"Chuck it over here."

"No way. If you want it, come and get it, big man."

Luke rolled his eyes. "Give it a rest, Jam. My mum will go mental if I get another detention."

"Calm down. It's only a bit of fun." The tall, dark-skinned boy roughly shoved the bright red rucksack into his companion's midriff.

"That hurt, you muppet."

"Serves you right for supporting a rubbish team."

"Give over, you two." The smaller of the three boys spoke up.

"Who rattled your cage, Charlie?" Jamal lunged at the boot bag slung over Charlie's shoulder.

"Grow up."

"Make me."

"Oi. Leave it alone." Charlie cast a protective hand over the bag, but it was too late. Jamal had grabbed it before sprinting into the distance, across Rotherleigh Road and towards a small copse of trees.

"Ah, crap. I've got football practice tonight." Charlie threw his schoolbag to the ground in disgust.

"Jamal's only playing. He's too unfit to keep that pace for long. We'll catch him in no time. Follow me." Luke sped off with Charlie at the rear, soon gaining ground on the taller boy in the distance.

By the time they caught him, Jamal had strung up the boot bag from a tree branch an inch too high for the shorter boys to reach.

"Idiot," scowled Charlie.

"I'll get it." Luke jumped, grabbed a handful of fabric, and the bag crashed to the floor.

"Thanks, mate."

"You're welcome. Now can we just go home with no more dickery from you, Jamal?"

"Where's the fun in that?" Jamal grinned and raised his hand. "What's over there?" he asked, pointing to a distant building.

"It's a cottage," said Luke.

"I can see that. Who lives in it?"

"How should I know?"

"I thought you knew everything."

"Well, I don't, and I don't care either. Can we go now?"

"Mrs Ballinger lives in the right-hand cottage," said Charlie confidently.

"Who?"

"Mrs Ballinger. She cleaned for us before she retired."

"Ooh, posh boy. I keep forgetting you have staff."

"Leave him alone, Jamal," said Luke.

"Does she live alone?" Jamal's eyes flashed mischievously.

"Yes. Why?"

"We haven't played knock down ginger for a while, and I vote you batter the door."

"No way. She knows me. I'd be in all sorts of crap."

"Coward."

"You do it then." Charlie stared defiantly, hands on hips.

"No point in keeping a dog and barking yourself."

"It's getting late. I'm off," said Luke, checking his phone. "And, Charlie, you'd better move sharpish, or you'll miss football practice."

"It's an hour later tonight. Mr Pearcey's got a council meeting."

"Good. Then you can still tap Mrs Ballinger's door," Jamal persisted.

"No. I'm not getting grounded to please you."

"Then try the one next door."

"No point. It's empty."

"Are you sure?"

"Positive. The Drewits left years ago."

"Double dare you to go inside." Jamal raised an eyebrow, and Charlie sighed.

"Why me?"

"It's your turn."

"When was it your turn?"

"I make the rules."

"For crying out loud." Luke scowled. "I've got better things to do, even if you two haven't."

"Run along home then," sneered Jamal.

"It's not like that."

"Isn't it? Sounds like you're scared."

"Like hell."

"Then prove it. Wait five minutes for Chazzer to get inside. We'll watch from the window to make sure he doesn't sneak off, and then you can go."

"Must we?"

"Yes," said Jamal firmly. "Otherwise, we're as boring as Freddie and his dragon-slaying nerds. He can listen to a real adventure next time he starts boring off about his stupid dungeon elves."

Charlie shrugged. "Do what?"

"He means Dungeons and Dragons," explained Luke.

"Whatever. Get on with it, Charlie. We haven't got all day." Jamal gestured at the stone path leading towards the cottages. "Talk about primitive. Don't they have cars around here?"

Charlie ignored him and stepped cautiously down the path. He advanced a few yards and glanced over his shoulder, hoping Jamal would call off the dare. But the taller boy stood grinning, casually sweeping a hand through his dark, curly hair, watching until Charlie was almost out of sight.

"Looks like he's going in," Jamal said excitedly.

"You didn't leave him much choice." Luke shifted uncomfortably, wishing he was anywhere else but there.

"Come on."

"Where are we going?"

"To the cottage, like I said. Charlie will weasel out of the dare if we don't watch him."

They sauntered towards the left-hand side of the shabby property ahead, Jamal narrowly missing a broken tile near what remained of the front garden. Two years of neglect had left the stone building covered with weeds while ivy crawled out of control across the front aspect. The boys squeezed past a large bush and pushed open the gate to find Charlie leaning against the wall on the other side.

"I knew you wouldn't go for it," said Jamal.

"Something's wrong."

"Yes. Your sense of adventure. You should be inside by now."

"The house is open," said Charlie, pointing to the unlocked door.

"Big deal. Nobody lives in it."

"But the door should be secure."

"That's no excuse for welching on a dare."

"He's right," said Luke, stepping forward. "Nobody leaves their house open for anyone to enter. Did you move the door at all?"

Charlie shook his head. "No. It was already ajar. I didn't touch it. And I'm not going to. We should leave well alone."

"Don't be daft. We're here now. Let's finish what we started."

"You bloody do it if you're so brave?" Charlie wiped his hand over his eyes, hoping Jamal wouldn't see his trembling fingers.

"It's just an empty house, chicken shit. Fine. I'll go." Jamal dropped his schoolbag by the door and strode inside. He returned moments later carrying a dusty milk bottle.

"Here," he said, thrusting it towards Charlie. "It's just an empty house with a few crappy bags of litter and stuff. Not worth wetting your pants over."

"Then let's go," said Luke, rechecking his mobile. "Crap. Message from Mum. She wants me to pick up a box of tea bags on my way back."

"I'll come with you. I want an energy drink."

Charlie smirked. "You're not allowed."

"What Mama don't know she don't care about," said Jamal.

"What was that?" Luke cocked his head to one side as Jamal pulled the door to.

"I didn't hear anything," said Charlie.

"Listen."

The boys stood quietly for a moment.

"Must be the wind," said Jamal. "Or at least the hot air coming from Charlie."

"Do one."

"It's there again. Shut up for a moment and listen properly."

A faint metallic tap reverberated from below.

"It's just the pipes," said Jamal.

"No. It's a regular noise. Listen."

The clanging continued between long silent gaps but with an undeniable rhythm.

"Something's down there," said Luke.

"Don't be an arse."

"Call me all the names you like, Jamal. Something's not right. We should check."

"Er, no. I've been inside. It's your turn."

"We'll all go. There's safety in numbers."

"It's getting dark." Charlie thrust his hands into his jacket pocket and tried to ignore the menacing sound.

"It'll only take a minute," said Luke. Then we can run home. The last man back is an arse."

Jamal glanced at Charlie, who closed his eyes and nodded.

"Okay then. Lead the way."

Luke licked his lips, pushed past Jamal, and headed into the tiny hallway, the other two trailing like shadows behind.

"Have you got a light?" he whispered.

"No. But look over there." Jamal pointed to a shelf running the length of the rear wall, housing boxes of light bulbs and a torch.

"It better bloody work," said Luke, clicking the button. A powerful beam swept across the hallway.

"Watch out," yelled Charlie, shielding his eyes. The clanging stopped, and the boys exchanged glances.

"They've heard us," hissed Jamal.

"Then let's get the hell out of here." Charlie stared owl-like, transfixed with fear.

Thud, thud, thud. The noise slowly resumed, every stroke sounding laboured.

"Not without checking. It's our duty," said Luke solemnly.

"I need a wee."

"Alright, Charlie. Go outside, empty your bladder, and stay put. If we're not back in five minutes, fetch our parents."

"Okay." Charlie disappeared, and Luke turned to Jamal.

"Ready?"

"Let's do it."

They followed the sound into the kitchen and towards a wooden door standing ajar.

"What's that awful smell?" Jamal raised the front of his hoodie over his nose.

"Over there. On the table."

"What is it?"

"It was milk. It's more like yoghurt now. I'm surprised you didn't smell it earlier."

"I didn't get this far," admitted Jamal. "The bottle was by the door."

"Never mind. Stand back." Luke approached the basement door and pulled it towards him before directing the flashlight beam down the stairs.

"What can you see?" Luke felt Jamal's warm breath on his neck as he hovered behind.

"Nothing yet, but the noise is louder."

"Jesus. We should never have started this. Let's call your dad."

"Not until we know what's down there." Luke's breath came in ragged gasps as he tried to conceal his fear.

Jamal wordlessly reached for Luke's trembling hand as they advanced downstairs. The groans began before they reached the bottom, a pitiful moan of despair keeping time with the metallic beat.

"Who's there?" whispered Luke, his voice rasping as Jamal shivered behind him.

The voice moaned again, this time more urgently, as if trying to speak.

Luke tensed, fighting the urge to turn tail and tear upstairs. He took a deep breath and composed himself, and then something clattered to the ground.

Jamal screamed. "What the fuck was that?"

"It's okay. I dropped the torch."

"It's not okay. I'm done here."

"Wait." Luke scrabbled on the earthy floor and retrieved the flashlight before switching the beam back to full. He swept it behind him, catching a glimpse of Jamal's wild-eyed face and flaring nostrils, and patted him on the shoulder. He was about to speak, to reassure his friend when another weaker moan stopped him, and he shone his torch to the side of the room. It flickered over a white-washed wall, illuminating an old paint-spattered table with the desiccated remains of a plate of food and onwards to a camping stove. Luke swallowed and slowly shone the light to his left, moving inch by inch, frame by frame. And there, at the end of the cellar, the torchlight settled on the iron-barred door of a man-sized cage, where it glinted against the metal. Hand in hand, the boys approached as the beam picked up a shadowy form on the dusty floor. A skeletal shape lay huddled in the corner, clutching a rusty chain, his hand moving like a clockwork automaton as it beat the link against an iron bar in a last desperate attempt to survive.

# You'll Never Escape Me: Chapter One

## Three years later

"I won't do it, and you can't make me." Sean narrowed his eyes and glared at me across the desk.

"Are you serious?"

"Deadly."

"Then we might as well shut up shop."

"It's tempting."

I sighed and pushed against my wheeled chair, steering it towards the water cooler Sean had reluctantly installed the previous month. I grabbed a plastic cup and filled it before scooting back again without spilling a drop.

"I can't help but admire your determination not to stand if you can help it. But I doubt your physio would feel the same way," he said smugly.

"Don't nag," I replied, anger welling inside me. Sean's supercilious recommendations were all very well, but he wasn't the one suffering excruciating back pain caused by the dead weight of a suicidal psychopath. Not only had I suffered multiple knife wounds, but my attacker had the poor grace to fall directly on top of me with his dying breath. The injuries had kept me in Cheltenham General for the best part of a month and although I could walk and probably run at a push, standing up often brought a particular brand of agony I was keen to avoid.

"You know I'm right." Sean winked as he flashed the okay gesture, and I fought to contain my irritation.

"Going back to the matter at hand," I said.

"It's still a firm no."

"Fine. I'll do it."

"Callie won't see you. She's far too busy and important."

"I don't want to hear it, Sean. Since you handed over the accounting, you've taken your eye right off the ball. Are you bored with getting paid? Or shall we just live off credit cards for the next few months?"

Sean's face fell. "Don't exaggerate. We've only just banked Doll Murphy's cheque."

"It paid the rent, your car insurance, and the electricity bill, which wasn't pretty, Sean. They weren't kidding when they said prices were on the rise."

"Hold fire." Sean tapped his mouse, and his PC sprang to life. A couple of clicks later, he was staring at the accounting software with a look of disgust.

"Fine," he said. "I take your point. But I would rather eat my spleen than go cap in hand to Callie."

"You say that as if we hadn't earned the money. It's not our fault their centralised accounts department can't get its act together."

"You could always speak to them again."

"Speak to who? I never get the same person twice, and the only one who sounded remotely competent said she'd need permission to expedite our payment from someone senior at Truscombe nick. And with Kim on long-term sick and the new inspector not yet onside, that's Callie."

"But you know what happened last time."

"Yes. Your ex-wife asked you out to dinner, and because you didn't have the guts to say no while you had the chance, you spent the next three months avoiding her. Which now makes everything harder. I'm only surprised we're still getting the work."

"They're overloaded," said Sean. "Another round of cutbacks. I haven't seen Tom in weeks."

"I wonder how he is?" I asked, despondency creeping over me. Although Tom had grown irritated with us during the final days of the Skin Thief debacle, he had been a good friend afterwards, visiting me in the hospital and texting regularly until last month. I'd messaged him a few times since to tumbleweed.

"I don't know," muttered Sean, staring distractedly at his computer. I shuffled my chair a few inches towards him as he quickly minimised a screen looking suspiciously like an online pet store.

"You don't need any more lizards," I said.

"No. But the ones I own require feeding."

I swallowed a snappy retort and changed the subject. As a guest in Sean's house, it wouldn't do to get between a man and his geckos.

"So, when are you going to the station?" I asked.

"How about when hell freezes over?"

"And back in the real world, where we still need to eat?"

"Oh, God. Tomorrow, I suppose," he said, putting his head in his hands. "It's just excruciating. I never minded the difference in rank while we were married. But being beholden to Callie is not high on my list of aspirations."

"It's up to her to play the game," I snapped. I'd never

met Callie, but she was already an irritant. Sean lost all sense of rationality in any dealings with his ex-wife, and I had a low tolerance for people who didn't pay their bills. And yes. Assistant Chief Constable Callista Hart might hold too high a rank to get down and dirty with BACS payments to third parties, but she carried responsibility for the smooth running of the southwest offices. As far as I was concerned, it was her bad.

"Fine. I'll eat my toad tomorrow first thing. But I warn you, Sass. If Callie gets snarky, she might pull the funding again."

"I'll take her to small claims."

"Don't be silly. I'll sort it out. Now can we do something more productive?"

"Such as?"

"What have we got?"

"A backlog of research for the station, which I'm unenthusiastically ploughing through, as it's not bringing any money in."

"I told you. I'll sort it."

I ignored him and continued. "A potential missing boyfriend, a couple of background checks on dodgy claimants for the DWP, and a request to quote for covert surveillance from the Truscombe bookies."

"I'll take that," said Sean.

"It's not a done deal. They've asked Jez Marley too."

"Bloody hell. He's only been in town five minutes, and he's getting all the decent jobs. There's not enough work for two PIs."

"It's not worth worrying yet. Doug Parmenter said he'd decide on Friday."

"I know Big Doug. Perhaps I should pop by."

"If you think it will help."

"I'll do better than that. Thorny Devil is running in the three thirty at Prestbury Park on Friday. It's about time I had a bit of luck on the gee-gees."

I rolled my eyes. Sean had a long list of fixations, starting with lizards and ending with virtually any sport, particularly those with gambling opportunities. Personally, I didn't get the excitement of horse racing. I'd only been once, finding the so-called atmosphere ruined by the tortuous car journeys at either end. I didn't do queuing. It simply wasn't worth it.

"Go for it," I said unenthusiastically.

"Right. That's a plan."

"For tomorrow," I said. "It's only two o'clock. I've got plenty to do. How about you?"

"Shopping, I suppose. What do you fancy for tea?"

I lowered my pen. "Anything you like, but you don't need to cater for me. I can do it." I took a deep breath and let loose the question I had been trying to avoid all week. A negative answer would be tricky to deal with, but it couldn't go unsaid for much longer. "I've been living at yours for a few months, Sean. Isn't it time I found somewhere more permanent?"

"Do you want to?"

"I really should. I'm paying a small fortune in storage costs. And you must be fed up with me by now."

"I don't mind. And it works for both of us. I appreciate the extra rent, and you are paying a damn sight less than you did at Bosworth House."

I shuddered at the mention of my former flat. After Sean had collected me from the hospital, I never went back. He'd packed and stored my possessions, made up his spare room, and I'd moved into his house in Carling Drive. Every few weeks, I went through the motions of volunteering to leave, but it suited me better to stay. We rubbed along together reasonably well, and I wasn't as lonely as I'd been in my flat.

"As long as you're sure?"

"I'd tell you if I wasn't. Now stop fishing and give me a steer on food, or we'll be dining on fish and chips again. I don't mind, but I know your aversion to brown food."

"Oh, I don't know. Just grab me a healthy ready meal. Or a quiche and salad."

"Gross," he said, pulling a face. "You're as fussy as Dhruv."

"That's unfair. Dhruv's not a fan of takeaways. He prefers to cook for himself."

"I wouldn't know. We pass like ships in the night, considering we work in the same building."

"Ah. Haven't you called round to see him?"

"No. Have you?"

"Not to his flat. I meant to the office."

"I'm not sure I'd be welcome. Dhruv's boss is a strange one."

"I know. We've met."

"When did you visit?"

"Last week. I probably should have said something, but things aren't straightforward, so I left it for another time."

"Said what? Is Dhruv alright?"

"More or less." I considered my words carefully. Sean had many positive attributes, but tolerance and understanding were not among them.

"What's that supposed to mean?"

"Look. It's not a secret, but best not to mention that we've spoken if you see him, right?"

"Mention what?"

"Dhruv is in therapy."

"Big deal. So are you."

I scowled. With great reluctance and after much persuasion from the hospital, I had consulted a therapist shortly after I was released. I attended once and studiously avoided his secretary's calls over the following weeks. I wasn't against therapy. Not at all. But it wasn't for me. I can only process my feelings with peace and quiet. It doesn't work if other people get involved.

"Dhruv is pretty much reliant on it," I explained. "He's going weekly."

"Blimey. That doesn't sound like him at all. Dhruv's always been pretty upbeat."

"Yes. Well, that was before Mill went off the rails."

Sean pushed his mouse away and looked directly at me, fully concentrating for the first time since we'd started the conversation.

"I don't understand."

"You know Mill's been in and out of hospital since contracting sepsis. He's lost a chunk of his foot, and it's badly set him back. Psychologically, I mean. Anyway. He's started drinking heavily, which isn't a good look for a teacher. God knows how it's gone undetected by the school. Dhruv tried everything to set him right, but Mill isn't listening, and their relationship is on a knife edge. Dhruv is gutted. He's in therapy for his sanity and hopes to arrange some relationship counselling."

"Doesn't that need both parties?"

"Exactly. And Mill won't have a bar of it. It breaks my heart. Two lovely guys, and they're tearing each other apart. More casualties of the bloody Skin Thief."

"Should I have a word?"

"I'd rather you didn't. Dhruv was open about everything. You know what he's like. He wears his heart on his sleeve. But I'd rather he told you himself."

"He might if I drop by."

"Sure. On a pretext. But don't mention me."

"That would seem odd."

"I mean, don't say I told you."

"Copy that. Might be better if Mill was out."

"He's always out, according to Dhruv. I—" But I didn't get to finish. Sean's mobile vibrated across the desk. He picked it up and smiled.

"Bloody hell. It's Tom," he said, accepting the call. "How are you, my old friend?"

# You'll Never Escape Me: Chapter Two

I went to the toilet while Sean took the call and returned to find him animatedly rifling through his desk drawer. "Where are my keys?" he asked.

"They're your keys. How should I know?"

"Doesn't matter. Yours will do."

"House keys or office keys?"

"Don't you keep them together?"

"No."

"How on earth do you remember them? Don't answer. It doesn't matter. Have you seen anything odd in town today?"

"Odd, how?"

"Police. In West Street."

"No. But we've been together all day. I've only seen what you've seen."

"Hmmm." Sean wasn't listening and continued opening doors and half-heartedly moving files as if overwhelmingly distracted.

"What is it, Sean?"

"We need to leave."

"When?"

"In about ten minutes."

"Then why the drama? You've got plenty of time to find your keys."

He stopped in his tracks and faced me. "Good point."

"Where are we going?"

"To see Tom."

"Business or pleasure?"

"Murder."

I stared goggle-eyed. "Wow. Where?"

"Grosvenor Street, last night. And that's all I know."

"Male or female?"

"As I said, I don't know any details."

"They must be sure of their facts to involve us."

"It's off the record, strictly off the record. Tom doesn't know how the new inspector would view our little arrangement, and it's not a straightforward question to ask. So, he's playing it as if Kim were still the boss. We must be careful not to press him too hard."

"I can't believe it—another murder in our sleepy little town. We've only just seen off one psychopath. Presumably, this is a domestic matter?"

"Presume all you like. I don't know, and I'm not prejudging."

"Are we meeting Tom at the usual place?"

"Yes. Assuming Fat Vi will still serve me. That troublemaking new waitress told her about our little nickname, and she wasn't impressed."

"I'm not surprised. It's rather childish."

"I think you mean humorous."

"I don't."

Sean raised an eyebrow. "Desist. I'm still the boss."

I smiled sweetly. "Glad you think so."

"Come on then," said Sean, grabbing his coat. He slid his hands into the pockets where they closed over a large bunch of keys.

"Found them."

"I never doubted you would.

**Grab your copy...**
**vinci-books.com/never-escape**

# About the Author

Jacqueline Beard crafts chilling crime thrillers and gripping mysteries that peel back the idyllic veneer of rural England to expose the darkness beneath. With roots in East Anglia stretching back to the 1500s and now settled in Gloucestershire, she draws on history, place, and the complexities of human nature to weave tales of suspense and deception.

A former military servicewoman and long-time estate agent, Jacqueline has a sharp eye for understanding ordinary people's virtues and secrets. Since 2017, she has penned two historical mystery series before turning her hand to regional crime fiction, with a thrilling new series set in the haunting beauty of the Cotswolds.

Her books are for readers who crave atmospheric tension, psychological depth, and shocking twists that linger long after the final page. Whether exploring the shadows of the past or the crimes of the present, her stories deliver the unexpected, revealing just how far people will go when pushed to their limits.

When not plotting her next sinister tale, Jacqueline will be researching her expansive family tree or wandering the Gloucestershire countryside with her dog, perhaps uncovering inspiration for her next dark and twisting story.